The Keeneston Roses

Bluegrass Singles #4

Kathleen Brooks

Dedication

This book is for my readers. I appreciate every email, every post, and every tweet I get. I've been lucky enough to meet some of you in person and have had a blast hanging out online at Kathleen's Blossom Café on Facebook. This book wouldn't be here without you and your love of Keeneston. Now, grab a glass of the Rose Sisters' Iced Tea and enjoy!

Prologue

Keeneston, Kentucky, a very long time ago . . .

"Stop touching me!"

"Mom! Tell her to stop touching me, too!"

"Touch. Touch. Touch," Violet Fae said as she used her finger to poke her sisters, Lily Rae and Daisy Mae.

"Girls! Stop it this instant, or I am turning this car around and busting your chops," Donald Rose yelled into the backseat of the Ford Woodie station wagon.

"She started it," Lily Rae whined and smacked the hat off of Violet's head.

Their father groaned and tightened his hands on the large steering wheel as he drove down Main Street in the quaint, small town of Keeneston, Kentucky. "Three girls. I fought a war for this country, and what do I get? Three girls."

"There, there, dear," Iris Rose said peacefully. She somehow tuned out the squabbling coming from the back seat. "You always said you wanted three children. God just granted you that wish before you left for Germany."

"Sure, I wanted three kids, just not all at once!" their father complained as he drove past the bank with the large columns carved from stone and the pale yellow, gray, deep red, and dusky blue buildings that lined the street.

"Touch. Touch. Touch," Violet Fae said in a snotty tone,

continuing to poke her sisters.

Lily pulled the white gloves from her hands and slapped them across Violet's face.

"Moooooom, Lily hit me!" Violet wailed as Daisy snickered.

Iris turned in her seat and narrowed her eyes. The girls gasped and bit their lips in unison. "If I hear one more word from any of you, y'all won't be allowed to listen to *The Adventures of Thin Man* on the radio for a month. Now, we have a wedding to attend, and I don't want to hear another peep from you. Lily, put your gloves on. Daisy, wipe that smirk off your face. Violet, straighten your hat. Donald, tighten your tie," her mother ordered like a drill sergeant as they pulled into the church parking lot.

An answering chorus of "Yes, ma'am" broke out.

Donald tightened his tie and hurried to open the door for his wife.

"Peep."

"Mom! Daisy said peep!" Violet yelled gleefully.

"Tattletale," Lily hissed.

"That's one week of no *Thin Man*. Do you want to push it?" Iris asked with a serene smile on her face and watched the three girls shake their heads. "You all are sisters. Someday you'll only have each other in this world. Remember that as you torture each other instead of being good sisters and loving one another."

Their father opened the passenger door and held out his hand for their mother.

Lily turned to her sisters and stuck out her tongue.

Daisy pinched Lily.

Violet put her thumbs to her ears and wiggled them while making a face.

The back door opened, and Lily turned to smile

innocently at her parents. The parking lot of Saint Francis Church was full. The daughter of the wealthiest man in Keeneston was getting married. The Shillings had moved to Keeneston with their brood of four kids right after World War II. They bought the bank and the house next door. They made both the house and bank larger. And like most families after the war, they had another child, Frank. Frank was also ten, and he thought girls had cooties.

Lily passed him as they walked into the church and stuck her tongue out at him. He stuck his out in return. Boys. Ick.

"Lily and Frank, sitting in a tree," Daisy whispered before Lily whipped around and pinched her side. "Ow! I'm telling Mom."

"You're such a tattletale," Lily said again as she rolled her eyes.

"But I'm your sister, and you have to love me. Mom said so." Daisy smirked.

Chapter One

Keeneston, Kentucky, some years later . . .

Lily Rae Rose pinned her long golden hair into a perfect, high ponytail. She fluffed her fringed bangs and tied off the ponytail with a colorful scarf that matched her yellow cardigan and skirt. She buttoned up her white shirt and tucked it into the tiny waist of the flared, calf-length skirt. There. She looked perfect for the first day of her senior year of high school.

Her door was thrown open as Daisy rushed in wearing nothing but a bra and a pink skirt. "I can't find my black sweater. The one that makes me look less like a boy and more like Violet."

"I found it!" Violet rushed in, holding the sweater. "I found it in my closet. I guess I borrowed it and forgot."

Violet's hair was cut to look like Grace Kelly's while Daisy had opted for a pixie cut. Needless to say, their father yelled a lot on haircut day.

"I want to look perfect," Daisy said as she slid the short-sleeved sweater on. "You know how badly I want to join the Belles, and with us all cheerleading and the fact that Jimmy is totally into me, I think I have a shot."

Lily curled her lip in a sneer. "A Keeneston Belle? Don't you want to do something more with your life than just hook the catch of the class and settle down to manage him?" The Keeneston Belles were technically a philanthropic group, but really their main goal was to snag the best of the bachelors Keeneston had to offer.

"What else is there to do in Keeneston?" Daisy grinned. "Besides, Mom is a Keeneston Lady. It's tradition."

Lily shook her head. Once a Belle got married, she moved into the Ladies' group, which literally ran the town. The husbands just never seemed to realize it.

"I want to go to Europe," Violet whispered.

"Europe!" The other sisters gasped.

"Don't tell Mom and Dad, but I want to go to cooking school and become a chef. Now, I just need to find a way to look into these schools."

"You'll figure it out, Vi," Lily said with a smile. "Although I don't know what I will do with you all the way in Europe. No Rose has left Keeneston except to fight for our country."

"Our sister the tradition breaker," Daisy teased.

"Well, don't tell anyone. Triple sister secret," Violet said seriously as she held out her pinky. The Rose sisters all joined in and shook pinkies.

"Girls! It's time for you to leave," their mother shouted up the stairs of the old Victorian that had been in their family for generations.

Lily grabbed her books and purse and ran down the stairs, followed by her sisters. She flew out the front door, jumped from the porch steps, raced past the rose bushes, and smashed into a solid mass of tight white T-shirt and rolled jeans.

"*Umph!*"

"Lily, are you okay?" she heard Daisy call from the porch.

Lily wobbled and would have fallen on her bottom if

strong hands hadn't encircled her waist and pulled her tight against a warm body. "I'm fine," Lily called back as she looked up into the molten-brown eyes of her neighbor, Frank Shilling.

"That you are." He smirked and Lily felt her heart tumble out of her chest and smash onto the ground at his feet.

For once in her life, Lily Rae Rose was speechless. The boy she'd had a crush on for the past three years of high school was now holding her in his arms. She saw the shine of the grease of his James Dean hair and smelled the leather from his black jacket.

"Thank you." She blushed and didn't bother removing her hands from his chest. She sent him a flirty smile and a wink. When Lily Rae wanted something, she went after it. And she had wanted Frank Shilling for years—except he had been going steady with Peggy Sue Jerwsky. But if the rumors Lily heard from her friend John Wolfe were true, Frank and Peggy Sue were kaput.

"So, are you going my way?" Frank asked with a wink.

"Well, considering there is only one school in Keeneston, I think it's a pretty good bet I am."

"Can I carry your books for you?"

Lily Rae heard her sisters taking the steps to their porch at the speed of a snail to give her time to talk to Frank. When she handed Frank her books, she could practically feel them squealing their excitement. They had known how much Lily had wanted to go steady with the cute boy next door.

"How was your summer?" Frank asked. They walked down the sidewalk with her sisters, keeping a safe distance behind them to give them privacy.

"It was good, even if I had a job."

"What did you do?"

"I helped with events at the country club. There were a lot of sweet sixteen parties," Lily said with a bit of a nervous laugh. "What about you? Your mom said something to my mom about you not being here all summer."

"That's right. I spent the summer in the Hamptons with my grandparents. Sun, surf, and sand for me. That and stuffy debutantes."

"I'm sure they were hurling themselves at you. It must have been dangerous. Thank goodness you weren't hurt," Lily teased.

The sound of a large engine revving drew their attention. A big, black convertible with flames painted on the sides cruised to a stop next to them.

"Frankie, what are you doing? Get in," Rex, the wannabe greaser, said as he pounded the side of the door with his palm. Three tough girls in satin jackets sat in the back of the car smirking, and Lily felt like sticking her tongue out at them . . . a habit she had given up a couple years ago. Well, at least when her mother was around.

Frank turned his back on the car and handed Lily her books. "I'm sorry I can't finish walking you to school. I sort of promised Rex I'd go with him."

Lily tried her best to smile but knew it fell short. "It's okay. Have a good first day at school."

Frank shuffled his feet.

"Come on. I'm getting old here," Rex called out.

"Just cool your heels," Frank shot back. "Are you going to the Back to School Sock Hop on Friday?"

"I hadn't decided yet," Lily said slyly. "It depends on if someone asks."

Frank's face lit up as he took the hint. "Would you go

with me?"

"I'd love to," Lily responded as calmly as she could.

"Great! I'll pick you up at seven."

Lily felt her sisters hurrying forward as she watched Frank jump the door and slide into the leather seats of Rex's convertible. As Rex drove off, Frank shot her one last grin. She had a date with Frank Shilling.

"Oh my goodness, you have a date with Frank Shilling!" Her sisters giggled as they linked arms and walked the rest of the way to school.

"Psst, Lily," Donna Odell whispered as the home economics teacher droned on about the proper way to clean a sewing machine. "Frank gave this to me to pass to you."

Lily looked around the room. When her teacher's head was turned, she grabbed the note from Donna.

Milkshakes at the drive-in after school?

"He said for you to tell me yes or no, and I'll pass it along to him since our lockers are next to each other."

Lily smiled as she folded the note and stuck it in her pocket. "Yes."

"Miss Rose, is there something you'd like to share with the class?"

Lily smiled. "There's a lot I'd like to share with the class, Mrs. Romstine." The class snickered. Mrs. Romstine did not look amused, so Lily smiled sweetly and answered, "But most importantly how wrong I have been in the cleaning of my sewing machine. Thank goodness you have shown us the correct way to do it."

Mrs. Romstine didn't look convinced, but the bell rang, and her attempts at discipline were overshadowed as the kids rushed from the room. Their first day of senior year was complete, and she had a date with the dreamy Frank Shilling.

"Lily, what did Donna want?" Daisy asked. Her sisters rushed to either side of her and linked arms as they walked to their lockers.

"I have a date with Frank. We're going to the drive-in for milkshakes."

Daisy and Violet shared smiles before placing their books in their lockers and grabbing the ones they needed for homework.

"Do you want us to go with you?" Daisy asked.

"That might be good. Then Mom and Dad can't throw a fit. You know how they hate us having any independence."

Violet rolled her eyes. "That's because you don't think you need their permission to do anything."

"So speaks the sister who wants to go to Europe," Lily quipped.

"Do you always have to be right?"

"Well, I am the oldest." Lily smiled to Violet.

"By six minutes. Give it a rest already," Violet laughed.

The girls headed out of school, waving to their friends and sharing the gossip of their first day back at school.

"I still can't believe Jimmy started dating Peggy Sue. That girl just waits to steal the boys we like," Daisy complained. "My chance at becoming a Belle is decreasing by the second."

"Peggy Sue is a Belle. Do you really want to join them? I know they say they are all about community service, but it's a long-standing tradition in Keeneston that their unspoken mission is to ensnare every eligible bachelor in town. Are you really that man crazy?"

"I don't plan on staying a virgin forever, so why not

join them?" Daisy winked as they giggled. "Look, there's Frank. We'll go sit at another table. I need to think of a new plan for the sock hop this Friday. I had been planning to go with Jimmy."

"We'll think of someone new, don't worry," Violet told her sister before turning to Lily. "We can't stay too long. You know if we're not home by dinner, Dad starts asking too many questions."

Lily sent a thankful smile to her sisters and headed to the table where Frank sat with a chocolate shake and two straws. The collar to his leather jacket was popped up, framing his chiseled face. He looked dark and dangerous and that sent tingles rushing through her body. What could she say — sweet, innocent Lily Rae Rose had a thing for bad boys.

"Hi, Frank." Lily stopped at a table under the metal roof of the drive-in. Cars were parked on three sides of the small rectangular court. Her sisters sat in a matching area on the other side of the small kitchen that stood in the middle of the drive-in.

"I'm glad you were able to make it. I didn't think you would say yes." Frank smiled and the tingles rushing through Lily turned to sparks.

"And why wouldn't I say yes?" Lily asked flirtatiously, then leaned down and placed her mouth slowly around the straw.

Frank swallowed hard. "I don't have the best reputation, and you're one of the perfect Roses whose beauty cannot be rivaled, whose manners are pristine, and whose innocence is as fresh as a new bloom."

Lily laughed. Her parents had let her and her sisters yell, squabble, and possibly shoot each other with BB guns at home. But when they were in public, they were perfection. Her parents were prominent citizens. Heck, her family had been one of the Keeneston founding families and insisted on remaining pillars of the small community — a community so small there were no stoplights and only three streets. But the people of Keeneston were proud of their town, so their parents had made sure their three girls lived up to their reputations.

"I'm not so innocent, but don't tell anyone."

"Oh, I bet you've dipped your toe into the pond of sin, but I doubt you've taken the plunge," Frank said with a quick glance down her body.

Lily felt herself fluster. She was a flirt, but she'd never actually done anything about it. She'd received stolen kisses behind the gym or under the bleachers. But no one had ever dared look at one of the precious Rose sisters with desire.

"Well, I guess we'll just have to wait and see if you're the one to teach me how to swim." Lily was rewarded with a grin that curled her toes inside her penny loafers.

"Lily," Daisy called as she rushed over. "Mom just drove by on her way home. If we're not home, she'll start to ask questions, and you know you don't want to answer them."

Lily felt her stomach plummet. Her mother hated the Shillings, especially Frank. "I'm sorry, but I have to go. I'll see you at school tomorrow."

Frank stood and handed Lily her books. "I look forward to it, my bloom."

Daisy rolled her eyes and tugged Lily's arm, but Lily felt her heart kick into overdrive. He called her his bloom. He must like her!

Chapter Two

Lily, Daisy, and Violet cut through the courthouse parking lot, climbed over their neighbor's fence, and slipped through the hedge into their backyard. They raced to the back patio, set their books down, and breathed in deeply.

"Hurry! I see her in the kitchen," Daisy whispered.

The girls sat down, opened their books, and tried to wipe the sweat from their foreheads before their mother opened the backdoor.

"Oh, here you girls are," their mother said sweetly. "What are you up to?"

"Just doing our reading for school tomorrow." Lily smiled up at her.

"Well, we're having lamb for dinner tonight. After all, you must be tired from running all the way from the drive-in after sharing a milkshake with that hooligan, Frank Shilling."

The three girls' eyes went wide, and Lily felt her breathing stop. "Frank?" she asked innocently.

"Yes, you know, the boy next door who is a vandal and always up to no good."

"Mom," Lily said, "Frank is a nice boy."

Her mother made a noise that sounded something like a snort. "Lily, at some point you will need to wake up and realize your mother may know a thing or two about the world. Frank Shilling is bad news. If I thought you would do as I say, I would tell you to stay away from him. But, I know you better, and you would just sneak off behind my back and see him anyway. And that, young lady, is when you get into serious trouble. No, if you want to see him, you can. But it has to be here where we can keep an eye on the two of you."

"Mom, I'm almost eighteen. You can't do this to me. It's so embarrassing. Are you trying to ruin my life?" Lily cried as she jumped up to face her mother.

"No, I'm trying to make sure you keep your good reputation. I know times have changed, but not that much. If he's really the good boy you say he is, then he won't mind doing it."

"Can I at least go to the dance with him on Friday?" Lily asked through clenched teeth. She couldn't wait to make her own decisions.

"Of course. Invite him over for dinner beforehand though. Maybe you're right, and he really is a nice young man." Her mother smiled as if that was the furthest thing from the truth.

"Fine. I will, and I'll show you that I am right."

"Lily Rae, it's not about being right. It's about doing anything you can to ensure the happiness of those you love. I'll be thrilled if you are right and Frank falls in love with you. After all, true love is the greatest gift in the world." Their mother smiled at them and turned back into the kitchen to unload the groceries.

Lily looked out over the yard shaded by large maple trees and lined with colorful flowers. It was peaceful, bright, and happy. But all those fuzzy feelings were crushed as Violet spoke up.

"Lil, what if Mom is right? He does run with a pretty bad crowd. Rex is repeating his senior year because he was suspended for half of last year. Is that really the kind of guy you want to go steady with?"

"It's not like Frank was part of what Rex did. He didn't spray-paint the school. I won't hold him accountable for something his friend did," Lily said stubbornly.

"I guess his dreaminess can make up for any deficiencies his friend has," Daisy joked to break the tension.

That Friday night Lily slid on her baby-doll shoes and tied a matching scarf around her ponytail — perfect for the dance. When the doorbell rang, she took one last look in the mirror and then raced down the large curving staircase.

As she rounded the curve of the banister, she looked into the large square entranceway at Frank handing her mother a bundle of roses.

"Thank you for inviting me to dinner, Mrs. Rose. I've smelled your cooking for years and have dreamt of this many nights, that's for sure."

Lily soaked in the sight of him in his button-down shirt with a loosened tie. His hair was freshly styled and his smile was anything but innocent.

"I'm glad you can join us. Did you forget your jacket?" Lily's mother kindly rebuked.

"How's it going so far?" Daisy whispered from where the three of them were spying.

"He brought Mom flowers and complimented her cooking, but she doesn't appreciate his dressing down," Lily whispered back as they watched their father glare at him. "Come on, we better get down there before they scare him away."

Lily rushed the rest of the way down the stairs. As she came into view, Frank turned and gave her an appreciative smile. "Hey, aren't you a classy chassis?"

Lily blushed and practically felt the breeze from Violet's eye roll behind her. "Thanks, Frank. I like your threads."

"Thanks. Hi, Daisy. Hi, Violet."

Her sisters murmured their hellos before disappearing into the dining room, leaving them together. Lily grew nervous. She knew this was a crush because she hurt when he wasn't with her. But when they were together, she felt so insecure. He ran with the cool kids, and it was rumored he had dated a Hollywood actress while he was in the Hamptons over the summer. Yet, he was here, looking at her like he wanted to rip off her clothes. No one ever looked at her like that. No one braved the Rose reputation to see the passionate person underneath the cardigans.

"I'm sorry you have to do this. It's just that my parents like to know who I'm going out with."

"I understand. Haven't you figured out I'll jump through all the hoops to go steady with you?" Frank asked in a low voice and stepped close to her, looking into her eyes.

"Dinner," her mother called from the dining room.

Lily blinked as she broke Frank's gaze. He had been about to kiss her; she just knew it. Maybe tonight they could sneak away from the dance. She certainly didn't want to get a reputation for being fast, but kissing Frank was what her dreams were made of.

Frank slid his arm tightly around her as they slow-danced to The Hilltoppers. The dance had been so romantic. Frank was a fantastic dancer, and Lily didn't miss the wishful glances from the other girls. They had danced slowly, and they had danced fast. They had laughed, they had talked with her friends, and she had loved every minute of it.

"Mr. Shilling, this is not the appropriate distance," their principal said with disapproval as he held out a ruler to demonstrate the appropriate amount of space required between their bodies.

Frank took a step backward and the principal moved on with a nod of his head. "Let's blow this joint," Frank said as he steered her from the gymnasium.

"And where are we going?"

"Lovers Pond sounds good to me. What about you?"

Lily gulped. She wanted to, but Lovers Pond was a sure way to ruin your reputation. "I'm sorry but with my curfew I don't think I can."

Frank gave her a lopsided grin. "There's my innocent bloom. Tonight I'll just dream about it. How about we go hang with my friends at the water tower instead? I promise I'll get you home in plenty of time to meet your curfew."

"I can do that. It will give me a chance to meet your friends. I don't know them very well." Lily thought about Rex and knew her mother would drop dead if she discovered Lily was hanging out with him. But her mother was wrong about Frank, and maybe they were all wrong about Rex. There was only one way to find out, and that was to decide for herself.

Lily waited as Frank jumped out of the car and walked around to open her door. There were six cars with their lights on next to the town's water tower. Some of the guys were trying to race each other up the tower while others were sitting in the back seats of their cars necking with girls.

She hated to admit it, but Lily had a sneaking suspicion

her mother had been right. Some of them were old enough to drink, but there seemed to be a lot of empty beer bottles scattered around for those few legal drinkers. Music blared from the car speakers. She'd only heard some snippets from Elvis Presley before, but she knew her mother thought rock n' roll would corrupt them.

"What are you doing bringing a square to our place?" Rex yelled from his car as he lifted his face from the neck of a junior with a very fast reputation, which was apparently well earned.

"Cool it. She's with me," Frank said with a sternness that made her feel protected.

"It's all right. If they don't want me here, we don't have to stay," Lily whispered as she grasped Frank's hand in hers.

"Well, I want you here, and that's all that matters. Come on, let's have a beer and talk."

Lily barely nodded her head and accepted a beer that was tossed at Frank. Rex gave her a look of disgust and went back to necking while Frank introduced her to his crew. Some were nice, but mostly they seemed to mock her. Lily was ready to go when Frank pulled her into the shadows of the water tower.

"I'm glad you're here. There's something I have been wanting to give you." Frank held up his hand and pulled his class ring from his finger. "We got interrupted earlier, but I was hoping you would agree to go steady with me."

Lily almost lost her breath as her dream came true before her eyes. As soon as she had turned thirteen and discovered there was more to the opposite sex than just being stupid boys, she had dreamed of Frank. She had watched him grow up into a dream. Tall, muscular, and with a smile that made her knees weak. And now he was standing in front of her holding out his class ring.

"Oh, Frank! Yes, I will go steady with you."

Frank slipped the ring on her finger, and it promptly fell off. They both laughed, and she undid her necklace and laced it through the ring. "I guess this will have to do for now." She smiled at him and then held out the ends of the necklace for him to take.

Frank leaned forward and fastened the necklace around her neck. Lily stopped breathing when his fingers trailed her collarbone and stopped at the top swell of her breast. She looked up with a mix of confusion and desire and saw his eyes devour her a moment before backing her against the cold metal of the water tower and covering her lips with his.

"I've been wanting to do that all week," Frank whispered before kissing her again.

Lily was lost in the taste of his lips, the pressure of his body against hers, the scent of his cologne, and something that was just Frank. But when his hand cupped her breast, the unflappable Lily flapped. She jerked her head back, hitting it against the water tower as she fought for breath.

"Told you she was a square," Rex chuckled as he emerged from the shadows.

Frank stepped in front of her and shoved Rex. "I told you to cool it, Rex," he growled.

"Don't have a cow. I was just bringing you another beer."

"It's okay, Frank. It's time I get home anyway. It was nice seeing you, Rex. I love the flames you had painted on your car," Lily said a little bit shyly. She'd never had anyone challenge her besides her family, and she wasn't familiar with how to handle it. It irked her that she fell back to what her mother taught her. She should always say something nice or not say anything at all.

"Thank you, young Rose. Now hurry home before you get eaten by the big bad wolf." Rex let out a howl and soon the field echoed with men howling.

By the time Lily arrived home, she was depressed. This was never going to work. His friends hated her, and she wasn't prepared to do what it took to fit in with them.

Frank pulled into her driveway and turned off the car. He turned in his seat and cupped her shoulder. His thumb gently rubbed her tightly wound muscles. "I'm sorry about my friends."

"It's not going to work, Frank," Lily said with tears in her eyes.

"Of course it is. They don't matter. All that matters is that you're wearing my ring. You're my girl, Lily. My rose who I want to watch bloom in my hands."

"But, Rex . . ."

"But Rex nothing. It's just you and me, doll. We're the only ones who matter. Let me prove it to you. If I can't, then you can give my ring back." Frank was so sincere Lily wanted to believe him. She had to believe him or her dream would vanish into the night.

"Two weeks."

Frank smiled. "These will be the best two weeks of your life. I guarantee it."

Chapter Three

Two weeks turned into three months. After the first month, Lily stopped thinking about giving back Frank's class ring. They were made for each other. He was the perfect gentleman. He had stopped hanging out with Rex and had dinner at her house with her family every Thursday night.

He took her out on dates each Friday and Saturday night. They went for ice cream, to sock hops and football games, and even to drive-in movies where they necked in the privacy of the back seat of his car. She was so madly in love and couldn't wait to tell him. It was part of her Christmas present plan.

These past couple months had been so dreamy that Lily let her hopes rise. She'd been wearing his class ring, and everyone knew they were the new *it* couple of Keeneston High. When they cruised down Main Street at night, Frank only had eyes for her. She wondered if the Christmas gift he kept on mentioning was a different kind of ring.

"Lily, did you hear me?" Daisy asked with annoyance.

"Hmm?"

"I asked if Frank was going to New York for Christmas next week?"

"Oh, yes. He leaves on Tuesday. We're going to exchange gifts a couple days before, though."

"Mom wants to know if he's going to join us for the Keeneston Christmas celebration on Saturday."

"We are going to the town celebration, but then we may leave early to exchange gifts."

Daisy looked down at the scarf Lily held in her hands. She'd spent the last month knitting the cashmere scarf and hat for him. "I'm sure he's going to love it. Well, I'm going to bed. I'll see you tomorrow for the first official day of Christmas vacation. We need to pick out what to wear to the party."

Lily watched her sister give one last wistful look at the scarf and then close the door. While Lily was basking in the good fortune of love, Daisy and Violet were not. Violet had plenty of men after her, but they seemed more interested in how she was stacked than in her as a person. And Daisy was too mature for the boys in Keeneston. All the mature ones had gone off to college. Lily hoped that Daisy would run into some of them while they were home for Christmas. Not that many men went to college, but the ones who did were the guys that would be interested in Daisy.

There was a soft knock on the door. Violet quietly opened it and stepped into the room. She looked nervously around as she closed the door. "Lil, I need your help."

"Of course, Vi. Did something happen?"

"Not yet, but I need a ride into Lexington," Violet said in a hushed whisper as she set the *Keeneston Journal* on the bed. "Look."

Lily set down the scarf and picked up the paper. *New Chef at Lexington Club Shines*, Lily read. "You want to go to dinner at some fancy restaurant?"

"No, look. The chef is from Lexington but went to culinary school in France. I have to talk to him and see if he'll write a letter of recommendation for me. I need to find a way to contact this school about a scholarship. Of course, I first need to find out if they even accept women."

"I don't have a car . . ."

"No, but Frank does," Lily cut in. "Can you talk him into giving me a ride to Lexington?"

"I don't see why not. When do you want to go?"

Violet bit her lip nervously. "Right now?"

"Vi, it's ten o'clock at night."

"I know. But we don't have school tomorrow, and the restaurant will just be closing when we get there. The chef will be cleaning up and won't have any customers to distract him. Please, Lily. It's my dream."

Lily let out a long breath. "Okay, but we need to make sure Dad and Mom are already asleep."

"They are. I checked before I came to see you. We already said goodnight to them, and they turned off their light twenty minutes ago."

"Well, we can't just waltz out the front door . . ." Lily pondered. "With their bedroom downstairs, they'll hear any of the doors, and we can't risk them locking us out."

Violet smiled. "It's a good thing we excel at climbing trees."

Lily turned to look out her window at the huge old maple tree in the front yard. This was going to be interesting.

"I see London, I see France . . ."

"Shut up, Violet, or I won't help you," Lily hissed as softly as she could. She slowly made her way down the tree. Violet had climbed out the window first and was almost at the last branch.

"I don't know about you, but this is the best view in all of Keeneston," the deep voice joked.

"Frank!" Violet and Lily gasped before shushing each other.

"Catch me," Violet whispered as Frank held out his arms. Violet dropped from the bottom limb, and Frank set her aside before reaching for Lily.

"Would you care to tell me what's going on?"

"Violet needs you to drive us to Lexington. She wants to meet a chef," Lily told him as she and Violet dragged him away from the house.

"Sweet Violet is dating a chef?"

"No. It's a secret, but I need to ask him about culinary school in Europe. I can't tell my parents. They won't understand. And I don't want to get my hopes up until I find out if they even accept women and offer scholarships."

Frank looked between the two sisters and nodded his head. "Then let's burn rubber."

Violet Fae sat nervously in the back of Frank's car as he sped down small country roads leading to Lexington. She tightened her fist as they passed the Ashton Farm and finally turned onto Broadway in downtown Lexington. She didn't know what she was doing. Could she really walk into a swanky restaurant and persuade the chef to talk to her?

Frank pulled to a stop in front of the restaurant, and Violet took a deep breath. She could do this. What did she have to lose? She straightened her hair and pinched her cheeks to put some color into them.

"Vi, you look great. They'd be crazy not to take you. Do you want us to go in with you?" Lily asked.

She was a good sister. Sure, they didn't always get along when they were growing up, but when they turned fifteen everything had changed. They stopped trying to push each other's buttons and turned into the best of friends. Their mother had been right; they were sisters, and they loved each other.

"That's okay. Thank you. It's something I need to do myself."

Frank got out of the car and pushed his seat forward for her to climb out. Wiping her hands on her skirt, she took one last deep breath and walked around to the back of the old brick building.

She heard the sounds of male laughter first. The back door was open as the men cleaned up for the night. Her heart pounded as she walked through the darkness toward the light spilling out of the kitchen into the alley.

"I can do this," she whispered to herself before stepping up to the door. "Excuse me, I'm looking for Chef Nichols."

Some of them let out catcalls while others suggested she look for them instead. But a second later she saw him walk from the office. He carried the air of confidence only a head chef had. "I'm Nichols. What do you want, kid?"

Violet swallowed and then stood as tall as she could. "I'm here to talk to you about your experience in culinary school."

"Are you a reporter?" Nichols asked as he hushed the men and sent them back to work.

"No. I want to be a head chef."

"A woman?" he snickered. "Betty Crocker comes out with a cookbook and suddenly everyone thinks they can be a chef."

"Julia Child just graduated from culinary school," Violet shot back. "Women have been the primary chefs in households since the beginning of time. Where did you learn how to cook? I bet it wasn't from your father."

Nichols smiled at her and then laughed. "You're right.

My father couldn't boil water. It doesn't matter, though; women are just not meant to run restaurants. They don't have the intelligence or the finesse to know how to make these complex plates."

"Chef, I'll make a bet with you. Give me two hours, and I'll make a dish that will prove you wrong. When I do, you will write me a letter of recommendation and give me the names of all the culinary schools that admit women."

"You're a plucky thing, aren't you?"

"I am. I'm also determined."

Nichols looked into her eyes, and Violet stared him down. "Fine. Two hours, starting now," Nichols said as he looked at his watch. "Gentlemen, clear the kitchen. I'll get the rest. You may go home now."

Clearly thinking she was here to neck with the chef, the men cheered as they left. Violet didn't let it bother her. She headed straight for the pantry and collected the nineteen items she needed to make her dish.

Just because she was from a small town didn't mean she didn't know how to cook. There were such things as books, and she had gotten a French cookbook for her birthday. While Violet preferred home-cooked comfort foods like her mother's fried chicken, she knew in order to be taken seriously she needed to cook like the French. And as she sprinkled flour on the beef, she knew without a doubt she would do everything she could to make her dream a reality.

Lily rolled her head to the side to allow Frank better access to kiss her. His lips started at her earlobe and followed a path down her neck and over her collarbone. Her sister had been gone for almost two hours, but Violet had told her to give her until one in the morning, and that was just fine with Lily.

Frank's hand started to slide up her stomach and hesitantly cupped her breast. When she moaned, Frank caressed them more ardently. So this is what she had been missing. No wonder some women were fast—it felt divine.

"Lily, I want you so badly."

"I want you, too."

"Really?" Frank asked with surprise as he pulled back.

"Really."

Frank kissed her quickly. "Oh, Lily. I love you. I think I have since you threw dirt at me for spying on you when I was six years old."

"Well, you deserved it," Lily giggled. "And I love you, too. So much, Frank. Say we'll be together forever."

"Forever, darling. I hate that I have to leave next week. But tomorrow is the Christmas party. I can't wait to share the evening with you. It's going to be magical."

"I can't wait. I love you so much, Frank."

Violet smiled as she set the beautiful beef bourguignon in front of Chef Nichols. She waited patiently as he turned the plate around in order to inspect it from all angles before cutting into it. He examined the coloring, sniffed it, and finally put it on his tongue and wrapped his lips around the fork. Violet held her breath and watched as his eyes widened in surprise.

"Miss Rose, I am stunned. This is fabulous."

"Thank you. Will you consider writing me a letter of recommendation then?"

"I'll do better than that. If you expect to enroll in culinary school, you need to prove your worth. It's hard being a woman in a profession dominated by men. This is our busiest season. You manage to work all of next week and not only will I write you a letter of recommendation, I'll call admissions and personally talk to them about you."

Violet couldn't contain her gasp. "Really? Thank you so much, Chef!"

"Don't thank me yet. You'll have to earn your recommendation. I'll see you here Monday at four. Expect to be here until eleven that night."

"Yes, sir!" Violet slipped off the apron and gave Chef Nichols one last smile before running out the back door. She had no idea how she was going to manage to get to Lexington every night, but if it meant having to ride her bike the fifteen miles, then she would do it. She wasn't going to let anything stand in the way of her dream.

Chapter Four

D aisy let out a long sigh as she flopped belly first onto Lily's bed. She buried her head in her hands and groaned. "Am I the only one who doesn't have a plan for after high school? Lily is probably going to get married, Violet is trying to go off to Europe, and I'll be left behind."

Lily and Violet exchanged a smirk at Daisy's dramatics. "There has to be something you want to do," Lily said as she tightened the bow in her hair.

"What I want to do has nothing to do with what I can do."

Violet shook her head in confusion. "What on earth does that mean?"

"I would love to own my own business, but I can't do that without a husband. I wouldn't know where to start."

"Well, maybe you'll find a husband at the Christmas party tonight," Lily suggested. The Keeneston Christmas party always had a huge turnout of eligible men.

"And maybe I can find one with his own car," Violet winked as she looked quickly to the door and then dabbed some perfume into her ample cleavage.

"Lily, Frank is here," her mother called from the bottom of the stairs.

"How do I look?" Lily asked her sisters nervously.

"Like a bride." Violet smiled before giving her a kiss on

the cheek.

"And I'm going to be the maid of honor," Daisy told them as she stood up.

Violet shook her head. "Are not. I am."

"I am."

"No, I am."

"I'm older," Daisy said, playing her trump card.

"Girls! Let me get engaged first." Lily laughed as she gathered her wrap and purse from the dressing table. She headed downstairs, no longer nervous, feeling full of love and rightness.

Lily didn't think she could stand it for one more second. The party was fantastic. A big band played music, people were dancing, and she had wished Merry Christmas to the entire town. Daisy was in the middle of men from the University of Kentucky barbershop quartet, enjoying being serenaded. Violet had found someone who had graduated from Keeneston High last year and worked in Lexington to drive her to town for the next week. But now that everyone seemed settled and happy to stand around chatting, Lily couldn't wait to leave.

She watched as Frank kissed his very uptight parents goodnight and promised to be home in an hour. Violet and Daisy, using their sisterly bond, looked over to Lily at the same time and sent her a wink. Finally Frank slid his arm around her.

"Are you ready to go, doll?"

"I have been ready forever."

Frank escorted her out of the party and down the crowded street to his car. As they drove through town, she enjoyed seeing the bubble lights on the trees and in the windows and the bright garlands decorating the town. "You missed our street." Lily laughed as they drove past the street they both lived on.

"I thought we could exchange gifts someplace more private," Frank said as he reached over and squeezed her hand in his.

"But your gift is at my house," Lily said, pointing back toward their street.

"That's okay. I really want to give you my gift first."

Lily's heart sped up. He was going to propose, and he couldn't wait to do it. She watched as they drove out of town and knew it was going to be the most romantic night of her life.

She envisioned the light dusting of snow surrounding the gazebo at the city park and Frank down on one knee. But they drove past the park. "Where are we going?"

Frank just smiled and placed his hand on her thigh. "Do you trust me?"

"Of course I do," Lily said instantly.

"We'll be there in just a minute. It's going to be the best night."

Lily smiled at his excitement, then felt her stomach tighten as they pulled onto the dirt road leading to Lovers Pond. But when Frank smiled at her reassuringly, she knew he had a plan. It was a very picturesque location, and it would be appropriate to get engaged here. They were in love, after all.

Frank pulled up and parked the car on the far side of the pond. Only one other car was there, and it was hidden behind a cluster of trees. The windows were steamed over, and Lily felt herself blush at what was going on in the car. She and Frank had necked before but never really played backseat bingo.

Frank turned on the Christmas music and faced her. His smile touched her heart as he looked at her. "I love you, Lily Rae."

"I love you, too, Frank. With all my heart." She spoke into the darkness as Frank bent his head to kiss her neck.

"Show me," Frank whispered against her delicate skin.

Lily laughed nervously. "What do you mean?"

"I mean, I love you, and I got you the most special gift. It's not like we just started going steady," Frank teased with a sly smile as he reached under her arm and slid the zipper to her red dress down her ribcage.

Lily gulped, but if she was going to be his wife, this couldn't be wrong. Not when it felt so right. She felt the coolness of the air against her chest as his hands moved to push down her dress. And then his mouth was there, and she changed her mind; this was wrong. Deliciously so.

"You are so beautiful, Lily. So sweet, so innocent. The perfect woman. And you're going to bloom against my body."

"Yes," she gasped as his finger touched a spot between her legs that made her forget she was in a car.

Her dress was pushed to the floor, her panties quickly followed as steam covered the windows. She was lost in the passion. Lost in the love. Her heart had never been so full. And when the door was flung open, she didn't even realize it. It was the blinding flash of the camera that jerked her eyes open.

"Rex!" she gasped as she tried to cover her nakedness.

The sound of Rex's laughter stole her breath. "Well, Frank, you did it. I hate to hand over my pink slip, but it was worth it to be able to post this around town. The most perfect Rose is nothing but a fast dolly. Do I get to go next?"

Lily shot her eyes to Frank who just gave her a shrug of his shoulders. "It was for a car. Of course I was going to take the bet. But you're a great kid. Someday you'll find someone who will overlook the fact you've lost your bloom."

"No one will believe you," Lily said with more courage than she felt.

"They won't have to. Rex has the picture."

Lily looked to where Rex stood wiggling the camera in front of her. Her heart turned to ice and broke in two. She didn't care that she was naked. She didn't care that her reputation would be ruined. She didn't care that she could be pregnant this very second, and she didn't care that she would have to leave Keeneston in disgrace. She only cared about the pain—the pain that made her shove Frank away, the pain that gave her the power to jump naked from the car, and the pain that tightened her fist and plowed it into Rex's smirking face. She ripped the camera from his hands and exposed the film before throwing it into Lovers Pond.

"You bitch! That cost me $6.95!"

"It'll cost you more than that," Lily yelled as in all her naked glory she kicked her leg up into his balls with such force that Rex fell to his knees. His falsetto scream could have broken glass, and then he promptly vomited.

Frank leapt from the car and grabbed Rex. He helped his friend into the passenger seat. He blew her a kiss and burned rubber around the pond, leaving her broken-hearted, naked, and freezing.

Tears came without notice. She gripped her chest to ease the pain in her aching heart. The betrayal made her nauseous. Surely no one would believe Rex . . . but they would believe her boyfriend. Her life was over.

"Lily," a soft, deep voice said from behind her.

Lily whirled around, ready to fight, only to find the concerned faces of John Wolfe and his girlfriend, Rhonda. John shrugged his broad shoulders out of his coat and handed it to her. Lily numbly took it and covered herself.

"Let us take you home," John said kindly. "My fiancée and I were just heading back to Keeneston."

"Congratulations," Lily mumbled as she let Rhonda wrap her in her arms and escort her to the car parked behind the trees. She was too numb. Her tears had stopped, and she didn't care if her heart stopped as well. "I'm ruined," she whispered to no one in particular.

Chapter Five

The Christmas party was in full swing. Daisy laughed as a member of the barbershop quartet cut in to dance with her. She'd never been the center of attention before and loved it. Violet flirted shamelessly with the friend of a friend who was staying in Keeneston for the break. And right about now, Lily would be getting engaged. It was a night of celebration.

Daisy looked at Violet, and the two shared a wink. But then she felt it. A pain shot through her heart. She looked back to Violet and saw her acting very different as well. They looked at each other and knew at once that something was very wrong.

"Excuse me, but I need to talk with my sister." Daisy smiled at the last member of the quartet. She let him escort her over to Violet who was already walking toward her.

Violet had never felt pain so acute before. The triplets shared a special bond and this was a feeling unlike any other they had ever experienced. They'd known from a young age if one of them was scared or hurt, but this was a feeling of absolute despair.

She smiled at the men as she grasped at Daisy's hand. "Thank you, gentlemen. We need a moment to powder our noses." Violet winked before dragging Daisy to the back of the building and out the door.

The sisters drew in deep breaths and then looked at each other. "Lily," was all they said before they took off running through town to get to Lily. They didn't feel the cold and didn't care that they left their coats at the party. They didn't care their parents would worry where they were. All they knew was Lily was at home and needed them.

The cold air burned their lungs as they raced down Main Street. They didn't talk to each other. They didn't have the breath to spare. Jumping the hedgerow, Violet fell to the frozen earth. Her knee cried out in pain, but she ignored it. The pain in her heart was driving her home.

Racing through their backyard, they saw the headlights coming up the street. They bent at the waist and gulped in air as the car pulled up to the house.

"That's John," Violet gasped as she and Daisy rushed toward the car.

"Rhonda! What's wrong," Daisy called out as Rhonda hurried from the car and around to John. John pushed back his seat, and out climbed Lily. She didn't blink. She only clutched at the large coat draped around her.

Violet and Daisy slid to a stop. Lily looked past them as if they weren't even standing there. "What happened?" Daisy asked unemotionally.

"Let's get her inside," Rhonda said quietly and cast a glance toward Frank's house.

Rhonda helped them walk her upstairs to her room. "It was Frank. John had just proposed, and we were, um . . . celebrating, when we heard the scream. We leapt from the car and saw her naked. It appears Frank had taken her virtue, and Rex had taken a picture to prove it."

"Rex? But they were no longer friends. I don't

understand," Daisy said quietly as they watched Lily step into the hot spray of her shower.

"It was all an act. Rex bet his hot rod that Frank couldn't take Lily's virginity."

"It was all about a car?" Violet asked, astonished. When Rhonda nodded, Violet looked to Daisy. "I'm going to kill him."

"It's okay," Lily said, stepping from the shower and into her bedroom. "I'm ruined, and there's nothing anyone can do about it. No one will want me now."

The girls encircled her. "That's not true, Lily. True love does exist. Do not let Frank or Rex win."

"I need to go to sleep. Thank you, Rhonda. And please thank John, too. I'm beyond mortified about tonight."

"It's not your fault, Lily. I've never seen John more upset. We are your friends; remember that."

Lily felt a tear slip down her cheek as she climbed into bed. She pulled the sheets up to her chin and closed her eyes. She heard them leave the room and close the door. She didn't know how long she would lie there, just existing in some kind of purgatory. She couldn't feel happiness or sadness. She couldn't feel at all.

The roar of an engine interrupted the still of the night as a car sped down the street. That was all her virginity was worth—the price of a car. Lily sat up and pushed aside the white lace curtain. She saw Frank with his new prize, pulling into his driveway next door. For the rest of her life, she was going to have to see him. She was going to know he was right next door. She felt so dirty, so violated. He had killed her dream of true love.

Lily was about to get back to bed when she saw two figures stalking across her yard. What were her sisters doing? In the first bit of emotion she had felt since the incident, she gasped. Her sisters! Lily ran from her room and down the curved staircase. She had to get to her sisters.

"Nice car, Frank," Daisy whistled.

Frank looked skeptically at her and Violet as they walked toward him. "Yeah, thanks."

"So, where's Lily? We thought she'd be home by now," Violet asked.

Frank shrugged. "We got in a fight and broke up. She left on her own."

"Oh, that's too bad," Daisy said as she frowned. "You know, there's something interesting about being triplets. We feel things."

"Feel things?" Frank asked and stepped onto his porch.

"Yes," Violet nodded. "Like when one of us is in pain."

Frank didn't say anything but stared at them in surprise.

"You hurt our sister," Daisy said with such menace in her voice his eyes widened.

"And we don't take too kindly to that," Violet said as they approached him.

Lily reached for the door at the same time it opened. "Lily Rae!" her mother exclaimed. "What is going on? I got a feeling something was wrong; I left your father at the party and hurried home."

Lily gulped and looked at her mother. Love and concern shown on her mother's face, and Lily couldn't take it. "I'm so sorry, Mama." She buried herself in her mother's open arms, sobbing.

"There, there, dear. It can't be the end of the world.

Come into the kitchen, and I'll make you some tea."

Lily forgot about her sisters as her mother's warmth comforted her. "I won't be able to hide it, Mama. I'm so sorry. I'm a disgrace."

"You'll never be a disgrace to me," she said kindly, then put an apron on over her beautiful dress and filled the teapot with water.

"It was Frank . . ." Lily found herself confessing everything—Lovers Pond, the proposal that didn't happen, the picture, John and Rhonda. "Oh no . . . Daisy and Violet. They were walking over there when you got here."

"Walking where?" her mother asked as gently as she could. Her mother had held her through the whole story not saying a word, only calmly stoking her hair.

"To see Frank. He just pulled in."

Her mother cupped her cheeks and looked into her eyes with a kind smile. "Stay here, dear, and enjoy your cup of tea."

Her mother stood up, opened a drawer, pulled out a rolling pin, and walked out the back door.

The sound of a spatula connecting with a cheek at full swing was a very satisfying sound for Violet. The way Frank's eyes bugged out almost brought a smile to her face.

"Did you think we'd let you get away with this?" Violet asked, pulling her arm back to smack him again. Frank grabbed her wrist but was rewarded with a hard *thwack* to the head by the wooden spoon Daisy held.

"No one breaks our sister's heart with no repercussions. Just because your family is powerful doesn't mean we will sit back and take it," Daisy growled and hit him over the head again.

"I didn't do anything she didn't let me do," Frank said

as he dropped Violet's arm and turned to grab Daisy's.

Violet grinned and smacked him with the spatula again. "Do you think that makes it better, you manipulative pig?"

Frank's face was growing red in the darkness, and Violet knew they were pushing him. She went to hit him again—the anger and pain of what he did to Lily overwhelming her common sense—when he managed to grab them both by their arms.

The sound of glass breaking startled them all. They froze and looked down the driveway at their mother, holding a rolling pin in her hand. The hot rod's windshield was shattered.

"Let go of my daughters right now," she ordered.

Frank gave a little snort of defiance. Their mother smashed the driver's side window. Frank let go. Daisy and Violet hurried from the porch to stand by their mom. Daisy turned and saw Lily, wearing only her nightgown and carrying a broom, racing across the yard.

"You dare hurt my daughter after I opened our house to you?" their mother asked in a tone they'd never heard before. Lily slid to a stop as Daisy and Violet encircled her waist with their arms in a show of support.

"She's nothing but a fast hussy," Frank spat.

Lily pushed away from her sisters, marched up the steps, and broke the broom over his head. The resounding crack filled the night air and seemed to echo down the street. A second later her mother was by her side.

"Do you feel better yet, dear?" her mother asked as she steered her down the stairs, never taking her eyes off Frank. Lily could feel his anger snowballing.

"Getting there." Lily had enjoyed the look of shock and

disbelief on his face when she broke the broom over his big head.

"This will help." Her mother handed her the rolling pin, and Lily gripped it in two hands. The headlights were smashed first. Frank raced down the stairs, but her mother simply held up her hands to stop him.

"It's a shame you've been drinking and destroyed your car," her mother clucked.

The hood was next. Lily beat it until sweat dripped from her forehead.

"I'll be telling the police about that when they get here. I saw you swerving all over the road. It was a good thing I had seen how much you drank at the party and decided to take Lily home myself."

"No one will believe you," Frank spat.

"Everyone will believe me. Girls, let's go. Oh, and you can keep the broom. It looks like you'll have a mess to clean up." Her mother held out her hands as Lily and Daisy each took one with Violet leading the way back to the house.

They were quiet as they walked across the yard. Their mother ushered them inside and pulled the teapot from the stove. "Everyone, go upstairs and get cleaned up. Then come down here for some tea."

Lily followed her sisters back up the stairs. Her heart may have been broken, but she was feeling again. With each dent and each broken window, she'd felt herself gaining control of her life again.

"Was anyone else completely dumbfounded when Mom broke his windows?" Violet asked when they reached the sitting room on the second floor.

"I couldn't believe it. I mean, she teaches Sunday school," Lily said as she shook her head.

"Did you see Frank's face?" Daisy asked before snorting. "His eyes bugged so far out of his head I was afraid they'd fall out."

Lily felt the dam break. She cried, she laughed, and she held on tightly to her sisters. They would get through this. She would get through this. Out of all that had happened, she was still filled with love. Her sisters' and mother's love gave her determination. She may never be ready to love again, but she would have love in her life.

Chapter Six

"**M**iss Rose, this is simply amazing." Violet beamed at Chef Nichols's praise. Her torte was a work of art. She'd not only survived Christmas week at the restaurant, her dishes had won the praise of customers and earned the respect of the head chef.

It hadn't been easy leaving Lily at home to come into Lexington. But after they had gotten cleaned up and had gone downstairs, Violet had decided to tell her mother about her dreams and her once-in-a-lifetime opportunity. The sisters had all agreed there was a side to their mother they had never seen before, and hoped that side would understand their dreams of exploring life outside of Keeneston.

She had understood, and a couple hours later, when their father came home, she had informed him she would be taking Violet into Lexington every night this next week and would need the car. Their father seemed confused, but their mother winked.

And so tonight was her last night at the restaurant. Her mother was her last customer. Chef Nichols sent the torte out with a waiter and turned back to Violet. "You did good, kid." He reached into his pocket and pulled out a thick packet of papers. "You'll find three letters of recommendation and a list of all the schools you should apply to. I will be calling them all personally first thing in the morning. And when you complete culinary school, you will have a job waiting for you here."

Violet flung her arms around his neck, surprising him and the rest of the kitchen staff. "Thank you."

"You deserve it. Don't be a stranger, and let me know which school you decide to go to."

"I will! Thank you so much, chef. You just made my dream come true."

Chef Nichols took off his white hat and set it on the prep table. "I didn't make it come true. You did that yourself. Now get out of here, kid."

Violet said goodbye to the staff and rushed through the swinging door that connected the kitchen to the dining room. Her mother had her eyes closed as she tasted the torte.

"Mom, I got the recommendation!"

Her mom's eyes popped open, and she stood up to hug Violet. "I didn't doubt it for a second. This is delicious. Come on, let's go home and tell the family."

Violet grabbed her mother's hand and walked out of the restaurant. "I hope Dad won't be too upset."

"Oh, he won't be. I know he's gruff on the outside, but underneath it all, he only wants you to be happy. He'll just worry about you constantly. I'm dreading the long-distance bill from him calling you all the time."

Violet closed the car door and only half listened to her mother's excited chatter on the way home. Her mind was filled with the streets of France. The hustle of city life, the smell of the freshly baked croissants coming from the small cafés that lined the old cobbled streets, and the endless possibilities. Before she knew it, she was home.

Lily and Daisy rushed out the door and down the porch

steps. "You won't believe it," Lily called out as Violet opened her door.

"Believe what, dear?" her mother asked.

"The Shillings aren't coming back. They're staying in New York. Their grandmother holds the purse strings to the family, and John Wolfe just stopped by and told us the news. Someone told old Mrs. Shilling what happened, and she was so mad she cut Frank off and ordered the family back to New York. There was a moving truck here all night, and a *For Sale* sign was just put up."

"Is that so?" Her mother smiled serenely. "What a pity."

"Mom?" the three sisters asked all at once.

"Yes, dears?"

"Did you call Mrs. Shilling?" Lily asked with disbelief.

"Of course. I wasn't going to let that hoodlum live next door to us. There's nothing I wouldn't do for my babies. Even if one of them is going to be all the way in France."

"Oh," Daisy and Lily gasped.

"Did you get the recommendation?" Daisy asked.

"Of course she did," Lily squealed before she and Daisy enveloped Violet in a tight hug.

"I did. He even gave me the addresses of where to apply. I'll be sending out my applications tomorrow, along with his personal letter of recommendation."

"I knew you could do it, Vi. But you better not forget us back home when you're off gallivanting across Europe," her father's slow, Southern drawl said from the door to the house.

"Never, Daddy!" Violet flew up the stairs and into her father's arms. She had her family's blessing. Now all she needed was an acceptance from one of the three schools she was applying to.

Violet ran out to meet the postman two months after
sending off her first application. It was the start of spring.
She hoped it was a new start for her, too. She heard the
front door open behind her and turned to see her sisters
running after her.

"Did it get here?" Lily asked.

"I don't know yet," she said as she grabbed the
mountain of mail from their bemused postman.

"Daisy, there's something for you." Violet handed her a
thick envelope. "It's from the University of Kentucky."

"Hurry! Open it," Lily said excitedly. "Mom, come
quick!"

Their mother hurried out the door with her new broom
in hand. "What is it?"

The sisters didn't say anything as they watched Daisy
tear into the envelope and scan the letter. "I got in," she said
with disbelief.

Her mother clapped her hands. "I have a daughter
going to college! I have to call your father at the store."

"Wait, did you get anything?" Lily asked Violet as she
sorted through the mail.

Violet's hands trembled when she saw the postage from
France. She dropped the other mail onto the ground, still
holding three envelopes in her hands. Their mother came to
her side and took a deep breath. "Open them, dear."

Violet slid her finger under the seam of the first
envelope. She scanned the letter and handed it to her
mother. "I'm so sorry. We didn't want you to go there
anyway."

Violet heard Lily and Daisy groan and murmur their
encouragement as she ripped into the second envelope. "I

got in!" Violet cried out. But just as fast she felt her heart plummet. "I didn't get any financial aid, and look at how much it costs."

"I'm sure we can manage," her mother said gently as she leaned in to look at the paper. "Oh my!"

"How much is it?" Lily asked.

"Two thousand five hundred dollars a year," Violet said with defeat.

"I could hold off on UK," Daisy offered. "I have a partial scholarship, so Mom and Dad could put the three hundred dollars they were going to have to pay for me toward your education."

Their mother shook her head sadly. "I don't think even that would help, dear. But it's so nice of you to offer."

"And I couldn't let you do that," Violet said as she turned over the last envelope. Her finger slid under the seal and she worried her lip as she pulled out the letter. She read it once and then read it again. "Oh my goodness."

"What is it?" her mother asked, no longer wanting to wait for an answer as she pulled the letter out of Violet's hand. "Oh my goodness! Lily, call your father and tell him to pick up a bottle of champagne on his way home. My daughter got into UK, and my other daughter got a full scholarship to culinary school!"

"Is this real?" Violet asked, stunned.

Lily and Daisy grabbed her as they jumped up and down in a circle and celebrated. "Okay, okay, I'll go call Dad." Lily laughed and hurried into the house.

Lily's heart still hurt, and she forced her lips into a smile. Of course she was happy for her sisters. They were following their dreams, and she would support them all the way, which was why she could never tell them how empty she felt inside.

Between the unknown power her mother wielded and an apparently very strong right hook John possessed, Rex hadn't breathed a word of the incident to anyone. Instead, he had expressed his anger by breaking the school windows. He was caught and had enlisted in the military to avoid jail time. With Frank and Rex both gone, there was no reason for Lily to still feel empty, but she did. Her innocence was gone, both figuratively and literally. However, her heart beat a little happier when she saw others in love. And for purely selfish reasons, she had started trying her hand at matchmaking. Just because true love didn't exist for her didn't mean it didn't exist at all.

Lily helped her mother clean the kitchen after the celebratory dinner. Daisy and Violet were upstairs trying to decide what they needed to get before heading off to college. Talk of graduating high school had turned into talk of life away from home, and Lily was sad to say she felt left out.

"Lil," her father said, startling her as she washed the final dish.

"Yes, Daddy?"

"I've been thinking. I know you don't want to go to college, but you're a real good people person, and you have great organizational skills. I'm swamped at the store, and I could use a gal with a good head on her shoulders to help me out. I know it's unorthodox, but I'd like you to come work for me."

"Work for you? At the drugstore?"

"I need help with the soda fountain after school. And I believe the ladies would feel more comfortable asking you for assistance with womanly matters. You would be a very big help to me."

Lily put the plate down and looked into the hopeful eyes of her father. It was true; she was great at running the drugstore and soda fountain. She didn't have anything else to do. She could always be a secretary. But taking dictation in Lexington didn't sound very exciting. Maybe if she worked with her father, then she would be able to earn enough money to get her own place. And maybe, just maybe, move away from Keeneston to start a new life.

"I would love that, Dad." Lily smiled and saw the relief in her father's eyes. His daughters all had a purpose in life now. He always liked having things in place. With Lily working for him, she was now situated like her sisters.

"What a wonderful idea, honey." Her mother smiled as she hugged her husband and then Lily. "Why don't you girls head to bed? It's been an exciting day, and I am sure you are all exhausted."

Daisy grabbed her hand and before Lily could say goodnight, Daisy had dragged her upstairs with Violet pushing her from behind.

"What's going on?" Lily asked.

"We are going to sneak out and celebrate," Violet whispered. "Get dressed up. Mary Jane is throwing a party since her parents are out of town."

"Men, liquor, and dancing. It's time for the Rose sisters to shed their perfect-girl images." Daisy grinned as she tossed an outfit onto Lily's bed.

"Hurry and change; we'll take care of the rest," Violet ordered as they hurried from the room.

In a loud voice, Daisy called out, "Okay, goodnight, Lily. See you in the morning."

"Night, Lil," Violet similarly echoed. She then leaned over the rail and bellowed down the stairs, "Goodnight, Mom and Dad. Love you!"

"Goodnight, dears. Love you, too, but do try not to scream so loudly. Manners at all times."

Violet rolled her eyes, and Lily clapped a hand over her mouth as she stood in her door and watched her sisters. "Yes, ma'am."

Violet turned to Lily and pointed to her room. "Go get dressed. Mom and Dad will be asleep in no time."

Lily turned and looked at the outfit on her bed. It was a little more daring than she had worn before. Her sisters had picked out a skirt that had become a little too short and a shirt with a V-neck that showed off her cleavage. With a sigh, Lily changed and waited to see what else her sisters had in store for her that night.

Violet jumped from the last branch of the large tree in front of Lily's window. The impact with the ground vibrated up her legs and made her teeth click together, but it was worth it. She and Daisy had talked just that morning about Lily. She had changed. Sure, Lily smiled but it no longer reached her eyes. Sure, she was still polite but she no longer seemed to care about life. It was time they changed that.

Daisy dropped to the ground, and then Lily finally landed with a soft *thump* onto the grass. Holding her finger to her lips, Violet led them to the driveway. With a smile of accomplishment, Violet held up the keys to the family car. Slowly she opened the driver's door and slid the car into neutral.

"I'll steer, you push," she whispered as her sisters stepped in front of the hood of the car and pushed. Slowly they turned the car and pushed it down the driveway. When they reached the street, the giggling sisters jumped into the car as it coasted downhill.

"Oh my, I can't believe we just did that," Lily laughed.

"We have a couple months left until we have to grow up. I say we enjoy every second of it together." Daisy held out her pinky for a pinky promise.

Violet pulled into the grass at Mary Jane's farm. The party was in her parents' barn. She could already hear music playing and the sound of happy laughter. She linked arms with Lily and Daisy and pushed open the barn doors.

People didn't exactly stop and stare, but there were plenty of raised eyebrows as they closed the door behind them and joined the fray. No one came to talk to them as they walked through the crowd to where bottles of beer sat. Daisy picked one up and handed it to Lily.

"Here's to moving on," Daisy said and handed a bottle to Violet. The sisters clinked bottlenecks, and the party was on. Lily smiled, batted her eyelashes, and the men came running.

As Violet was swung around in swing dance after swing dance and jive after jive, she saw Lily flirting her way through the party. Even if she wasn't over Frank, it was at least a start. And now that her sister was settled and on the road to mending her heart, it was time for Violet to enjoy her last few months in Keeneston. She would miss her sisters, but she had a life of her own to experience. And experience it she would.

Chapter Seven

Paris, France
One year later . . .

V iolet breathed in the hot air of the kitchen. She lived
for nights like this. The chaos of the kitchen, the chefs
yelling, the frantic rush to fill orders. It energized her, and
she knew this was what she wanted out of life. Her entrée
was going to be featured in the restaurant owned by the
culinary school. And somewhere in the crowd was one of
the teachers who would grade it for her final exam.

One more month of classes and she would give her final
presentation. One more month and she would graduate.
Then she could go public with her romance. One more
month and she could be a chef in her own kitchen with the
love of her life by her side.

It was true. Paris was known for food and romance, and
it had lived up to its reputation. The first day of culinary
school she had looked up from her seat and into the eyes of
the man she would spend the rest of her life with. They
took it slowly, knowing it was a mistake to get involved.
But they couldn't stop themselves any more than one could
stop the earth from spinning.

Needless to say, there had been plenty of late nights in
the kitchen. And she'd learned that there were a whole lot
of things you could do on a prep table that didn't involve

food. Violet basked in the freedom of living abroad. The pressure to always be the perfect woman and the perfect daughter she felt in Keeneston was gone. Instead, she lived life to its fullest without a care in the world . . . except for her heart and her cooking.

"You're doing great. They love it," he whispered into her ear as he came up from behind her. "I plan on showing you how much you made my mouth water tonight. I'll meet you back here after everyone has gone."

Violet felt her face flush, and she grinned as she plated one of her entrées to look as beautiful as it tasted. "Yes, chef," she answered saucily back to her teacher. She heard his satisfied chuckle as he headed back into the restaurant.

She knew it was wrong, but at this point she didn't care. True love was true love and nothing was going to stop it. There was only one other woman in her class of seventeen. Violet and Luc had been careful that no one else knew or even suspected their connection. It had started off innocently enough when she needed help with her crêpes. It had escalated to passionate moments in both his office and the practice kitchen in the early morning hours. But one more month and they wouldn't have to be careful anymore. As soon as she graduated, they could bring their relationship out in the open and claim it had just started.

Violet set the plate on the counter and hit the bell indicating the table was ready to be served. A waiter swept through the swinging door and took the plates into the restaurant. Entrées were completely served, and it was time to work with her classmates on the desserts. In just one more hour the restaurant would be empty and cleanup complete.

Violet moaned happily as Luc pulled away and tossed the

condom in the trashcan. "You did great tonight, *mon chouchou*," he told her as he pulled his shirt on over his broad chest and started to button it up.

Violet nibbled on her lip as she watched him dress quickly and efficiently. "Are you in a hurry?"

"*Oui*, I have a student coming in early tomorrow to go over a menu."

Violet sighed as she watched his flat stomach and impressive buns disappear under his clothing.

"I've been thinking about when I go home . . ."

Luc's dark eyes met hers, and Violet stopped her thought. How could she want him again so soon?

He smiled, and she had her answer. "*Oui*?"

"I wondered how you would feel about a trip to America. I've sent out my résumé to restaurants here and in Kentucky. I'd like to stay here. However, I want to go home for at least a visit and have a backup plan in case I don't get a job here."

"It sounds divine, but let's not plan anything until you graduate and then finally we can be a real couple."

Violet giggled and buttoned her dress. "I'm pretty sure what we just did was us being a very real couple."

Luc grinned back at her before leaning forward and kissing her. "I'll see you in class tomorrow. Get some sleep."

Violet finished getting dressed and grabbed her purse from the office. She locked up the kitchen and enjoyed the walk through the historical streets of the city. Paris never slept. It was so different from Keeneston. She didn't know if she ever really wanted to go back home. Her sisters wrote her every week, and they called each other once a month.

Daisy was enjoying the University of Kentucky. She'd

opted to join a sorority instead of trying to impress the
Keeneston Belles. Her sorority focused on charity work,
studying, and hosting parties. Daisy was really coming into
her own. When Violet had asked her about dating, Daisy
told her she'd gone out on a couple dates but hadn't been
too serious about anyone yet.

Lily had written to tell them about their new neighbors.
She was glad when Frank's house had sold to newlyweds,
and she had hoped it would ease some of the bad
memories. The husband, Mr. Schniter, was older than his
young bride, Edna, who was just a couple years older than
Lily. Mr. Schniter was a traveling salesman and, having
been in the military, had taught his young wife how to
shoot his service pistol so she would be safe while he was
gone. Lily wrote about how he had tried to get her to try it,
and when she finally had, she had shot out the windshield
of his car parked to the right of the women. Mr. Schniter
had taken back the pistol with a shake of his head and
handed Lily her broom. He joked that he felt better leaving
his wife at home knowing Lily could wield a broom like a
police baton.

When Violet had talked to Lily about her dating again,
Lily had grown quiet.

"I don't think I'll ever be able to trust another man, Vi.
After feeling the pain of a broken heart and the betrayal I
suffered at Frank's hands . . ." Lily had said before changing
the subject.

So much was changing around Violet. They were
growing up and growing apart. They were no longer the
inseparable Rose sisters but now just Violet, just Daisy, or
just Lily. It was sad but, at the same time, empowering. To
only be known as part of a whole and then experience life
as just yourself was inspiring.

Violet passed couples pouring out of the cinema and smiled at them holding hands. Soon she would have that with Luc. He wasn't much older than she was. He was twenty-eight to her nineteen. That was nothing compared to her parents' thirteen-year age difference.

Violet turned down the alley that led to her apartment. The night air was warm, and she took a moment to soak in the noise of an active city before pushing the key into her door. The door pushed over that day's pile of mail, and she bent to pick it up. There were letters from her mother and sisters and some bills that she tossed on the small table. But her hands shook when she saw two more envelopes from restaurants where she had applied for work.

One was covered with stamps and postage marks. It was from a restaurant in Louisville, the top gourmet restaurant in the state. She cracked the seal and hurried to open it. Her excitement plummeted when she read that they had no need of a woman chef. Unfortunately, it was still unheard of for a woman to run a large kitchen. Baking and putting out cookbooks, sure. But ordering men around and putting out exquisite cuisine instead of casseroles — no way.

Violet crumpled the paper and tossed it in the trashcan. She opened the letter from a small luxury restaurant outside of Paris and gasped with excitement. She had a job offer! She didn't bother to notice it was only six in the morning at home when she picked up the phone and called.

"Is someone dead?" her father's sleepy voice asked over the long-distance call.

"I got a job!"

"Who is this?"

"Your daughter," Violet laughed.

"Which one?"

"The only one who would call you this early."

"*Humph.* So, my baby girl got her first job. When are you coming home?"

Violet nibbled on her lip, unsure how to break the news. "Well, I didn't get the job in Louisville. I got a job here in France."

"Who is it? Is someone dead?" Violet heard her mother mumble.

"It's our daughter."

"Which one?" She heard her mother ask.

"The one that's left us and isn't coming back," her father told her before turning his attention back to Violet. "What about the job offer with Chef Nichols?"

"It's my last choice. If I work at one of these restaurants for just a couple years, I can come back and run my own restaurant. I could own it, run it, and cook for it. It's what I've always dreamed of."

"Well, then I guess I need to say congratulations. I am proud of you, Violet. We just miss your smiling face around here."

"I know. I miss you all, too. I should be home to stay in a couple years, but I'll be back after graduation to visit."

"You better be. Although I'm sure we won't even recognize you. Here, your mother wants to talk to you."

Violet felt a tear roll down her cheek as she waited for her mother to take the phone. She missed her parents so much. "You got a job? That's fantastic! Tell me all about it."

By the time Violet talked to her mother and promised to tell Lily all about it, she was still too excited to sleep. She pushed open her window and sat at her table. Looking out over the streets of Paris, she wrote letters to her sisters.

She stamped them and walked downstairs to place them in the mailbox. When she made it back upstairs, she saw it was already two in the morning. She hurried to get ready for bed, but just as she feared, she couldn't fall asleep. Images of cooking in the small luxury restaurant and coming home to Luc filled her thoughts. They could be married first here in France with his family and then again in Keeneston with all her friends and family surrounding them.

The two of them had talked about marriage when things turned serious. She had let him know she wasn't someone who took their special times together lightly. Luc had promised he loved her, and they would marry as soon as she graduated. He cautioned that if they let their relationship be known before that, Violet might be asked to leave culinary school. Neither of them wanted to take that chance.

As the sun began to creep through the window, Violet gave up trying to sleep. Her grade from the night before would be posted at the school, and if she got to class early enough, she could catch Luc right after his students left and tell him about her job. Violet hurried to get dressed, and when she walked the streets to school, she found herself skipping.

Chapter Eight

Violet pushed open the glass doors to her culinary school and walked into the lobby. She passed students studying at the round tables and headed upstairs to Luc's office. Nadine, the other woman in her class, came hurrying down the stairs with a cake balanced precariously in her hands.

"Nadine, do you need help?"

"*Oui!* I am afraid I will drop this beautiful cake Monsieur Luc helped me with. I just could not get the frosting to taste correct, but Monsieur Luc had just the right touch to fix it."

Violet smiled at her friend and grabbed the books she was carrying in the crook of her arm along with her bakery kit. "Let me take these to your locker for you."

"*Merci!* I am going to run this cake home real quick. I'll see you in class."

Violet watched as a rumpled and harried Nadine raced out of the building and down the street as fast as she could with her cake. Violet turned and walked down the stairs to the back of the building where their lockers were. She would see Luc soon enough to tell him the good news.

"That's fantastic, *mon chouchou*!" Luc smiled from behind his desk. "I wish I could kiss you, but there are too many people around. Tonight I will make sure to kiss you everywhere."

Violet blushed and tried not to giggle. Even though she was not so innocent anymore, his candid talk always heated her face . . . and other places.

"Now that I don't have to worry about a job, I can focus on my final exams and be completely prepared to make my dishes for the teachers."

"As if you need much practice. You'll do wonderfully," Luc told her as he stood up and slid into his white chef's coat.

"Oh, I forgot, I wanted to see if you would like to join me this weekend at the film festival. It looks like great fun." Violet had the festival article she had cut out of the paper in her purse. It would be so romantic and carefree. They could just be boyfriend and girlfriend there. No cooking, no worrying about school . . . it would be perfect.

"I am sorry, *mon chouchou*, but I've warned you this last month of school is always crazy for me. Everyone needs help on their dishes in preparation for their exams. Unfortunately, I will be here all weekend, handling confectionary calamities and duck disasters."

Violet tried to remain smiling, but she was sad that they never seemed to be able to be together in public. Less than a month, she told herself over and over again as she went to her first class.

Violet was deader than a doornail. The next day was her crêpes exam. She had to prepare breakfast, lunch, and dinner crêpes in both sweet and savory. If the pan was too hot or the batter too thick, she would fail her exam. And right now she didn't know what was going on, but her practice crêpes were completely wrong. There were bubbles and tears and . . . they were just a disaster.

Violet looked around for Nadine, but the kitchen was empty. She had been so engrossed in her work she hadn't even heard her friend leave. Everyone else had perfected their dishes and had gone home. That made Violet feel even worse about her crêpe catastrophe. She glanced at her watch and was surprised to find it was after midnight.

She grabbed her cast-iron crêpe pan with the mangled crêpe still on it and went in search of a teacher. She just hoped someone was here. The hallway was lit for the custodians to polish the floors. Her heart dropped as she passed darkened office after darkened office.

Tears formed in Violet's eyes as she walked farther down the hallway that housed the teachers' offices. She was going to fail. A year of hard work and some flour and eggs were going to be her demise.

"Oh, thank goodness!" Violet audibly gasped as she saw a sliver a light coming from under Luc's door.

Hurrying the rest of the way down the hall, Violet didn't stop to knock on the closed door. She turned the knob and burst in.

"I need your help, Luc," Violet called out in panic as she looked miserably down at her crêpe pan. "I can't get my crêpe to—"

The woman's shriek broke through Violet's harried plea for help. "Nadine?" Violet managed to stammer. Her friend hadn't left after all. Instead she was naked and splayed out on Luc's desk with Luc's mouth feasting on her.

"Oh hell," Violet cursed as Luc's head popped up.

"Violet," Luc and Nadine cried at the same time.

"Please, Vi, don't tell anyone. We're in love and—"

"And you'll be together once you graduate," Violet finished for Nadine. She watched as Luc's eyes went wide, and Nadine shot a glance between them.

"*Mon chouchou*," Luc cooed.

"Yes?" Violet and Nadine responded at the same time. Nadine turned red and spouted a slew of rapid-fire French cuss words before kicking Luc in the nose.

"I'm so sorry, Violet."

"So am I," Violet said as an angry and tearful Nadine made her way out of the office with her clothes clutched against her chest.

Luc stood and grabbed his shirt from the floor to press against his bleeding nose as he turned on Violet. "*Mon chouchou*, it's always been you I loved. She bewitched me," Luc pleaded.

Violet held out her pan. "What did I do wrong with my crêpe?"

Luc froze in the act of pulling up his pants and with wide eyes stared at her in confusion.

"My crêpes? What did I do wrong?" Violet asked again as she shoved the pan under his nose.

Luc looked down at the pan and touched the crêpe. "Too much butter and too high of heat."

"Thank you," Violet said with a nod before turning for the door.

"Ah, *mon chouchou*, don't leave. I love you. I didn't want her. I want you. Please, don't you have anything to say?"

Violet felt her hand tighten on the handle to her crêpe pan. "Yes, I do. Kiss my grits!" Violet swung the pan and was rewarded with a resounding *thunk*. Luc stood so still Violet thought he was stunned. For a moment she thought about swinging the pan again to erase the stupid grin stuck on his face. But then his eyes rolled back into his head, and he crumpled to the ground.

"Good riddance," Violet said as she sauntered back to the kitchen.

With a flick of her wrist, the crêpe folded perfectly as she presented it to one of her teachers. Violet held her breath as the serious-looking teacher cut into the dessert crêpe. She'd received pleasant nods from the other teachers who had scored her breakfast, lunch, and dinner crêpes, but it was well known among the students that Chef François was the toughest nut to crack.

Violet bit down on her lip as Chef François fingered the texture of the crêpe and then wrote something down on his pad of paper. He held the fork up to the light and studied it from all angles before taking more notes.

"And what makes your crêpe any different from the others I have tried this morning?" Chef asked with something akin to a sneer on his face.

Violet smiled nervously as she wiped her hands on her apron. "It has a little bit of home in it."

"The United States?" he asked with a snort of disdain.

"Yes, sir. Kentucky."

"I fail to see what Kentucky can offer fine dining, Mademoiselle Rose."

Violet gulped as he finally put the forkful of crêpe into his mouth. His eyes closed as he worked his palate. Chef narrowed his eyes at her and slid his fork back onto the crêpe before cutting off another bite. He chewed and his eyes rolled upward in contemplation.

"Interesting. The chocolate is very smooth, but there is an interesting bite to it. I though it was cayenne pepper, but it's not."

"It's Kentucky bourbon, Chef."

Chef François's lips thinned as he stared at the now-offending crêpe. "*Humph*," was the only sound he made before walking away.

With shaking hands, Violet set the plate aside and cleaned her station. She was going to fail. She was going to lose her job and go home with her head hung low. Not to mention she was no longer virtuous. Golly jeepers, she was done for.

"Attention! Your grades will be posted tonight in the lobby for this portion of your exam. Tomorrow you will prepare us a breathtaking duck. Dismissed."

Violet hurried from the kitchen before Nadine could catch up with her. Glancing over her shoulder, she saw Nadine with bags under her eyes, trying to get her attention. Violet pretended not to notice as she bolted out the door. She was not going to talk to the woman who inadvertently crushed her dreams and her heart. Violet knew Nadine was just as much a victim as she was, but that didn't make the pain in her chest ease.

Violet turned left out of the school and wound her way back to the apartment with hopes that Nadine had given up and had gone back to her place. Sighing with relief when no one was standing by the door, Violet dug into her purse and pulled out her keys. There was only one person she could talk to right now.

She picked up the phone and asked the operator to place a long-distance call. Violet crossed her fingers and hoped her sister picked up. She didn't feel like talking to her parents right now.

"Rose residence," Lily's voice said from an ocean away.

"Oh thank goodness it's you," Violet said before great sobs broke forth.

"Vi! What is it?"

"It's my heart. I thought he loved me," Violet wailed into the phone.

Lily sucked in a breath, and Violet heard her curse. "I'm so sorry, Vi. So Luc broke up with you?"

"No! I caught him with his head between Nadine's legs! He told her everything he told me — that he loved her and after graduation they could be together. I'm such a fool."

"I am so sorry, Vi," Lily whispered.

"Why didn't you tell me?" Violet yelled at her sister.

"Tell you what?"

"How much love hurts," Violet said, curling up on her bed and crying.

"It's how you know it was real."

"I'm never doing it again then. It feels as if the whole world is pressing on my chest while every person in it is laughing at me. How could I have been so stupid? Well, never again. I will never trust a man, let alone love one again."

"You're not alone, Vi. I'll be right there with you as we get old together. Are you going to come home?"

"And let him win? Never. I have my dream job lined up, and I'll be home when I am good and ready."

"Good for you, Vi," Lily cheered. "Are you done with your exams?"

"One more. Duck. So far I've gotten all A's except for one B. How are you doing?"

Lily chuckled as if thinking of something. "Good. I miss you. Our new neighbor is very entertaining. She's our age, but married an older man. She seems to really love him, but she always likes to act younger. We went skinny-dipping at

Lovers Pond and were almost caught by the sheriff."

"Skinny-dipping! That sounds terrifyingly free. I just might have to try it."

"You should. And I'm letting my hair grow out more. Daisy loves UK. She's been dragging me along on all these double dates, but my heart isn't in it. And honestly, neither is Daisy's. She's just having a great time learning and doing charity work."

Violet smiled as the tears slowed, although now she was feeling a bit homesick. "How is work going for you? What's it like working with Dad?"

"It's not bad. He's been giving me more and more responsibility. I've started working with the doctors to make sure prescriptions are right, and I'm now completely in charge of the soda fountain. Oh . . . and I'm a bridesmaid in another wedding coming up. I fixed up Donald and Suzie. Now they're getting married."

"It seems you are quite the matchmaker," Violet laughed.

"I think it's easier when your heart is no longer in it. You can see the way couples look at each other and know if it's real or not."

Violet looked at the clock and gasped. "We've been talking forever! I'll need a second job to pay for this. I better go, but thank you for being there, Lily. I love you."

"I love you, too!"

Violet hung up the phone and grabbed her cooking supplies. She raced out the door and almost barreled into Nadine. "Jeez Louise!"

"I'm so sorry, but I had to talk to you. Luc is in the hospital." Violet just snorted at Nadine's announcement. "I went to see him, and his wife was there."

That got Violet's attention. "Wife? What wife? Luc wasn't married."

"He used us, Violet. He was married the whole time with three kids at home."

Empty. That's what Violet was. She was empty. She would never allow another man to take advantage of her. From now on she would be in charge. "Well, I guess we shouldn't really be surprised. Although now I don't feel bad about hitting him with a crêpe pan."

Nadine laughed. "So, that's what happened to him. He told the doctors and his wife he fell down the stairs at the school. I giggled, and his wife narrowed her eyes at me so I left."

Violet let out a deep breath. Nadine was still a friend. And boy, did she need a friend who understood what she was going through right now. Violet laced her arm through Nadine's and smiled at her. "Come on, let's go get our grades and then do a practice run on our duck for tomorrow."

Nadine smiled back, and while Violet's heart was still broken, at least she had a friend to help her through it.

Chapter Nine

Violet hung the framed diploma in her new flat just outside of Paris. Today marked the one-year anniversary of culinary school graduation, and she'd just been promoted to saucier. She was now in charge of all sauces and sautés at the luxury restaurant where she worked. It was a huge accomplishment. If she worked hard, it was possible to make sous-chef in another couple of years.

With the title of saucier came a higher paycheck. She looked around at the packed boxes in her new flat and smiled. She'd immediately started her job in the restaurant at the winery after graduation. It was an amazing place to work, and she'd learned so much. The head chef was supportive and really enjoyed teaching her how to mix flavors and add the local wines to sauces to enhance the meal.

As she opened another box and started unpacking, Violet could admit to herself she was lonely. Yes, there were people all around her. And yes, she worked twelve-hour days, but she was alone. She'd tried dating, but her heart wasn't in it. Instead she found herself flirting her way through life and then coming home alone. She knew it was strange being a single female who worked outside the home, but she didn't care. Cooking was the one thing that brought her happiness.

Her newly installed phone rang, and Violet jumped across her bed to reach it. "*Allô?*"

"Listen to my sister speaking French now," Daisy teased.

"Daisy! It's so good to hear from you." Violet sat up on her bed and smiled into the phone at her sister's voice.

"It's good to hear your voice, too. I have news." Daisy was practically giggling over the phone.

"What is it?"

"I met someone."

"Daisy, you're on a campus full of thousands of people. Of course you met someone."

"No, I met my soul mate. I just know it!"

Violet's grin slid from her face. "How do you know it? How long have you been together?"

"We're not together. At least not yet. But I met him when my sorority and his fraternity had a mixer. He's a senior and is so cute." Daisy giggled and Violet tried not to roll her eyes. She'd been this way before. So in love she was blind to the world. Well, not anymore.

"You don't even know him. I think it's a little early to be calling him your soul mate. Date him for a while first and stop simpering. He's just a man and puts his pants on just like you and me."

The line was quiet, and Violet regretted saying anything at all. "Daisy?"

"Just because you suffer from a broken heart doesn't mean the rest of the world has to suffer, too. This isn't about you, and I'm not you."

Violet sighed. She felt horrible, but she couldn't see where she was wrong. They weren't even dating, and Daisy, who had never had a serious boyfriend, was head over heels in love with this guy already. But she didn't fight her sister on it. "I'm sorry. You're right. Tell me about him."

Violet sat back against her headboard and listened about this perfect man. She was jealous. That's what it was. She was jealous Daisy could still be so innocent and so naïve about love. Violet wished she could be that way again. She and Lily had talked about it. Talked about how they acted their way through dates and flirting. It was just a way to keep control and keep their hearts safe.

"Violet? Did you hear me?"

"Yes, he sounds divine."

"No, I asked if you were coming home for the summer. You haven't been home in almost a year, and we'd love to see you."

Violet's lips thinned. She didn't want to go home yet. It would take too much energy to act as if she were happy. "I don't know my schedule yet. With my promotion it may be harder for me to get some time off."

"Well, we miss you. I need to get to class, but promise me you'll think about coming for a visit."

"Of course." Violet said her goodbyes and sat staring at the brown boxes that needed to be unpacked. She should go home but not right now. Now was her time to grow and explore in France. She was respected and gaining valuable knowledge. Plus she hadn't had to hit anyone with a spatula or a crêpe pan in the past year. Maybe she'd get home next year.

The sound of a horn honking sent Violet scrambling off the bed and out onto her narrow balcony. Looking down, she saw tall, handsome Jacque. He was a waiter where she worked and had bragged about his new car the other day.

"My fair lady," he called up and removed his

sunglasses, looking up at her. "It's a great day for a cruise around the hills in my new car."

The sun was warm, a sexy Frenchman was waiting, and he had a convertible. "I'll be right down," Violet called, hurrying back into her bedroom.

She opened box after box until she found a scarf. Tying it quickly over her hair, she raced out of her flat. Violet might not be as naïve anymore, but that didn't mean she couldn't have a good time.

Daisy smoothed her dress and straightened her pearls before rushing down the stairs of her sorority house. Tonight was the best night of her life. Robert had stopped her on the way to class and asked her to dinner. She had spent hours getting ready, and now she looked perfect.

Robert was standing beside her housemother in the front entryway. He was so dreamy with his blond hair and blue eyes. His navy suit was pressed, and he held a bouquet of daisies in his hands. When he saw her coming down the stairs, a smile stretched across his face and went straight into her heart.

"Hi, Robert."

"You look lovely, Daisy. I know it's kind of cheesy, but I brought you some daisies."

Daisy reached out and took the flowers with a smile. It was the first time a boy had gotten them for her. "Thank you; they're lovely."

"Here, dear, I'll put them in water, and they'll be in your room when you get back. Remember, curfew is ten o'clock," Mrs. Fitzsimmons, a widow who had lived in the house for the past ten years, said with a smile.

"Thank you, and I'll have her back at the house, safe and sound, by curfew." Robert sent her a wink as Mrs. Fitzsimmons took the flowers and headed for the kitchen.

"I thought we could go to the drive-in movie tonight. I have a basket packed in the car, and we could make a night of it." Robert held open the door for her as they left the sorority house.

"That sounds wonderful." All Daisy could think about was the dark drive-in and the semi-privacy the car afforded them.

Robert closed her car door after she settled herself on the leather seat. She glanced into the back and saw a large picnic basket sitting on the seat. Daisy had always been overshadowed by her other sisters, but now a man was courting her. A man wanted to spend time with her, not the curvy Violet or the saucy Lily. She felt more alive than ever before.

The two years she had been in college had been life-changing. Daisy loved being a third of the perfect Rose triplets, but being in the middle, she always felt as if she were the invisible one. She missed her sisters — missed seeing Violet and missed having Lily across the hall from her — but she had grown. Daisy had discovered she loved business courses, and someday maybe she could manage her husband's business. One of her sorority sisters left after her first year of college and was now keeping books at her husband's furniture store. Another one of her friends had gotten pregnant and eloped. Now she was at home with their baby while her husband finished school.

Lily looked at Robert as he paid for the tickets and drove to an open speaker. He was handsome and already a senior. Could she be leaving school to get married and work with him by next year? The thought warmed her, but she also felt a pang of discontent. She wanted her own business. She didn't want her husband to have to open a credit card for her. She didn't want her husband dictating what she did with the money from her business. Would Robert do that? Maybe he'd want her to have a job outside of the home.

"So, are you excited about graduation?" Daisy asked when he put the car in park.

"I am. These past four years have been the best of my life. It's hard to believe graduation is just in three weeks."

Daisy felt the pitter-patter of her heart as Robert slid his arm along the back of the bench seat and rested his hand on her shoulder. "What do you plan to do after graduation?"

"My father owns RB Advertising. I'm going to join the family company."

"That's so nice. My sister Lily works with my father and loves it."

"That's nice of your sister to help out. I'm sure her husband wants her home, though."

"Oh, she's not married," Daisy said, trying to hide her grimace. After what happened with Frank, she worried her sister would never trust a man enough to get married.

"Wow, that's so progressive. Do you plan to do that, too?"

"What, work?"

"Yes."

Daisy shrugged as the pitter-patter of her heart slowed. "I don't know. Right now I just want to graduate college."

Robert smiled down at her, and her heart sped back up, especially when he pulled her close to his side. "I would be proud of a wife with a college degree. Not many men can say that."

Daisy gulped at the feel of her body pressed against his,

his warmth heating her. Now she fully understood how Lily could have thrown all caution to the wind with Frank. The movie started on the screen, but Daisy couldn't tell which one it was. She was lost in Robert's gaze, and when his eyes dropped to her lips, she stopped breathing. He slowly leaned toward her and smiled before placing his lips on hers. It was a short, sweet kiss that left her heart pounding.

"Let's have dinner. I brought a nice bottle of wine for us to share," Robert said as he released her. Suddenly Daisy felt empty as he moved away from her. He had to be the one. Her body recognized his.

Daisy brought the glass to her lips and the bold ruby liquid danced along her tongue before she swallowed it. The wine was nothing like the bourbon she and her sisters had snuck sips of from their father's liquor cabinet. "This is excellent." Daisy smiled and took a bite of her dessert.

"You deserve only the best. As soon as I saw you, I knew I had to get to know you. I know that sounds silly . . ."

"Not at all. I felt the same." Daisy felt her cheeks heat and didn't know if it was from the wine or their conversation. Either way, she felt happy. She loved feeling as if she were his sole focus.

"I don't want to, but I did promise to get you back to the house before ten." Robert took her now empty glass and placed it in the basket before starting the car.

"Do we have to?" Daisy asked as she laughed. She had enjoyed tonight so much she didn't want it to end.

"I'm afraid so, but how about we meet tomorrow after class to study and then get dinner when we are done?"

"I would like that." Daisy grinned as she started to

think maybe she could have it all. She could have the man, finish college, and have a career. If what she felt tonight was any indication, she had been right when she saw Robert from across the room at their mixer — he was the one.

Chapter Ten

Daisy opened the porch screen door and looked around for her sister. The summer was almost over, and she couldn't wait for the remaining days to pass. It had been hard being away from Robert so much. He was busy with his new job, and she was working in Keeneston. She lived for the twice-weekly dates they went on. He came to Keeneston every Wednesday night to have dinner with her family, and then every Saturday she spent the whole day with him in Lexington.

"There you are, Lily." Daisy had been looking everywhere for her sister. She took a seat on the porch swing next to Lily and smiled.

"Why the goofy face?"

"Don't tell anyone, promise?" Daisy looked around to make sure their parents weren't around.

"Of course," Lily said as she closed her notebook.

"Robert just got his own place and wants me to help him decorate it."

"Okay . . ." Lily said with confusion. "And this is a secret because?"

"Because if he has his own place, then I am going to be alone with him at his apartment from now on. Things may become *intimate*."

"Do you need the sex talk? I mean, I know Mom didn't

give it to us, but it's pretty easy to figure out. A man has a penis and he sticks it . . ."

"Lily!" Daisy squeaked before lowering her voice. "This is serious."

Lily rolled her eyes. "Fine. Do you love him?"

"Of course!"

"Does he love you?"

"I think so."

Lily's eyes widened. "You *think* so? He hasn't told you?"

Daisy suddenly didn't feel so giddy. "No, he hasn't."

"Well, it's your choice. Do you have a condom? I can sneak you some from the pharmacy."

Daisy turned bright red. "I don't think I can do this."

"If he loves you, he won't make you do this until you're married or ready."

"You're right. I don't think I'm ready yet. Have you done this more than once?" Daisy asked suddenly suspicious.

Lily didn't answer but instead reopened her notebook. Daisy leaned over and saw two names at the top of the list. "What are you writing about Roger Burns and Sue Atwater?"

Lily slammed the notebook shut. "Nothing."

"You're lying to me. I told you about maybe losing my virginity to Robert and you won't tell me what you've been doing all summer with that notebook!" Daisy reached for the book and grabbed it out of Lily's hands.

Opening it she found page after page with people's names at the top. "Daniel and Diane, they got married last month . . . what is this?"

Lily let out a breath in frustration. "Fine. If you have to know, Miss Busybody, it's my Cupid book."

"Cupid book?"

"That's what I said, isn't it? After my incident with Frank, I discovered I have no interest in anything beyond casually dating a person. My heart is irrevocably broken. But, I also noticed that I can see love all around me." Lily shook her head at Daisy's disbelieving face. "I know it sounds strange, but I can see how a woman will lean closer if she's interested, and I can see that spark in a man's eyes when he is looking at someone he likes. All I do is play Cupid a little."

"You're matchmaking?"

"Yes, and very successfully if I may say so. I have fourteen couples married so far, and Mr. Burns and Miss Atwater are my next targets. Miss Atwater works at Mr. Burns's law office, and she comes to the soda fountain every day to pick up his favorite drink. All she can do is gush about how great he is."

"So, she's interested, but is he?"

"That's what I am trying to find out."

"I want to help," Daisy said with excitement. What a way to end the summer — helping two people find the love she felt for Robert.

"Really? You don't think I'm silly?" Lily looked down at her notebook. Daisy was struck by how alone her sister really was.

"No. I think it's wonderful."

Lily's face lit up with excitement, making Daisy feel reconnected to her sister. This was going to be fun and help pass the time until she was back at school for her junior year. "What do we do first?"

Daisy and Lily crept down the narrow alley of the old building on Main Street. Because the town was built over a hundred fifty years ago, only a foot or two separated the buildings. Roger Burns's law office was painted a dusky blue, and Daisy was sure her shirt was now that color as they brushed the side of the building.

"We're almost there," Lily whispered.

A window appeared on the corner of the building, and they smiled at each other. She hated to admit it, but Lily was right about coming down the alley as opposed to walking through the open parking lot in back of the building. There would be nowhere to hide if he looked out the back window of his office.

Lily and Daisy stopped side by side below the window. The alley was on one side of them. The garbage cans blocked them from the view of anyone in the back parking lot. Acting as one, they slowly rose up and looked inside. They saw Sue sitting and taking dictation while Roger looked over documents as he talked. Sue nodded, her hand flying over the page. Finally, Roger set down his papers and looked up.

Sue smiled at him and set down her pad and pencil. "Oh, she's so into him," Daisy giggled in a whisper.

"But is he? Look, he's unsure about himself," Lily commented as they watched Roger fidget with his tie, stand up, and walk around his desk.

Sue blushed and batted her lashes. Roger leaned against the desk and knocked over the container of pencils, scattering them on the floor.

"This is not going well," Lily muttered.

"Look, they're nose to nose, picking up the pencils," Daisy said excitedly. "Kiss her!"

"Shh," Lily said, but not soon enough. Roger and Sue

both stood up and looked toward the window.

Lily and Daisy jerked back and stumbled right into the two large metal trashcans. Their arms pinwheeled as they reached for each other to no avail. They fell to the ground in a *crash* of metal, hitting pavement and squishing discarded food.

"Get up," Lily urged Daisy as she scrambled to her feet ignoring the smushed, week-old cake on her bottom. She reached for her sister and hauled her from the trashcans as they ran up the alley, darted across the street, and disappeared down another alley.

"Do you think they saw us?" Daisy asked, catching her breath. "And, *eeeew*, what is this?" She pulled something unidentifiable from her hair.

Lily pulled her lip back and cringed at the goo in Daisy's hair. "I don't think we want to know. Come on, let's sneak home and change before anyone sees us. We need to regroup."

Hiding in the doorway of the courthouse, Daisy looked at her watch. She had a good view of the law office a block away. Through the large windows of their father's drugstore across the street, she saw Lily trying to usher their father out. After what seemed like hours, he finally left Lily in charge of closing up and headed for home.

When Lily gave her the signal, Daisy walked up the street toward the law office. She took a deep breath and pushed the glass door open. The bell overhead chimed, and Sue looked up from her desk to smile at the newcomer.

"Hiya, Daisy," Sue said cheerfully as she set her purse back down. Phew, Daisy had timed it just right. They were getting ready to leave the office for the day.

"Hi, Sue!" Daisy stepped closer to the hallway that led

to the offices and called out, "Hi, Roger!"

A minute later Roger stepped from his office to see who was calling him. Roger was a little older than she and Sue, but age was just a number. Roger was one of the most eligible bachelors in Keeneston. All the Belles were after him. He was a well-respected attorney, and his family had long held top political positions in the town. That alone would send the Belles bouffant hair spinning. Add in that he was twenty-six years old with a killer smile and twinkling eyes, and they were just uncontrollable around him.

"Daisy, this is a surprise. What brings you here?" Roger asked as he stepped closer to Sue.

"Well, Lily sent me. They held a drawing for a free dinner and sundae for two at our soda fountain from a list of our most loyal customers. Lily drew Sue's name. I was hoping Sue was free tonight to claim her prize."

"Really? Wow, that's so nice of y'all," Sue said excitedly. "But, I don't have anyone to share it with. I don't have a beau right now."

Daisy felt horrible at the way the smile slid from Sue's face. "Oh, that's too bad. The prize is for two."

Daisy didn't say anything for a moment and then snapped her fingers. "Roger, why don't you be her date so Sue can claim her prize?"

Roger put his hands in his pockets, and Daisy saw he was trying very hard not to smile. "Well, if it helps Sue. Sure. Let me go get my coat."

Sue, on the other hand, was over the moon. She pulled out her compact and checked her makeup before giving her neck a spritz of perfume. "Thank you so much. Do we just go down there now and claim our prize?"

"That's right. Well, congratulations. Enjoy the dinner

and dessert, you two."

Daisy made it out the door before a huge smile broke free. She had done it. Now the rest was up to Lily.

Lily skipped home that night. Her heart had been full, watching Sue and Roger fumble through their first date. But it was when the date ended and their eyes locked that Lily knew there would be another wedding soon. Tonight she had made up her mind to not bother trying to find her "one" but to help others find theirs. And with Daisy helping, she felt like she could fix up the whole town.

"How did it go?" Daisy asked from the porch steps.

"They have another date planned for Friday." Lily and Daisy gave each other a high-five and took a seat back on the steps.

"What's so exciting?" their neighbor, Edna Schniter, asked as she cut across the yard to join them on the steps.

"You can't tell anyone, but we played matchmaker tonight." Lily grinned as Edna smoothed out her dress and took a seat next to Daisy.

Over the summer, Daisy and Lily spent most of their time with Edna. Her husband was so rarely home, and it seemed right for the three of them to be together. While no one could replace Violet, it was comforting for Lily and Daisy to have a third person around.

"I can't believe you're leaving us again," Edna said as she put a cigarette in her mouth and pulled out a gun.

"Do you always have to pull out that gun?" Daisy asked and shook her head.

Edna pulled the trigger and Lily gasped. "It's just a lighter." Edna chuckled. "My husband gave it to me the last time he was in town."

Daisy let out a sigh. "I am so glad I'll be closer to Robert soon."

"Why aren't you all hitched yet?" Edna asked as she took a puff of her cigarette, causing Lily to cough.

"He has to do a lot of wining and dining for his job as an advertising exec, and I think being single helps with that. No wife to have to hurry home to. Plus I want to finish college."

"I wish I had done that," Edna said. "Don't take me wrong, I love my husband, but there's so much to learn out there. I just think it would be neat."

"It is. I'd be happy to lend you any of my books if you want them. Lily's read them all and has them anytime you want them."

Lily understood what Edna was feeling. She felt it, too. But she didn't feel good about Robert. Of course she'd warned Daisy, but all that did was cause them not to talk for two weeks. So now Lily kept quiet and hoped it was just her fear and mistrust of men in general coming forward. She hoped Robert wasn't giving off some silent signal that would someday cause Daisy heartbreak. She knew firsthand that when you became blinded by love you didn't see the signs that were flashing "danger."

"Well, speak of the devil," Lily said, pasting on a fake smile. Robert's new car drove up their street and parked.

Lily watched Daisy glow under his stare as he walked toward them. "Good evening, ladies."

Edna and Lily murmured their hellos, and Daisy stood up and grabbed her purse. "I'll see y'all later."

"Have a good night," Lily called as she watched her sister walk away with what she hoped wasn't the biggest mistake of Daisy's life.

Chapter Eleven

Keeneston, Kentucky
Two years later . . .

Violet was finally home. She stepped out of the airport
and into the waiting taxi. It had been four years since
she'd called Kentucky home. She was sure the Belles
thought she would come home pregnant and ruined within
a month of leaving for France, but she hadn't. She had lost
her heart in France, but she had lived and breathed her
passion. However, when her meals starting turning from
culinary masterpieces to home-cooked meals of fried
chicken and grits, she knew it was time to go home.

"Where to, miss?"

"Keeneston, please." Violet slid into the back seat as
suitcase after suitcase was loaded into the trunk. She had no
idea what to do now; she just knew she needed to go back
home.

The emerald grass played along the rolling hills as they
drove out of Lexington. Foals frolicked in their pastures,
cows chewed on bluegrass, and new leaves unfurled
toward the sun. Spring in Kentucky had always been her
favorite time of year. It took thirty minutes, but soon Main
Street was upon her. Fresh flowers were planted in front of
every window, and the people outside painting their fences
stopped to stare at the unfamiliar sight of a taxi driving

through town.

"Right here, please," Violet told the driver. The screen door opened and her mother stepped onto the porch to see who had arrived.

"Violet?" her mother asked softly. "Violet!" she yelled when she realized it really was her.

Violet smiled and felt the tears fill her eyes. "I'm home, Mama."

Her mother raced down the steps, and they met in a tight embrace in the middle of the yard. Tears and laughter mixed with joy; she was in her mother's arms once again.

"Oh, look at you. You're so grown up. Of course by the time I was twenty-one, I already had you three, so I have to stop thinking of you as my little baby. It's so good to have you back. Are you back for good or just to visit?" her mother asked as she ran her hand over Violet's cheek.

"For good. Do I still have a room?"

Her mother laughed as more tears spilled. "You'll always have a place here. This is your home. Now, let's carry this luggage inside. I can't wait to surprise your father and sister."

Daisy closed her book and stood from the desk in the lecture hall. It was her last class of the day. It was April, and she would graduate the first week of June. She was so close she could taste it. She would be a college graduate and a wife shortly after. She and Robert had talked about it for the last year. He was making a name for himself in the advertising world, even getting a couple national campaigns. By the time Daisy graduated, Robert would have a nest egg big enough to buy a house.

She pushed open the wooden doors and stepped onto campus, breathing in the budding flowers and freshly cut grass. People walked all around her, heading to and from class. Some laughed, but despite the flowering dogwoods and daffodils, the campus wasn't as cheerful as it had been. Everything changed in a split second one early afternoon on November 22, 1963. Shots fired in the faraway state of Texas had reverberated through their campus in Kentucky. Women had fallen to the ground in tears. Men stood rooted in shock as the news broadcast the assassination of President Kennedy.

Time had marched on, but the veil of sadness had not lifted. Instead, troops were being sent to a country halfway around the world and the shroud of the Vietnam War now covered the campus. Not just hers, but the whole country's innocence had been lost that day, and they could never go back to how things were before.

Daisy looked up and down the street and then waved as she saw Robert pulling up. "Hi! Thanks for picking me up. Are you sure you can leave work early?"

Robert hurried from the car and opened her door for her. "It's no problem. I actually need to talk to you about work and about us. Want to head to my place?"

"Sure," Daisy said with a feeling of dread. "Is everything all right?"

"Actually, something pretty big has happened. It will be good for us in the long run, but I am afraid you might not want to stick it out. Let's just talk about it when we get to my place. Tell me about your day. Are you ready for graduation?"

Daisy gave a weak smile and managed the small talk until they pulled in front of his apartment. Her palms grew sweaty and it felt as if someone were clog-dancing in her stomach. She tried to remember to breathe as Robert unlocked the door and turned on the lights.

"Here, let's have some champagne. The situation calls for it." He smiled as he headed for the refrigerator.

Well, that had to be good, right? Maybe he wanted to get married sooner. Whatever it was, it was killing her. "Just tell me. You've turned me into a nervous wreck."

Pop went the cork. Robert poured two glasses and handed her one. "I got a huge promotion."

Relief washed over her. "Congratulations! Your father is making you second in command?"

Robert shook his head. He'd been battling with his father for the past year for more control over the company, but his father had been keeping him on a tight leash. "No. My campaign for that new detergent that went national, well, it caught the eye of the Pentagon. They called and want me to work with them on the war effort."

Daisy set her glass down and shook her head. "I don't understand."

"They want me to work on war propaganda. They need more men to volunteer to go to Vietnam. I'm headed to Washington, D.C., to work for the Secretary of Defense. My salary has been tripled, and my work will be seen all over the country."

"You're moving to Washington?"

"It's just for one year. They think they can win this stupid fight in the jungle, and I'll be back here as soon as they do." Robert took her hands in his and looked down into her eyes. "But I have to leave in two days. I won't make it to your graduation. I'm so sorry, Daisy."

"I could join you after I graduate. I mean, we had talked about getting married soon. We could just speed up our plan," Daisy said with a shaky voice. All their plans and dreams were slipping away.

"I want to, my love, but they told me I got the job

because I wasn't married. Apparently, I will just about live at the Pentagon, and I will have to travel to military bases as well."

Her hand flew to her heart. "Do you have to fight in Vietnam?"

Robert smiled kindly down at her and shook his head. "No, thank goodness. But we can write, and I will call you every week. I had meant to give this to you under different circumstances, and I understand if you don't want it anymore, but . . ."

Robert dug his hand into his pocket and dropped to one knee. He opened the box, and Daisy gasped at the beautiful ring.

"Daisy Mae Rose, I have loved you since I set eyes on you. You are kind, passionate, and strong. I couldn't wish for anyone else to be my wife and the mother of my children. Will you marry me?"

Her heart sang, and she felt tears pressing for release. "I thought you said the Pentagon didn't want a married man."

With a sly smile he held out the ring. "Technically, I wouldn't be married. I would be engaged. And this is my promise to you that I am yours. No matter how far away, my heart is always with you. Can you do it, Daisy? Can you wait until this war is over to become my wife? I'm sure with my advertising the American people will be behind us in no time and victory will be coming along shortly."

Daisy smiled and then nodded. "Yes! I love you, Robert. Of course I will wait for you."

Robert slid the ring on her shaking finger. It was too loose, but she could get it resized. It was beautiful. And it was a symbol of their love and commitment to each other. "You've made me the happiest man in the world today. I love you."

Daisy flung her arms around his neck, and when he kissed her she knew she would wait forever for him.

Violet waited in the kitchen as her mother brought dinner to the dining room. She quietly snuck to the door and put her ear to it. Her sister and father had just gotten home from work and were sitting down for dinner.

"Who is coming to dinner?" Lily asked. Violet was sure Lily was gesturing to the extra plate setting on the table.

"Oh, Mom," Lily groaned, "you're not setting me up with another blind date, are you?"

"Would it be so bad if I did? Do you have any idea how many weddings we have been to in the past couple of years? It's like the whole town of Keeneston is getting married except for my daughters." Her mother paused. That was Violet's cue.

"So what if we don't get married? We just get to live with y'all longer," Violet teased, walking into the dining room as if she'd been there every night for the past four years.

Lily's eyes were comically round as she screamed and jumped up from the table. She hugged Violet so hard, Violet was worried she might not be able to breathe. When her father wrapped her and Lily in a bear hug, she felt the first tear roll down her cheek. Soon the whole family was a blubbering mess, standing in one big group hug.

"I can't believe you're here. Please tell me you're staying for longer than a week," Lily ordered and refused to let go of Violet's hand.

"I am. I'm here to stay. I'm going to send out résumés

next week to restaurants in Lexington. I'm hoping Chef Nichols hasn't forgotten about me," Violet told them as they finally let her take her seat at the table.

"We have to call Daisy. Does she know you're back in town?" Lily asked as she grabbed Violet's hand once again.

"She doesn't. Maybe you can call her and try to get her home this weekend."

Lily rubbed her hands together and smiled mischievously. "Subterfuge — my favorite pastime."

Dinner was a happy blur for Violet, listening to her sister and father tease each other about work, while her mother shook her head as if this happened every night. And it probably did. She's just missed out on it over the past four years. The rightness of being back in Keeneston hugged her. She would miss France. She would miss the fancy clothes and the fast-paced life of a top chef. But this was home. This was where she belonged.

"I'm declaring sister time," Lily called out. She pushed her seat back from the table and grabbed Violet's hand once again.

Her mother smiled and dabbed her eyes with her napkin. "I'll get the dishes tonight. You girls go have fun. I'm so happy to have all my babies nearby again."

"Come on. We're going to be late if we don't hurry," Lily whispered as she pulled her out the front door and down the steps. "I hope you still have air in your tires."

Violet watched as Lily pushed open the shed door and pulled out her bike. She disappeared again before coming back out with Violet's purple bike from high school. "The tires are pretty soft, but it will have to do."

"Where are we going, and why are we riding our bikes? Can't we just take Dad's car?"

"We are picking up Mona Crosby and our mission requires stealth, hence the bikes." Lily grinned and Violet couldn't help but return the smile.

Chapter Twelve

"Hurry," Lily called over her shoulder.

"Why?" Violet asked as she panted after her sister.

Lily didn't answer until after they climbed the hill on their street and left behind the cluster of large Victorian houses. As they cruised downhill and passed row after row of corn, tobacco, and soybeans, Lily slowed down to talk.

"We need to get Mona to go for a bike ride, crash her, and then you and I will head off to 'get help.'"

"Won't Mona be hurt? And that's horrible to leave her on the side of the road by herself," Violet said, aghast.

"She won't be alone for long. Kevin Stokes gets off work in twenty minutes from the farm. He'll be driving a pickup, perfect for putting a bicycle in the back," Lily said with a wink and a mischievous grin.

Violet laughed as she looked at her sister. She was glowing. When Lily had told her over the phone about all the weddings she had attended and about how she had *helped* the couples along, Violet had no idea Lily had actually orchestrated their relationships.

"You seem like your old self, Lil," Violet called out. Lily held her hands up in the air as she sped down the hill.

"Matchmaking makes me feel alive. It makes me happy to give others what I can't have myself. It's very rewarding to see their love spark and grow. It's a way of experiencing love without any of the pain. Now, hurry up. There's Mona's house."

"What a great idea to go for a bike ride. It's so pleasant out here before the summer heat sets in." Mona smiled as she pedaled between Violet and Lily. Her long blond hair was tied back in a ponytail, and she wore a bright blue scarf tied at her neck.

"That's what I thought, too. And I thought it would be nice for Violet to see the countryside again. She's been gone too long in France." Lily gave her sister a wink. It was the key to cause the crash. They had just ridden down a hill and were starting to pedal uphill near the farm where Kevin worked.

Violet took a deep breath and hoped love was worth the physical pain Mona was about to experience. One thing she knew was it wouldn't be as painful as her broken heart. Violet nodded to her sister, and they both angled their bikes toward Mona, who was pedaling unsuspectingly in the middle. Giving her bike one last push, Violet headed straight for Mona. Violet saw Lily coming from the other side and closed her eyes, knowing impact was coming soon.

"Oh no," Mona called out a second before Violet collided with her sister. The bikes crashed head-on, and Violet opened her eyes and shot over the handlebars, straight into her sister's surprised face.

Violet and Lily met midair. Forehead cracked into forehead, and they grabbed at each other and held on as they fell with a hard *thump* onto a pile of wrecked bikes. Lily groaned and Violet closed her eyes and tried to remember to breathe.

"Jumping Jehoshaphat! Are you two hurt?" Mona's

voice called out from above the wrecked sisters.

Violet opened her eyes to see a completely uninjured Mona standing over them. "Ow," Violet groaned and pushed herself up to sit. "Are you hurt?"

Mona shook her head. "No, my chain came off, and I had to stop to walk my bike up the hill. What happened? You two just veered and collided at the exact same time."

Violet saw Lily roll her eyes and barely heard the curse she couldn't contain. "We must have popped our tires. Maybe something was in the road," Lily said as she struggled to get up.

"Yeah, that's it. Must have run over something," Violet groaned as she slowly managed to stand up.

"I'll go get help. You two just sit on the side of the road. I'll be right back!" Mona helped the sisters to the side of the road before hurrying to her bike. Violet collapsed against the bed of bluegrass and waited until Mona had slid her chain back on her bike and pedaled off before turning to her sister.

"Of all the harebrained schemes. I have an egg on my head where you flew into me. My elbow is bleeding. And I'm pretty sure I have an imprint of a pedal permanently engrained on my hip."

Lily kept her eyes glued to the setting sun and tried moving different body parts. "That didn't go as I planned, but at least nothing seems to be broken. I'm more upset that Plan A didn't work. I thought for sure this was the perfect way to get Kevin and Mona together. Every woman loves a knight in shining armor coming to her rescue."

"What are you going to do now?" Violet asked. The sky was turning shades of blue, yellow, orange, pink, and purple.

"Plan B."

"What's Plan B?"

"I'll kidnap her and send a ransom to Kevin?"

Violet was about to respond when the sound of a car engine reached them. Violet propped herself up and felt her mouth drop open. "Son of a . . . your plan worked, Lily." Inside the truck was a smiling Kevin and a calf-eyed Mona.

"Thank goodness. I didn't want to go to jail for kidnapping," Lily said with relief as she sat up and watched the infatuated couple heading toward them.

Kevin finally tore his eyes from Mona and looked down at the two disheveled sisters. "Lily! Violet! What happened? By the way, it's nice to have you back, Vi."

"Kevin is my hero! He saw me biking down the road by myself and pulled over to offer to escort me to my destination. He told me he couldn't live with himself if he let a woman go off into the night by herself. Isn't he such a gentleman?"

Kevin blushed as Mona looked at him like he hung the stars and the moon. "Shucks, Mona. Any man would do the same."

Mona reached out and placed her small hand on his muscled forearm. "And when I told him about you two, he grabbed my bike, put it in his truck, and insisted on rushing straight here to check on you two."

Violet looked at Lily and tried not to laugh. The two lovebirds had totally forgotten about them sitting on the ground bleeding. They were lost in each other, just as Lily had planned. Well, not exactly how she had planned it, but the end result was all that mattered.

Kevin placed their bikes in the bed of the pickup and helped Lily and Violet climb onto the tailgate. Violet dangled her legs as Kevin went to open the cab door for Mona.

"Are you sure you two don't mind riding in the back? There's just not room for everyone up here," Kevin asked with only a slight hint of remorse.

"Of course not. We're just glad Mona found you," Lily called out.

"I'll get you home in a jiffy."

Kevin started the truck, and Violet grabbed the side of the truck bed to hang on as he drove over the rolling hillside and back into Keeneston. "Don't you dare tell anyone about this," Violet warned her sister.

"We'll be dancing at their wedding and laughing about this before you know it," Lily said, full of cockiness. "Besides, we won't have time to dwell on the little hiccup my plan took—we'll be too busy on our next project."

"What do you mean, Robert left?" their father asked. Daisy had come home, and Lily and Violet enjoyed surprising her. But the happiness quickly turned to frustration when Daisy had announced Robert had left that morning for Washington.

"It's an amazing opportunity. As soon as the war is over, he'll be back and we'll get married," Daisy said with a smile plastered on her face. She pressed her hand to the necklace she had hidden under her suit top.

"But, you've been together for years. It's time to shit or get off the pot," her father muttered, flicking the newspaper closed.

"Dad," Daisy gasped.

"It's true, dear. There's no reason he couldn't have married you before he left. Or at least set a date for a wedding. He didn't even come to talk to your father about your future. A true gentleman would ask permission to marry you or to set a date. Instead he ran off into the night. It's not right." Her mother shook her head as she placed the main course on the dining room table.

"He did make a commitment," Daisy defended as she pulled out her engagement ring.

"*Humph*," her father grunted. "Did he come talk to us? No. Did he tell you to start planning a wedding? No. Did he even tell you when he was coming back? No."

Lily could no longer stay quiet. "I told you not to trust him. I don't like this at all. He's just stringing you along."

Violet nodded her agreement, and Daisy lost her temper. "What right do you have to agree to anything, Vi? You haven't been around for the past four years, and you think you can waltz back in here and give me relationship advice? I'm the only one of us who even has a marriage prospect."

"You're right, but you've told me all about your relationship, and I think he's using you. His loyalty is questionable at best, and it's obvious he's a social climber."

Daisy threw down her napkin and stood up from the table. "If you all don't like him, fine. But I'm not going to sit around as you bash my fiancé."

With an air of righteous indignation, Daisy stomped from the room and out the front door. The sound of her car starting made Violet jump from the table. Her father reached out and grabbed her arm to stop her.

"Give her time to come to terms with our dislike of her fiancé. With him gone, she'll discover quickly how much she depends on us for our unyielding love. Call her next week to let her know you two love her. We'll do the same in a couple days. We'll ride this out as a family. While family may disagree, we never abandon."

"Yes, Daddy." Violet sat down and took in her parents' worried looks. "Do you think he'll ever marry her?"

"I don't. He's all smiles and polish on the surface, but there's something very calculating underneath. However, it's something Daisy needs to discover for herself, much like you two had to," her father told them as he cut the pork tenderloin.

Tears threatened to spill from their mother's eyes as she passed out the plates. "It's the hardest thing about being a parent. We have to give you enough space to learn your own lessons. She needs to learn this on her own and realize we will be here with open arms anytime she needs us."

Violet sniffled. "Thank you for giving me space to grow and the love to know that even if I failed, you would be there."

Their mother rushed around the table and wrapped them in a hug a second before their father's strong arms encircled them all.

Chapter Thirteen

D aisy couldn't stand the silence. It had been one week since she stormed out of her house and headed back to campus. She busied herself with studying, but her heart just wasn't in it. Her sisters were home, and she missed them. She missed Robert, too. He'd called her last night to tell her about his job and his new apartment. He laughed that he'd only been able to sleep there twice. Otherwise he was at work, creating propaganda to support American troops in Vietnam.

The phone rang at the end of the hall in the sorority house, and a second later her name was called. Pushing herself off her bed, she walked to the phone and took it from one of her housemates.

"Hello?"

"Hey, sis," a duo of laughing voices called out. Daisy felt her heart leap. Of course her sisters knew when she needed them the most. "We miss you. Can you come home this weekend? Mom's baking your favorite pie, and Lily and I have a new target."

"Mom's making pecan pie?"

"With chocolate chips," Lily called out with glee.

"You have a new target, huh?" Daisy smiled as she leaned against the wall and twisted the phone cord around her finger. "Who's the poor, unsuspecting couple?"

"They're not a couple yet. That's the problem," Violet lamented as if someone had just told her that her apple pie was too tart. "It's Louis and Bernadette."

"Louis, who owns the repair shop?" Daisy asked as she tried to place who Bernadette was.

"That's right," Lily told her. "And you know Bernadette. She's the daughter of the preacher over in Lipston. Their church is near the county line, and sometimes they come to the soda fountain after Sunday school."

Daisy laughed as she felt the loneliness float away. "Pie and matchmaking. What could be better?"

Crash! Violet felt the reverberation of the impact all the way up her arms. She pulled her arms back and shook them out before hefting the crêpe pan back and slamming it into her bike once again.

"I'm a little scared of her. She looks kind of happy, bashing the bike with that pan," Daisy whispered to Lily.

Violet smiled and turned around. "It's been a while since I smashed something with this. It feels good. Maybe I should play softball."

"You're so violent. Violent Violet is your new name," Lily teased.

"You didn't seem to mind when I smacked Fred with the spatula." She swung the crêpe pan as if hitting a softball and smiled. "Maybe I should join the Lipston church league to meet Bernadette."

"You have to hit the ball with a bat, not a large pan. No, I think you'd do well with tennis," Daisy laughed.

"And besides, we already have a plan to get Louis and

Bernadette together at the soda fountain." Lily looked the bike over and nodded her approval. "Great job, Vi. Now, lets put our plan into action."

The three sisters walked side by side down the street and turned right to walk out of town. Louis's repair shop was only a half-mile away. The small concrete building appeared around the bend in the road. Bright blue letters over the garage door spelled out the name of the shop. Marvin Gaye played over the radio.

The tail end of a Buick Riviera came into view first. Next came Louis's tapping boot from under the car. The three sisters walked through the garage and gathered around the pair of knees sticking out while Louis belted out the song.

When the song ended, the three women clapped and whistled. Louis's body jerked, and the sound of a wrench dropping to the concrete reached their ears, along with a curse, as Louis hit his head on the undercarriage. They tried not to laugh, but it didn't work.

As he scooted out from under the car, the sisters could see a deep blush forming on his dark cheeks. His black hair was fashioned in the stylish conk that all the singers were wearing, and a small lump was forming on his forehead.

"Sorry for sneaking up on you like that, but we had to hear the next member of The Temptations," Lily teased. Daisy smacked her.

"Are you hurt? We're really sorry." Daisy cringed as Louis rubbed the lump.

"Nah, I've got a thick head."

"That's right. I remember hearing you took a baseball to the head at the state championships a year ago," Violet said. She remembered reading the article about the Keeneston

High School's first state championship in baseball. Some of the opposing team's parents didn't like the fact that Louis had played. But Keeneston had stood behind him and cheered loud enough to drown the others out.

"I can still tell you when rain's comin' on," Louis joked and looked at the bike Violet was holding. "What on earth happened to this?"

"I know you work on cars, but I didn't know if you could fix it. I left it in the parking lot of the market, and someone ran over it. It's been years, but I still don't think Dad has forgiven me for bringing his car back without a bumper," Violet said with a grimace. "So I've been riding this bike since I got back to town."

"And with her bike broken, Vi now has to sit on my handlebars. We're a little too old for that. So, we were hoping you could fix it," Lily said with a bat of her eyes.

Louis lowered himself to the bike's level and started looking over it. "It shouldn't be too hard. I have to finish the mayor's car, and then I can get to this tomorrow."

Violet sighed and put her hands over her heart. "Thank goodness. How long do you think it will take to fix?"

"I should be done by tomorrow evening. And I can probably fix it for under eight dollars."

The three sisters cast worried looks at each other. "We promised Dad we would help out at the soda fountain. His regular cook is off tomorrow night, and Violet said she would fill in."

"Grill cookin' will be quite the change for you after all that fancy cookin' you've been doin' in France." Louis took the bike from Violet and set it against the wall.

"Yes, but I'm looking forward to it. I've been missing some good home-cooked meals."

"Well, if you throw in a burger, I'll deliver it to you at

six."

Violet's smile spread. "If you deliver it at six, I'll even throw in a milkshake."

Louis held out his hand, and they shook on it. "Deal."

Lily hurried around the soda fountain's counter and pretended to wipe it down. With a nudge of her elbow, she got Violet's attention when the beautiful young woman strode into the shop and looked for a place to sit. Her dark blue and white polka dot dress emphasized her small waist and flared over her hips, stopping just past her knees. Her black hair was fashioned elegantly under a hat and her light brown complexion was flawless.

"Bernadette! It's nice to see you again. How was teaching Bible school this afternoon?" Lily asked, resting her hands on the counter.

"The children were full of it today. They know school's coming to an end and are too excited to stay still," Bernadette said. She laid her small clutch purse on the counter and took a seat on the padded stool.

"Bernie, this is my sister, Violet. Vi, this is Bernadette. She's one of our most loyal customers."

Violet stepped forward with a look of happy surprise. "Really? Have you tried every flavor of ice cream my daddy has?"

Bernadette smiled and nodded. "Sure have. Every ice cream, shake, and cookie in the place."

"And she's not afraid to tell us when we didn't get the recipe right either," Lily laughed.

"Do you think she could help us?" Violet asked Lily as Bernadette listened on.

"She'd be perfect!" Lily turned from her sister and reached across the counter to grab Bernadette's hands. "Bernie, do you think you could do us the biggest favor?"

"Of course, what is it?" Bernadette looked worriedly between the sisters.

"Violet just came back from her job as a chef in France." Lily paused so Bernadette could make the appropriate *oohs* and *aahs*. "They made all these fancy kinds of sorbets over there, and I don't know how much our customers would like them. Do you think you could come in around 5:45 tomorrow and do a taste test for us?"

"A free tasting? Are you kidding? Of course I'll be here. But for today, let's start with double chocolate chip."

The three sisters huddled together in the storage room as they waited for Louis to arrive. Bernadette was sitting excitedly at the counter, awaiting her first taste of Violet's sorbet. The sisters had made their excuses to delay serving it until Louis arrived.

"What time is it?" Daisy asked impatiently.

"One minute since the last time you asked," Violet shot back as Lily eased up on her toes to peek out the small square window.

"He's here! Go!" Lily jumped out of the way, and Violet grabbed the largest bowl on the shelf.

Hurrying to follow their sister, Lily and Daisy pushed through the door only to skid to a stop in an attempt to walk nonchalantly to where Louis was taking a seat next to Bernadette.

"Sorry to keep you waiting, Bernadette," Violet called as she spooned scoop after scoop into the large bowl. "We seemed to have run out of bowls. Hope you don't mind using this one."

Bernadette's eyes went wide, and Louis snickered when Violet set down the bowl with no fewer than six scoops of different flavors of sorbet in it. "I can't eat all of that!"

Violet looked surprised as she looked between the bowl and tiny Bernadette, sitting primly at the counter. Then she looked at Louis, who was trying hard not to laugh. "Oh, well, I guess I got carried away. I think it's the best I've made. I'd hate to waste it." Violet set her hands on her curvy hips and stared at the sorbet.

"Looks great," Louis commented.

Violet snapped her fingers. "That's it. While we make your dinner, Louis, would you mind starting with dessert? You could help Bernadette taste it. It would be a big help to me to see if I should make a larger batch and offer it to our customers."

"I'd love to. That is, if Bernadette doesn't mind sharing."

Bernadette blushed and tittered a nervous "Of course not!"

"Great! Here's another spoon. I'll be back with your burger in the shake of a lamb's tail."

Violet shot her sisters a wink as they headed back into the kitchen. They had to cook the world's slowest burger, but judging by the looks and whispered giggles coming from the couple at the counter, Violet knew they wouldn't mind the extra wait.

Chapter Fourteen

Four Years Later . . .

Lily slid the notebook onto her bookshelf. It was the tenth one she'd filled since she started matchmaking at eighteen. Last week she and her sisters had turned twenty-six, and sadly, they were all still living at home. Lily looked around her room and noted the changes she had made a couple years ago to make it more womanly. Gone were the Elvis Presley posters, replaced by watercolors of the house and the roses out front.

Her door burst open, and Violet staggered in. She'd worked that one summer with them at Dad's place, but now only Lily worked there. Daisy was an assistant to the president of the bank, and Violet was a chef at a fancy place in Lexington. She'd even bought her own car a couple years ago.

"I'm so tired I could sleep for a week," Violet called before falling face first onto the bed. "Between working all night and matchmaking all day, I'm exhausted." The words were muffled by the comforter.

"I just put away our tenth notebook, and Mom brought in some mail. We have three wedding invitations and eight baby showers." Lily giggled and tossed the invitations onto the bed next to Violet's head.

"Eight baby showers? We need to get crocheting more

baby blankets. But, it does warm my frozen heart to see all this love and family about. It almost makes me think I can one day fall in love again," Violet said absently, flipping through the invitations. "Bernadette and Louis are having their second child. How exciting."

"Violet, Lily, where are you?" Daisy called from downstairs. "I got another letter from Robert."

Lily and Violet looked at each other and rolled their eyes. "We're up here," Lily yelled. "I swear, six years he's been keeping her dangling. How much longer do we have to pretend to like him?"

"Forever, if Daisy has her way," Violet whispered. They pasted smiles on their faces when Daisy ran into the room. She jumped onto the bed, and Lily sat down next to Violet as their excited sister ripped open the letter.

"I've been so worried," Daisy babbled while unfolding the letter. "It's been months since I last heard from Robert. I hate that they sent him to the Philippines two years ago in order to drum up more support for this war. The mail has slowed down so much since then."

"Well, don't keep us in suspense; what did dear Robert say?" Violet asked with forced enthusiasm. Lily shook her head silently as Daisy pored over the letter.

"He said he's been offered a position at the embassy, and he took it. Oh, wow, Robert's a diplomat! That's so wonderful. Can't you see us traveling the world together?" Daisy giggled as she continued to read. "He goes on to say that as soon as the war is over he'll be back to marry me, and we'll move to the Philippines. He's been given a house with large porches and open-air rooms larger than his apartment. Oh, it sounds divine," Daisy sighed.

"Is there any reason why you can't get married now?" Lily asked.

"Yeah, you've been waiting years to get married," Violet pointed out for the hundredth time.

"Y'all know it's too dangerous for me to live there now. It's practically next door to the war. Robert is just looking out for my well-being. And how selfish would it be to demand we get married when a *war* is going on? All these brave men putting their lives in danger and me planning a wedding? I just couldn't do it."

"Knock, knock." Lily looked up to see her parents standing at the door.

"Mom said you got a letter from Robert," her father said with the same false smile Violet and Lily had. Lily listened as her parents murmured their excitement for the contents of the letter, coming farther into the room.

"Your father is taking me out to an early dinner tonight. Will you girls be all right on your own?"

Lily and her sisters all laughed. "Yes, Mom. We're not kids anymore. I think we'll manage for a night."

"I'm a mom. I worry. It's what we do. Now come give us a kiss good-bye."

Lily and her sisters jumped from the bed and kissed their mother's cheek before being wrapped up in a tight hug by their father. The sisters followed their parents down the stairs and out onto the porch to wave them off.

"Have fun, you two!" Lily called out.

"Don't stay out too late," Daisy teased.

"We love you!" Violet called as all three blew them a kiss.

They stood waving on the porch as their parents drove down the street in a light spring drizzle. Lily turned to Violet and batted her eyes. "I bet you want to make crêpes for dinner."

Daisy put her head next to Lily's and stuck out her

lower lip. "Pleeeeease."

Violet laughed, and Daisy sniffled. "Fine! I give. I'll make crêpes. How about an early dinner, and then we can go to the drive-in. I think Paul Newman has a new movie out, and he's so dreamy."

"Then y'all need to help me in the kitchen. I think if someone looked at me with Paul Newman eyes, I would catch fire." Violet sighed and the sisters headed inside.

Daisy handed another plate to Lily to dry as they stood at the kitchen counter. Lily jumped at the lightning and thunder crashing to the ground. What had started out as a spring shower had turned into a massive thunderstorm. Nature was putting on a light and sound show that cancelled their Paul Newman night.

"Why am I washing all the dishes?" Daisy asked again.

"Because you are the one who asked Violet to make so many crêpes," Lily reminded her as Violet mixed a new batch of sweet tea.

"As soon as this cools, we can sit on the porch and watch the storm. Mom and Dad should be home soon. It looks like the rain may be letting up a little." Violet put the wooden spoon in the sink, and Daisy snatched it up to wash.

With an exaggerated sigh, Daisy handed the wet spoon to Lily to dry. "Done."

Violet set three glasses on a tray and filled them with ice. "Lil, will you get the door?"

Lily walked ahead of her sister and pushed open the front door. Violet had been right; the rain was slowing down. Violet set the tray down and pushed her hair back. The wind was strong, but it felt good. They all took their favorite seats on the porch.

"So, who will be the first entry in the new notebook?" Daisy asked as she poured herself a glass of sweet tea.

"I don't know yet," Lily said slowly, her attention drawn to nature's show. "Do you all hear something?"

Her sisters stopped their chattering and listened. Wind rushed over her and the smell of rain filled her nose. In the distance, thunder rumbled over and over again in a continuous grumble. The grumbling turned louder and grew nearer as they listened. The second Lily comprehended what it was, the church bells all across town began to ring, followed shortly by the siren used to warn people of a nuclear attack.

"Tornado!" Lily gasped as she dropped her glass. What she thought was thunder turned from a rumble to a roar as the wind quickly picked up. "Close the door!"

Daisy rushed forward and slammed the front door closed. The three sisters ran from the porch, down the steps, and into the yard. Lily looked down the hill into Keeneston and froze. A thick gray funnel was reaching from the heavens and ripping apart everything in its path. Debris flew through downtown as the freight train of wind nearly knocked them down.

"Come on!" Violet shouted, but her words were ripped away by the wind. Instead, she linked her arm around Lily's waist and pulled. Daisy similarly linked her arm, and they formed a chain in order to battle the wind around the side of the house.

Lily screamed as the *crack* of a tree splitting was the only warning they had to leap out of the way of the falling branch. "Hurry!"

The sisters pulled each other to the door at the far side of the property. "I can't open it," Daisy cried as she tugged at the handle to their storm shelter.

Violet and Lily wordlessly grabbed the door and pulled. As the sound of the tornado grew louder, the rain pelted harder, and the debris flew around them, the door finally gave way. "Go," Lily ordered. She braced the door with her body. Violet hurried down the stairs, followed by Daisy. With her sisters safe, Lily stumbled into the darkness, the door slamming shut behind her.

"Here," Daisy yelled over the noise of the raging storm above them. She held up the flashlight so Lily could lock the door. She slid the bolt into place, and they all stared silently at the door, willing it with their prayers to stay shut.

Daisy took Lily by the arms and stepped backward into their underground bunker. The smell of the dirt and the sound of the storm door banging against the frame as the lock fought to hold had the sisters clinging to each other in the dark.

It felt as though it lasted hours, though it was probably just seconds. Lily didn't know which. But then it was over. A steady, light rain began to fall, and she strained to listen for any signs the tornado was still near.

"Is it over?" Violet asked, her voice shaking with fear.

"I think so," Lily whispered, hoping not to wake the beast again.

Daisy took a wobbly step forward and slowly unlocked the door. As she pushed it open, Lily held her breath. They didn't know what they would find. Was their house still standing? Were the neighbors safe? "Mom! Dad!" Lily gasped as she pushed past Daisy and burst from the underground shelter. The house was mostly intact. Shingles had been ripped from the roof, tree limbs littered the yard, and Edna's convertible lay upside down in the middle of the street beyond their house.

The three sisters ran as one for the street. Lily didn't

want to look at the front of the house. She didn't want to see the damage. All she wanted was to know was where her parents were. The sound of police and fire sirens filled the air, their neighbors called for help, cried over destroyed possessions, and looked for lost pets.

"Mom! Dad! Has anyone seen our parents?" Lily yelled as Edna stood staring at her car in the middle of the road.

No one seemed to hear her. They were staring at what had been but was no longer. The house across the street was gone. It just wasn't there anymore. The owners stood staring in complete shock as they gripped each other for dear life. The open door to their underground shelter was the only explanation for them being alive.

"Dad! Mom!" Violet yelled, her voice choking on tears.

"They would be coming from Lexington. Let's go," Daisy yelled and took off, running down the street.

Lily looked around in disbelief at the destruction left behind by the tornado. Some houses looked untouched. Some were missing roofs, windows, or shutters. Cars were overturned, and fallen trees made the roads impassable. As they ran down the hill, the damage became worse. Main Street was full of people wandering in a daze; some screamed for help. People were bleeding; some just sat on the curb shaking. Firefighters, police, and some townspeople were putting out fires caused by downed electrical lines, bandaging injured people, and helping clear the rubble, looking for anyone missing.

The tornado hadn't made a straight path through town. It had zigzagged, cutting the town in half before roaring up their street and dissipating as if it had never been there.

"Do you think they could be at the store?" Lily wondered as she ran down Main Street.

"I hope not," Daisy whispered, conveying the fear they

all had. Their father's pharmacy was on the part of the street hit hardest.

"At least it's still standing." Violet took a gulp as the store came into view. The front windows were blown out and the roof was torn off. The sisters stood hand-in-hand, stopped in front of their father's life's work. Part of the roof was across the street at the courthouse, the rest had collapsed inward. Water was spewing from a broken pipe and the counter was caved in under the weight of an old maple tree that had been uprooted by the tornado.

"You don't think . . .?" Lily couldn't finish her thought.

"No. I don't see their car," Daisy said quietly. "They would have been coming from Lexington. Let's just run down the road a bit to see if the roads are even passable."

Violet and Lily agreed with a silent nod and took off at a slow run down the street, heading out of town. They ran together, never saying a word, and took in the damage all around them. Trees blocked roads and crushed fences, houses, and tractors. Lily saw William Ashton and his parents outside, wrangling loose horses as they ran by. The sisters rounded a sharp curve and stopped. Sheriff Mulford's squad car blocked the road in an eerie silence. A large pin oak lay across the road.

"No!" Lily shouted as she broke free from her sisters and raced forward. She couldn't see the entire car, but saw enough to know it was her parents'. She didn't need to see everything to know the tree had landed across the driver's seat.

"Mom! Dad!" her sisters shrieked from behind her.

"Lily, no," Sheriff Mulford said in a calm steady voice. He caught her up in a hug. "Don't look."

"Nooooo!" Lily screamed, kicked, and punched Sheriff

Mulford. He stood quietly, holding her tightly. Her sisters skidded to a stop next to them. Lily didn't hear their cries over hers and they all fell to the ground, clinging to each other. No one said it, but they all knew. Their parents were gone.

Chapter Fifteen

A rm in arm the Rose sisters stood and watched the double casket lowered slowly into the ground. All of Keeneston stood behind them as the sisters stepped forward and one-by-one placed a pink lily, a white daisy, and a purple violet onto the casket as it disappeared into the earth.

They turned with tears in their eyes to their friends and townspeople. Edna stepped forward with a single red rose and let it drop into the grave behind the sisters. One by one others stepped forward. Louis and Bernadette, Roger and Sue, and couples from all ten notebooks dropped a single rose into the Roses' grave.

Lily let the tears roll down her face until she had no more tears to shed. She was wrung dry. "Come on, Miss Lily, let's get you ladies home," Kevin Stoker said kindly as he and his wife, Mona, each took an arm and led her up the hill to their house. Daisy and Violet were similarly escorted up the street with the whole town processing behind them.

The house stood empty. The pitcher of sweet tea they had been drinking three days ago still sat on the porch. Destruction surrounded it, but the single glass pitcher was left untouched. The sisters hadn't been able to set foot in their home since that night. They'd been staying with Edna and her husband, but today they were coming home. Today they had to start living again.

Edna opened the front door and stepped out of the way. Lily and her sisters looked around. The house had been cleaned. The shattered windows were covered with board or plastic, waiting to be replaced. The roof was covered with a tarp, but otherwise, the house looked just as they'd left it.

"Thank you," Violet stammered through a fresh wave of tears.

"It was the least we could do for you, Miss Violet," their classmate, Caesar Tabernacle, said softly.

"Thank you, Tabby," Daisy said kindly and placed a shaky hand on his arm, stepping over the threshold.

Arms linked, the sisters made their way to the living room and sat as one on the couch. Behind them, the window was covered with plywood. But inside there were no signs of the storm that had changed their lives. Their friends had taken care of that for them.

"Miss Lily, Miss Daisy, Miss Violet. I'm so sorry for your loss. I brought you a chicken casserole . . ."

"Miss Lily, Miss, Daisy, Miss Violet. I'm so sorry for your loss. I brought you a broccoli casserole . . ."

Lily lost count of the people who had come by to give their condolences and bring them a casserole or a pie. The dining room table was covered with food and their kitchen was filled with women doing anything they could think of to help. Outside, the plywood was pulled down and the men carried a new window up the steps of the porch.

The world continued to turn around them as Lily clung to her sisters. She didn't feel time go by. She didn't see the changes the town made to their home. All she felt was emptiness seizing her and dragging her into darkness. Only the pain of loss kept her awake.

"Miss Lily, Miss Daisy, Miss Violet," Roger Burns said gently as he knelt in front of the sisters.

"Thank you for the casserole," Daisy mumbled.

Roger cracked a small smile. "I didn't bring a casserole. I brought the insurance company that is paying for the window and roof repairs. Sue is in the kitchen to organize freezing all the food your friends and neighbors brought by. And Edna is upstairs washing all the bed linens."

"That's so nice of y'all," Violet said and blinked as if just now noticing all the activity going on around them.

"Miss Lily? Do you need anything?" Roger asked, putting his hand on her arm.

Lily jerked and looked around as if seeing the world for the first time. "Who are all these people?"

"That's what I am here to talk to you about. I notified the insurance company, and they are paying for all the repairs the town is doing. The women have you stocked up on food for the next month. I need to talk to you about your plans. I have your parents' will with me. I'm the executor, and I will take care of everything. You will receive your father's life insurance policy in thirty days, and the house and store will be transferred to you three as well. Your father left you well provided for."

"I hadn't even thought about the future," Lily mumbled as her eyes started to glaze over again.

"You don't have to right now, but eventually you will need to. I will stop by tomorrow and check on you." Roger stood up and gave each woman a pat on the shoulder before collecting his wife and heading out.

Slowly, people trickled out of their house until only Edna was left. "Come on, dears, let's get you into bed."

"Thank you, Edna." Lily took her friend's hand and felt the warmth and strength in it. "We'll be fine tonight."

"Yes, thank you. We couldn't have made it through these past three days without you." Daisy stood and hugged their friend.

"Would you like a casserole?" Violet asked as she stared at the mountain of casserole dishes still laid out on the table.

Snort. Lily's hand covered her nose as her eyes widened. A giggle escaped, and she moved her other hand to cover her mouth. Daisy looked at the table, and a smile spread over her face a second before she broke out in laughter. Lily gave up the struggle to conceal her laughter and let loose. Violet started next, and soon the three of them were leaning on each other with tears of laughter rolling down their cheeks.

"Well, now that I know you three are all right, I'll say goodnight. I'll see you tomorrow." Edna closed the door with a smile on her face.

Lily and her sisters finally straightened back up and wiped the tears from their faces. Violet's stomach rumbled so loudly Lily and Daisy broke out in peals of laughter again.

"What? I'm starving, but I don't think I'll ever be able to look at another casserole without laughing. Where are those pies?"

"Wait for me, Vi! I want a pie, too," Daisy called after her sister.

"A pie for each of us," Lily declared as they made their way into the kitchen.

Pies in hand, the sisters sat on the front porch and looked up at the stars. They ate in silence, remembering the last time they were sitting on the porch together. Daisy set her plate down and looked at her sisters.

"What do we do now?"

Lily leaned back on the swing and set down her fork. "From what I remember Roger saying, we now own the house and the store. But none of us is a pharmacist."

"But one of us is a chef," Violet said with enthusiasm.

"So?" Daisy asked.

"So, who says we have to keep the store the way it was? I've always wanted to be the chef at my own restaurant."

"Dad and Mom would like that," Lily said quietly.

"I guess I could still work at the bank, and we could all still continue to live here," Daisy said as she took another bite of pie.

"That doesn't sound like enough anymore, does it?" Lily asked without looking at her sisters.

"No, it doesn't," Daisy said with relief. "I was afraid to admit it. I want to run my own business."

Violet sat up so fast she almost dropped her pie. "I know how to run a kitchen, but not the business side. We could open our own place. I cook and you handle all the business."

Lily clapped her hands excitedly. "It would stay a family business just like Dad wanted."

Daisy and Violet clasped hands and smiled. "What should we call our new place?"

"I don't know," Violet answered.

"Rose Garden?" Lily suggested.

"I like something with a new start. Life handed us a trial. But it's not going to destroy us. We'll bounce back in time," Daisy said and used her other hand to reach out to Lily.

"That's beautiful, Daisy. Just like a rose blossom. So fragile, but they come back year after year," Lily said as she placed her hands in her sisters' hands.

Violet gasped. "That's it! Rose Sisters' Blossom Café!"

Tears filled Lily's eyes. "It's perfect."

Daisy and Violet smiled, but Violet's smile slipped. "But what about you, Lily?"

"I don't know. I've never gone off like you two have. I've just had this home or the soda fountain."

Violet turned and looked at the house. "The house . . ."

"What about it?" Lily asked.

"It's so big. And eventually we will all want to get our own places. I mean, when Robert comes home and marries Daisy. I'll be working so hard starting the café I may make a little apartment above the café to stay close while we're getting it all put together. But the house . . . the house has seven bedrooms."

Daisy grinned. "And there are no hotels in Keeneston."

Lily sucked in a breath of excitement. "And Mom always said it would make a beautiful bed-and-breakfast. Oh, would you girls mind if I did that?"

"No!" they shouted, wrapping Lily up in a hug.

"You know how to cook and if you get stuck, the new Blossom Café can provide the food. You can open the downstairs, convert the den and master bedroom into your own quarters, and then offer six rooms out. What do you think?" Daisy asked.

"I love it," Lily said quietly. She reached out and took her sisters' hands in hers. "We are going to get through this together."

The sisters leaned forward and wrapped their arms around each other in a tight hug. "Come on. Tomorrow we start moving forward. Tonight we'll sit in Lily's room and tell stories about Mom and Dad," Violet said as she stood up.

They walked up the curved staircase and into Lily's

room. None of them had been back up there since the tornado. The room had sustained some water damage. A broken window had let rain and wind in. But with Edna's help, it wouldn't seem too overwhelming to fix. At least the bed was dry.

"Look!" Violet called out as she rushed into the room. "Everything got wet and all your books and papers were destroyed by the rain, but not these."

Lily's eyes went wide as Violet turned around with the ten matchmaking notebooks in her hands. "How on earth?"

"That's a sign if I've ever seen one," Daisy laughed.

"It sure is. And think of all the nice young men we'll meet when we start rebuilding," Violet giggled.

"Then, we better start making a list of eligible women in town," Lily said as she jumped onto her bed with her sisters. Life would be different now. They would feel the emptiness of their loss every day. But by following their dreams, they knew they would be honoring their parents' memory.

Chapter Sixteen

One year later . . .

Lily pulled open the screen door to the Blossom Café and rushed inside. She waved to all the people enjoying dinner and hurried into the kitchen. Violet was busy frying chicken, and Daisy filled plates with fresh-cut French fries and green beans.

"Wow, y'all got a crowd out there," Lily commented. She joined in to help Daisy set the plates on a serving tray.

"Since we opened six months ago, every night is a little busier than the night before," Daisy told her as she placed the last of the French fries on the plates.

"I heard you have three rooms rented out for the Keeneston Spring Festival," Violet said, placing the chicken on the plates.

"Sure do. The house seems so alive when I have guests in it. I put an ad in the thoroughbred magazine and have a full house booked for the entire fall Keeneland racing season."

Daisy picked up the tray and pushed open the door with her bottom. "I'll be right back. Don't start anything without me."

Lily watched her sister head into the restaurant to serve dinner with a healthy side of gossip. It had been a tough year, but the Rose sisters had stuck together and really bloomed into more mature women. They knew what they wanted, and they were going after it.

"She got another letter from Robert," Violet whispered.

"About time. He's only written her twice since Mom and Dad died last year."

Violet growled. Robert was a touchy subject. "He says he's been traveling the region on behalf of the U.S. Embassy."

"When is he coming home?"

"He claims the war is heating up. There're even whispers in the higher ranks of needing more men. He swore again that they'd be married as soon as the war was over. Daisy gets so excited about each word she doesn't see he's just stringing her along."

Lily sighed. "We've done everything we could to show her he is using her."

"I know. It's just frustrating."

The door was pushed open, and Daisy rushed back in. "Y'all wouldn't believe what I just heard out there! The Belles have made a list of the most eligible bachelors in the Class of 1968 and both Jake Davies and William Ashton are at the top."

"But they are both dating women already," Violet protested. "When did the Belles start going after men with girlfriends?"

"That's why I'm here," Lily said anxiously. "I heard from John Wolfe about their change in plans. There's not enough men around. If they aren't married, then they're fair game. But, I know of a way to get at least one name off that list. We'll need our bikes . . ."

As soon as the café closed, the sisters hurried back to the bed-and-breakfast. Lily pulled out the bike Louis had repaired and handed it to Violet before pulling out Daisy's bike and then her own.

"We are picking up Betsy Milner and taking her to Lovers Pond. We will need to make a quiet escape," Lily explained, pedaling down the driveway, leaving Violet and Daisy scrambling to catch up.

"Betsy Milner? Who's that?" Violet called out as she peddled hard enough to pull up next to Lily.

"She's just about to graduate high school. Blond. Taller than us. Been dating William Ashton forever."

"Oh, yeah. I remember her. She's one of the girls the Belles are trying to unseat. But, why are we going to take her to Lovers Pond?" Daisy was beyond confused.

"We need to get her to skinny-dip."

Violet temporarily lost control of the bike and had to slam on the brakes to keep from falling. "What?"

"William hasn't popped the question yet, and they've been dating for three years now. People are starting to talk. And as you just learned tonight, some of the Belles are going to try to angle in on him. They think they can separate him from Betsy and get him to marry one of them."

"And you've taken an interest why?" Daisy asked.

"See, I'm the one who introduced them. They're madly in love, and he just needs a little encouragement to pop the question." Lily shot her sisters a sly grin, and Daisy and Violet laughed in return.

"Sounds like fun. What do you need us to do?" Violet called out.

"Here's what I need you two to do . . ." Lily grinned as she began to explain their roles.

Lily waved at Betsy as they rode up her street. She didn't

know if she would be able to pull off her plan, but if she did, Lily knew another wedding would be just around the corner. Betsy was a cute little thing, and Lily felt old as she looked at her.

"We're celebrating our first six months of business. You've been such a great supporter that we want to take you with us. Grab your bike and let's go," Lily said, turning around in Betsy's driveway and coming to a stop.

Betsy smiled at the sisters with such kindness Lily knew she had decided to help the right couple. "How wonderful! And I still want to hear all about France, Miss Violet. You're a woman of the world, and I'm so jealous."

"But of course," Violet said in her best French accent.

Betsy whizzed past them on her bike. "So, where are we going?"

"It's a surprise. It's something just we sisters do, so you have to pinky swear you won't tell anyone," Lily said with such seriousness she heard Violet and Daisy choke down a giggle.

"I swear. This is so cool. I wish I had a sister. Y'all are so lucky. Marcy Faulkner, my best friend, and I are like sisters, though," Betsy rambled as Lily led them out of town and toward Lovers Pond.

Violet cursed in French while Betsy's eyes grew to the size of saucers. "You want me to get . . ." Betsy looked around and dropped her voice to a whisper, ". . . *naked?*"

Lily just laughed. "You can't skinny-dip without taking off your clothes. Violet, Daisy, and I do it all the time. It's the perfect way to celebrate our success. Right, girls?"

Violet smiled innocently. "It's tradition," she said as she started to unbutton her blouse and unzip her jeans.

Lily slid off her skirt while Daisy unbuttoned her capri

pants. Betsy looked nervously around at the deserted pond. Biting down on her lip, she slid out of her oxford step-in dress and then giggled. "I've never done anything like this before. It's pretty thrilling."

The women all slipped out of their undergarments and headed for the water. Lily cringed as she stuck her toe in. It was still cold. It wasn't hot enough outside yet to warm it to summer temperatures.

Linking hands, the four women looked at each other and, with a scream, jumped. The cold, dark water covered Lily's head as she kicked her way to the surface. She gasped as soon as her head broke through into the night air.

"Let's race to the other side to warm up," Lily suggested, and Betsy nodded with chattering teeth.

"Ready, set, go," Lily called as Betsy took off. "Come on, let's get out of here. We only have seconds to spare."

"Seconds until what?" Violet asked, but the sound of a car coming toward them answered her question. The sisters scrambled from the pond.

An old pickup truck came into view right as Lily, Daisy, and Violet grabbed their clothes and jumped bare-bottomed behind the honeysuckles. They didn't have time to put on their clothes before the door to the truck opened. "Lily? What did you need to see me about?" the deep voice called in a whisper.

Lily grabbed Violet's hand to stop her from making a sound as she shivered naked in the cool night air. Splashing water drew the man's attention, and they heard him head to the other side of the pond.

They heard a whistle of appreciation as Betsy called out, "I won!" before letting loose with a shriek that could be heard all the way into town.

"What is Tabby doing here?" Violet whispered as she

looked at the man standing at the other side of the pond. He was looking good for someone who enjoyed pig mud over dances. All the work on the farm had paid off. While he was just average height, his longer hair was pulled back in a ponytail. It shined from the lights of his truck. His shoulders were broad, and his arms stretched the sleeves of his sports coat. Plus, he was a great guy and had been a big help since they lost their parents.

"Just wait," Lily replied as she nodded with her wet head to the second vehicle driving down the path.

As the sisters peered around the honeysuckle, they saw the second car bouncing down the dirt path at the same time they saw Tabby lean over and haul a naked and shivering Betsy from the pond in order to warm her.

Daisy covered her mouth to muffle the gasp as she saw William Ashton shoot from the car and race toward Betsy. His hands balled into fists at the sight of her in Tabby's arms.

"He thinks . . ." Violet started to say.

Lily grinned with victory. "I know what he thinks. Hurry, let's get dressed while they are distracted."

"Get your hands off my wife," William bellowed as he ripped Betsy from Tabby's arms. The sound of a fist connecting with a jaw reached the sisters a second later.

"Oh dear," Lily worried and snuck another peek around the bush. Tabby's head had snapped back, but he hadn't fallen. He also didn't look too worried about the situation.

"I was just trying to warm her up."

"I know what you were trying to do," William yelled. He shoved Betsy behind his back and yanked off his coat to cover her.

"Wife?" the small, shivering voice said from where she

was slipping on the coat.

"Yes, wife. Do you think I wasn't planning on marrying you? Why else would I date you for so long?" William snapped, turning on Tabby once again.

"Well, I guess it was worth a shot. I just took advantage of the situation. She wasn't here to meet me. In fact, she didn't even know I was here. May I be the first to offer my congratulations," Tabby held out his hand. William took a deep breath and then shook it before bundling Betsy away.

"What were you thinking, skinny-dipping?" William asked Betsy, who was frantically looking around for the Rose sisters.

"I was . . . um . . . I mean," she stuttered as Violet, Daisy and Lily held their breath.

"When I saw you naked . . . golly, Betsy. It's taken all my restraint to be the perfect gentleman for you, but no more. No one gets to see you naked but me. Ever." William reached down and scooped up her clothes in a huff. "And then to see you in the arms of another man. I thought I was going to murder him. I love you, Betsy Milner, and I want you to be my wife more than anything in this world."

"I love you, too," Betsy said, tears threatening to roll down her cheeks.

"I'm not going to do it tonight, but soon. When I ask you to marry me, I want it to be a story we can tell our grandchildren." William chuckled. "And this is definitely not that story. But when I ask, you will say yes, won't you?"

"Yes," Betsy said with such excitement she jumped into his arms, the coat falling from her shoulders and giving William a good view of her naked body.

William groaned. "Soon. Very, very soon." He handed over her clothes and groaned again as she bent to get into his car. As he drove off, the only thing he was watching was

Betsy getting dressed and not the road.

"We did it," Lily cheered, jumping out from behind the honeysuckle.

"You sure did. Now will you tell me the reason for the sore jaw? Ashton has one hell of a punch," Tabby asked as he walked over to them rubbing his jaw.

Before Lily could say anything, Violet eyes widened, and she grabbed her sisters' arms to keep them from talking. "You poor thing. Lily just wanted to surprise you with a picnic for all the hard work you've done for us this past year. But we, um, forgot it at the café."

"That's right." Daisy smiled. "It was my fault. I was so afraid we were late, we ran out with that pie sitting right on the table cooling."

"And here we are with no pie and you with a sore jaw. You poor thing," Violet cooed. "Lily, did Catherine ever finish nursing school?"

Lily's smile widened. "Why, yes, she did. Let's put our bikes in the back of the truck and have her take a look at that jaw."

Tabby shook his head. "It's fine. It'll just have a bruise on it tomorrow."

Violet put her hand to her heart. "Bless your heart, you're such a strong man. I would just feel so much better if Nurse Catherine looked at it. Will you do that for me?"

Tabby blushed a little and then gave in. He put their bikes in the truck bed, and the sisters climbed into the cab. "That was brilliant." Lily giggled.

"Well, it looks like you're not the only sister with the matchmaking gene," Daisy teased Lily as the girls giggled.

An hour later the sisters took their bikes out of the back of Tabby's pickup at Catherine's house. Catherine had ordered

Tabby to sit at her kitchen table with a cold compress on his jaw for another hour. When Lily and Violet had left, Catherine and Tabby were giving each other moon-eyes.

"Tonight was so much fun," Violet giggled as she pedaled up their street.

"You're a natural." Lily laughed as they pulled into their driveway. "Daisy, not so much."

"Hey," Daisy yelled.

Violet and Lily giggled. "Tonight's the first time you didn't fall into a trashcan, a mud puddle, or some other dirty object," Lily teased.

"So I'm not as good at it as y'all are, but I still enjoy it," Daisy said, sticking out her tongue and pedaling away.

Violet turned serious as she and Lily pedaled after Daisy. "It's because her heart hasn't been broken. We are no longer invested in men the way she is. We can see their motives and look at them through jaded eyes."

Lily nodded. "True. We know the signs to look for in the bad ones and the symptoms of those who are really in love. This makes me happy, though."

"After tonight, I feel the same. I had been depending on flirting to control a man and make me feel good about myself, but this is a lot more fun. So, who's next?" Violet asked conspiratorially as they hurried after Daisy.

"I think we need to keep an eye on Betsy's best friend, Marcy. I heard she and Jake Davies were in jail together . . ."

Chapter Seventeen

D aisy couldn't stop smiling. With all the tension and worry about the Vietnam War, this was a week to remember all the happiness and love in the world. After the skinny-dipping episode last year, Lily had told her and Violet about Jake Davies's interest in Marcy Faulkner. They had decided to wait and see what happened between them. Before too long, the sweet young couple was ripped apart by the draft.

Facing the choice of moving to South Carolina with her family or staying with her love, Marcy had decided to stay in Keeneston and marry Jake as soon as she turned eighteen. One day after the wedding, her husband left for the war, and her parents moved to South Carolina. For the past year, Marcy had worked with Daisy and Violet at the Blossom Café, and they soon thought of her as their little sister. Each day was agony, waiting to see if Father James, the new priest at Saint Francis, would accompany a soldier to deliver a death notice to Marcy.

Daisy had seen too many deaths reach their small town. Everyday she gave thanks Robert was safe in the Philippines. He'd been made deputy ambassador and wouldn't be forced to go into the hot zones. But this week, one of their own had been reunited with them.

Jake Davies was home with his wife, and Daisy had bet

that in nine months there would be a little hazel-eyed Davies born. At least she hoped so. She pulled out the small notebook she carried and grinned at all the bets that had been placed recently. They had enough bets on weddings and births to fill one whole notebook.

Daisy pulled out her keys and unlocked the door to her house. She set her purse on the table and bent down to pick up the mail. She walked to the kitchen as she thumbed through the bills and letters. She almost missed it. It was so thin she thought it was a bill, but the extra postage gave it away. A letter from Robert. Not bothering to find her letter opener, Daisy tore it open.

Daisy-

I am sorry to have to write this, but I will not be returning to the United States. I have fallen in love over the years here. Today I have learned the woman I fought hard not to love is pregnant. We are to be married this evening. I tried to stay true to you, but I am sure you understand the temptations I was faced with and the desires a man has.

I still can't believe it. I'm going to be a father! I know you send your congratulations, as I am sure over our long separation there is another man in your life by now. I am breaking our engagement to let you be with him. You're welcome and the best of wishes for your future.

-Robert

Daisy folded the letter and put it in the middle of her copy of *Little Women* before closing the thick book and putting it away forever. Her heart was broken. The life she had planned was not to be.

Violet hung up the phone. That bastard. Daisy had sounded numb when she called to tell her it was over. Violet had asked what happened, but Daisy would only say that it was over. For years, she and Lily had pressed Daisy to break up with that user, but Daisy had been staunch in her support of their relationship.

Violet picked up the phone again, and using the rotary, called Lily. "Daisy just called. Robert ditched her."

"That bastard," Lily growled. "What happened?"

"I don't know. She wouldn't tell me. She just said she heard from him, and it was over. Her heart is broken."

"We need to get over there. She shouldn't be alone. We know how hard it is to suffer a broken heart alone." Lily moved her hand to her heart and felt the emptiness that lived there.

"I'll make some Arnold Palmer drinks and get over there right away," Violet said and poured some lemonade into a pitcher of iced tea.

"I'll grab something stronger. I'll meet you there."

Daisy felt disconnected from her body as she walked through her small, tidy house. She picked up college pictures of her and Robert from her fireplace mantel and looked at her smiling face and Robert's smug grin. How had she been so stupid? The evidence was right in front of her. Her look of utter infatuation and his disregard were clear as day.

As she meandered through the house taking down pictures of Robert, she felt betrayed. She felt angry. She felt devoid of the love and trust she had constantly flaunted to her sisters. And deep down, she was embarrassed. Her blind trust in Robert had caused more than one fight between Daisy and her sisters. Now Daisy was going to have to face her sisters and tell them they had been right.

Daisy put the last picture into a box and closed the lid. She ran her hand over the box top and sighed. Robert may have destroyed her heart, but she wasn't going to let him destroy love. She would prove love existed in every couple she matched up. They would be her heart from now on.

Her door flung open, and Violet burst in. Daisy tried to put on a brave face as Violet set down the drinks but when she wordlessly opened her arms, Daisy collapsed into them.

"I'm here," Lily called as she rushed through the door. "And I brought reinforcement." Lily looked to a tearful Daisy and opened her arms. Like Violet, she didn't say "I told you so" — she simply held Daisy as she cried.

Violet mixed the Arnold Palmer drinks, and Lily set down the bottle of bourbon. "What happened?" Lily asked.

"I don't want to talk about it. Suffice it to say, it's over, and I don't know if I'll ever love again. I just want to forget the pain and the loss. Just for one night, I want to forget everything." Daisy followed her sisters' eyes to where they were staring at the bourbon sitting next to the drinks Violet was stirring.

With a mischievous grin, Lily stood and hurried to the counter. She picked the bourbon bottle up, gave her sisters a wink, and poured half the bottle into Violet's pitcher. Violet stirred the bourbon in the tea and lemonade mixture, and Lily poured the concoction into glasses.

"To my sisters," Daisy toasted.

Her sisters joined the toast, clinked glasses, and took a big sip.

"Add a little more bourbon," Daisy suggested as she gulped down the evolving concoction.

"There," Violet said as she finished mixing it. "That

should do it."

Daisy took another gulp and grinned. "Perfect. I hardly even remember Wobert's name. Wobert? Rrr-obert," Daisy said slowly. "I still can't believe he did this to me."

At the sound of a sniffle, Lily refilled Daisy's glass. "Bottoms up."

Daisy gulped it down and sighed. She had great sisters. They were getting her drunk and the whole time had never said "I told you so." But now things made so much more sense. She had tried to get Lily and Violet to date again to no avail. Now she understood. A traumatic injury to the heart was not something you easily recovered from. For now, she had her sisters, her café, and her town. Her heart could wait.

Daisy moaned and threw her arm over her eyes. The morning sun was blinding. She and her sisters had spent the night perfecting and sampling their new special iced tea. The last she remembered, they had finished off the entire pitcher, and she had stumbled fully dressed into bed. She hissed as a ray of light snuck through and blinded her. Her head throbbed, her mouth felt as if it were made of cotton, and her stomach was in a fit. As she ran for the bathroom, the last thing on her mind was Robert.

Lily felt as if she were rocking in a boat. Why would she be on a boat? But her stomach was rolling back and forth and there was a breeze in her hair.

"Dear me! Lily Rae? Are you alive?"

Lily felt Edna shaking her. "Oh, stop or I'm going to hurl."

"Oh, thank goodness," Edna sighed in relief. "What are you doing sleeping on your porch swing?"

"Huh?" Lily grumbled. She didn't want to open her eyes. She had a feeling it would hurt, so she rolled toward Edna's voice.

Lily fell from the swing, Edna screamed, and Lily's eyes were forced open as she felt a draft where her miniskirt rode up. She was sprawled on the patio.

"Miss Rose. Mrs. Schniter. I was just heading to church to give my morning sermon. I believe it may be beneficial for you to join me this morning."

"Oh hell," Lily whispered in pain. "Is that Reverend Hamilton?"

"Uh-huh," Edna murmured with a false smile pasted on her lips. The new reverend was notoriously uptight, and gosh knows what he was thinking with Lily sprawled on the porch with her skirt up, showing her panties to all who passed by.

"Good morning, Reverend. Watch out, there's a very aggressive bee about. Lily had to dive for cover to keep it from stinging her. I thought I might have to pull out my gun and shoot it. Luckily, it was drawn away by the wonderful nectar of Lily's prize roses."

Reverend Hamilton made what sounded like a snort of disbelief, but Lily couldn't tell for sure as she covered her head with her arms.

"He's gone," Edna said, leaning over and hefting Lily from the ground.

Lily took one look at the spinning earth and ran for the bathroom. What had they done last night? They'd created a recipe that should be outlawed. That's what.

Violet awoke to the sound of church bells ringing. It felt as if they were ringing inside her skull and reverberating through her head. What was poking her? Was it raining? Why was she outside?

She opened her eyes, but all she saw was green. Green leaves surrounded her and damp green grass was beneath her. She rolled onto her back and looked up, but there wasn't a cloud in the overly bright sky. The steeple of Saint Francis was above her, and its bells were ringing. The rain fell again and soaked her, but within seconds it was gone.

Why was she so cold? Violet went to wrap her arms around herself and gasped. Her eyes widen as the sound of cars arriving, doors slamming, and people talking reached her ears. What the hell happened? She was next to the church . . . naked . . . and in the bushes. And why was it raining on her again?

Rolling back onto her stomach, she crawled forward slowly, trying not to make the bushes all around her move. Slowly she pushed a branch aside and looked out. She saw a sprinkler, a statue of the Virgin Mary, and the church parking lot. Double hell. She was naked in the bushes of Father James's little parish house.

"Daisy! Open the door! Hurry up!" Violet pounded against the back door.

Daisy groaned and pushed away from the toilet, feeling the world spin. "Don't yell so loud," Daisy whispered as she made her way out of her bedroom.

She stumbled and looked down at the clothes scattered about. Were those hers? Daisy looked down and stared at the hot pants and blouse. Nope, those weren't hers.

"Dang it, Daisy! Open the door!"

Daisy started forward again and kicked aside a bra that was definitely not hers. She flipped the lock to her back door and flung open the door. "What?"

The question died on her lips as she took in a naked Violet, trying to cover herself with a single leafy branch. Violet pushed past her sister and ran inside.

"My clothes! What are they doing on your living room floor?" Violet asked as she quickly dressed.

"What happened to you?" Daisy was so confused.

"I have no idea. But . . ." Violet turned and pointed at the empty pitcher, ". . . that is a very special drink."

"Sure is. I haven't thought of Robert since you all arrived."

The front door opened and Lily stumped in. "What did we put in that drink? I woke up on my front porch with my skirt up to my waist and flashed Reverend Hamilton on his way to give his morning sermon."

"That's nothing. I woke up naked in Father James's bushes," Violet grumbled as she zipped up her boots.

"We need to destroy that recipe," Lily grumbled and headed toward the counter.

"No!" Daisy and Violet yelled as they leapt forward.

"Why not? Look at what it did to us." Lily pointed at their disheveled hung-over state.

"Yes, but what if we use it for the power of good?" Daisy asked.

Violet nodded. "Small doses of that could be helpful in our matchmaking. And I know just the couple to try it on."

Chapter Eighteen

Several years later . . .

The years in Keeneston passed before Lily's eyes. The war ended, their boys came home, and matchmaking was in full force. Daisy never mentioned Robert's name ever again. As time passed, they all forgot their own heartaches; they were too busy focusing on matchmaking.

Lily wiped the kitchen counter clean for the night. The muffins for her guests were ready to be put in the oven first thing in the morning. She walked through the living room, her bell-bottoms swishing, and across the entrance hall to her private den. An entire bookcase was now full of notebooks. Those pages contained so much love. Lily smiled and took a seat on her couch. The ringing phone interrupted her reaching for the latest notebook.

"Hello?"

"Miss Lily, it's William. Betsy is in labor! We're on our way to Lexington, but she said we had to call you before we left," William's panicked deep voice said over the phone.

"A baby! Oh William, I am so excited for you both. Go! We'll see you at the hospital where you can introduce us to your son or daughter." Tears filled Lily's eyes as she hung up the phone. She might never have had children of her own, but all the babies of the couples she had gotten together felt like hers.

Lily picked up the phone and called her sisters. Within minutes, they happily entered the kitchen of their old home. Just like when they were children, they sat on the counters with mixing bowls in hand. Lily sat at their kitchen table and crocheted as fast as she could.

"I wonder if it will be a girl or a boy?" Violet asked for the tenth time.

"I don't know, but I can't wait to hold another Keeneston baby," Daisy said, joy radiating from her smile.

"I think it's wonderful. First Betsy and William, and I'll bet you Marcy and Jake will have an announcement to make any day now. Did you notice she seems a little rounder in certain places?" Lily asked, working on the last couple rows of a baby blanket.

"I sure did. And I saw that goofy look on Jake Davies's face about three months ago," Daisy said as she poured the batter into the cake pan.

"Me too. And this time we know it before John and Rhonda," Violet joked while whipping the chocolate frosting. "Although it may take me a little while to get used to this trend of waiting to have children. It's messing with my bets."

"There. All done," Lily smiled, holding up the baby blanket for her sisters to examine.

"Perfect. Taste this, I think it's ready, too." Lily leaned forward and accepted the spoonful of chocolate frosting.

"Yum. This is delicious."

"Vi, do you ever miss France?" Daisy asked as she cleaned up the kitchen.

Violet looked contemplative for a moment. "Yes and no. I miss the ambience of Europe and the chaos of a fully staffed kitchen. But then I'll go to the hospital, hold this new precious baby, and know real happiness. I had a hand in its parents finding love and will have a hand in this little child's life. That gives me more joy than cooking in France ever did."

Lily and Daisy leaned forward and wrapped Violet in a hug. "Our lives sure haven't turned out the way we thought, but I don't know if I would change a thing about them," Lily whispered.

"I know I wouldn't. I'm exactly where I should be." Daisy smiled as the timer dinged.

The sisters jumped apart. "No, where we should be is at the hospital. Let's get this cake frosted and go meet this little one," Violet said as she wiped a stray tear from her eye.

On the drive to the hospital, they took bets on whether the baby was a boy or girl, how big he or she was, and possible names for the little one. The sky was dark and the stars twinkled as they drove through the countryside. The dark figures of cows could be seen in the pastures surrounding them, but all too soon the pastures gave way to city lights. Lexington, while not big by city standards, was huge compared to Keeneston.

"There's a parking space." Daisy pointed to the open spot and Violet pulled into it.

"I wonder if the baby has been born yet," Lily said, clutching the blanket tightly to her chest.

"I hope so. I can't wait to meet the little one," Violet said, pressing the elevator button.

When they walked off the elevator, a nurse sitting behind a desk greeted them. The maternity ward was hopping at five in the morning. Lily looked around, taking in some men waiting in the lobby. She didn't see William so maybe that meant the little one had arrived.

"May I help you?" the nurse asked.

Lily stepped forward. "Yes, we're here for Betsy Ashton."

"Name?" The nurse asked.

"We're the Rose sisters."

The nurse nodded her head. "They told me you were coming. It's not visiting hours, but when that handsome man smiled at me I couldn't say no." The nurse sent them a wink as she looked at her master list. "Ah, here she is. Room 405A."

"Thank you," Violet said before hurrying toward Betsy's room.

The sisters walked excitedly down the hall, counting off room numbers. Finally they came to Betsy's room and heard the soft sounds of a baby coming from inside. Lily felt her heart swell and pushed back the tears that threatened to spill free. "Knock, knock," she said loud enough to be heard but not so loud as to startle the baby.

"Come in," William called out.

Lily and her sisters walked through the door to find Betsy sitting up in bed with a blue-blanketed bundle in her arms. She smiled and looked up at them as they came to stand beside her.

"It's a boy," she said with a serene smile.

"Oh, he's so handsome," Lily whispered, running a finger down his downy cheek.

"We brought you a cake to celebrate. No nasty hospital food for our new mother," Violet said.

"See, I told you it was a good idea to call them," Betsy teased William, who practically drooled over the cake. "Now, why don't you introduce your son to three of the most important women he'll ever know?"

William leaned over and carefully took his son from his

wife. He pulled back the blanket so they could all see his face. "Ladies, please meet William Ashton, Jr. Will, my young man, meet Miss Lily, Miss Daisy, and Miss Violet."

William stepped forward and held Will out to Miss Lily. Lily held him close to her. He smelled like baby powder and milk. He looked up at her, and Lily smiled down at him. "Hello, young Will. It's a pleasure to meet you."

Before Lily knew it, the morning sun was streaming in through the windows and there was a soft knock at the door.

"May we come in?" Marcy Davies, their former waitress and Betsy's best friend, asked.

"Of course. Come meet Will," Betsy said as Lily showed him to Marcy and Jake.

"He's so small," Jake whispered. "Aren't you afraid of dropping him?"

Lily laughed. "You better get used to it, and fast," she said with a pointed look to Marcy's stomach.

Marcy gasped. "How did you know?"

"You're pregnant?" Betsy practically shrieked.

"Yes, I'm fourteen weeks along, but no one knew," Marcy stammered.

"And you didn't tell your best friend?" Betsy sounded hurt but was also too excited to stay hurt long.

"You had so much going on with little Will being born—"

"Oh, who cares? Get over here and give me a hug," Betsy ordered, holding out her arms for her best friend.

Daisy sniffed beside Lily as Violet pulled out her handkerchief. Lily looked down at the round face in her arms and smiled at him. "Well, Will, it seems we have a whole new generation of children to see to. I'll be looking forward to the great things you accomplish. And never worry, we'll be here, helping you along the way."

She passed Will to her sister and stepped back. The room was full of joy and new beginnings. It seemed it was time to start a new chapter in their lives — one filled with happiness, matchmaking, and babies.

Chapter Nineteen

Keeneston, 37 years, 99 marriages, and 246 babies later . . .

M iss Lily sat on the front porch swing at her bed-and-breakfast and gave a disgruntled sigh. She looked down at the notebook in her hand, her fortieth, and stuck her tongue out at it. Darn that Morgan Hamilton for coming back to town and messing everything up. How can the town's reverend have a pair of daughters that differed so much? Pam was an angel; Morgan was not. Written at the top of the page was the name *Miles Davies*. It was about time Marcy and Jake's oldest son found love.

Flipping back through the notebook, Lily's smile returned as she stared at her accomplishments. Little Will had grown into a strapping young man who played in the NFL for years before coming back to Keeneston to take over his parents' horse farm. He'd even bred and raced a Kentucky Derby winner. He also fell in line and got married to McKenna Mason, or Kenna as she was commonly known. She was a bright lawyer from New York City . . . bless her Yankee heart.

After that, Kenna's best friend, Danielle, or Dani as she insisted on being called, followed her from New York. It just went to show that she too had good sense. Lily smiled as she looked at the earlier pages in her notebook. She ignored the fact that Kenna and Dani were on the run from dangerously powerful men. They had found their way home to Keeneston, and Dani had found love with a sheik. Mo was the prince of the island country of Rahmi and had come to Keeneston to raise racehorses.

And bless that sweet girl, Kenna had already given birth to a bouncing baby girl, Sienna. Some day, God willing, she'd find the perfect match for her like she had for her father. Lily turned the page and looked at Paige Davies's name. She was Jake and Marcy's only girl. Five boys and beautiful, talented Paige rounded out the Davies family. Paige had helped Kenna and Dani and, in turn, found love with FBI Agent Cole Parker. She had just given birth over Christmas to a handsome baby boy, Ryan. Hmm, that gave Lily an idea for Sienna.

Turning another page in her notebook, she came to Cade Davies and DEA Agent Annie Blake. Annie had come to Keeneston as an undercover agent and with Cade's help stopped a drug ring targeting teenagers. Annie had since left the DEA to work at the Keeneston sheriff's office. She, too, had taken the long road home, but home was here now in Keeneston with Cade and their baby girl, Sophie.

Lily flipped to the next section and traced her fingers over the names of Marshall Davies and Katelyn Jacks. Katelyn's grandparents, the Wyatts, had raised her in Keeneston, but she had gone off and had seen the world as a model. She had just recently come back to start a career as a veterinarian. Marshall had found peace as the new sheriff after coming back from Special Forces with his brothers, Miles and Cade. They had been a tricky match, and Lily and her sisters had to resort to giving Katelyn a glass too many . . . okay, three or four glasses too many . . . of their special drink. But it had worked out in the end, and they were now happily together.

In between the Davies pages, she smiled at she passed the deputy sheriffs' pages — Noodle and Dr. Emma, Dinky and Chrystal. That led her to her current page. *Miles Davies and Julie Bryant.* Julie was from the next town over, was four years younger than Miles's thirty-six years, and was as sweet as could be. She would have been perfect for Miles until the bad girl of Keeneston showed back up. Morgan Hamilton was darker than Miles, and Miles hid a lot of darkness from his time in Special Forces. That's why he needed someone sweet like Julie. But no, Morgan drew him in with her violet eyes and a take-no-crap attitude.

The screen door opened and Daisy and Violet came out carrying glasses of iced tea and a plate of brownies. "How's it coming?" Violet asked.

Lily blew out a breath and pushed back her now-white hair. "Not good. I just know that bad seed, Morgan Hamilton, has her claws in our Miles. This is my one hundredth match, and she's going to ruin it just like she did my rose bushes when she was a teenager."

Daisy handed her a glass of tea and took a seat. "Lil, for one night let's just not worry about it. This has stressed you out so much, your muffins this morning were dry. Dry!"

Lily sneered at her sister and thought about sticking her tongue out, but Violet stopped her. "Tonight is Marshall and Katelyn's wedding. Let's just go and have a good time."

"But if John beats me to this mystery, I don't know what I'll do." Lily slammed her hand onto the swing's cushion.

"Ever since Rhonda passed away, you two have been at it. For years now, we've watched you two play this gossip game. I think y'all are hot to trot for each other," Violet said, taking a giant step away from the daggers Lily was shooting her.

"You think I like John Wolfe?" Lily cried out.

"I think so, too," Daisy said softly before leaning back in her chair. Lily jumped to her feet and began to pace the verandah.

"You two are crazy. If anyone in this town understands why that is impossible, it should be you two."

"Lil," Violet started, "it's been decades and decades since Frank. I've longed to move on—to find love again. But I know it's not a probability for me. Look at us. We're not twenty-five anymore."

"Shoot, we're not even fifty-five anymore," Daisy said under her breath.

"And you have a shot at it. John has known you your whole life. He was the one who rescued you that night. He knows all about your secret pain. If he loves you, then why not give him a chance? You have always spoken so highly of him," Violet took a deep breath, "and I think you love him, too."

Lily gasped and Daisy raised the brownie plate to hide her face. "How dare you say that?"

Violet put her hands on her still curvaceous hips. "Because you do. Mark my word; this isn't over yet. You will have to face your feelings someday, Lily Rae."

"We'll just see about that," Lily stormed into the house. "I have a wedding to get ready for."

Lily, Daisy, and Violet stood by the refreshments at Marshall and Katelyn's reception. The wedding had been beautiful, and the couple was so in love. Lily's heart was bursting with happiness.

"Butter my butt and call me a biscuit, Morgan Hamilton just walked in," Daisy gasped.

"Well, that just cooks my goose," Lily growled as she stomped her way toward the growing scene.

"Lily, give her a chance. Remember, Annie believes there's a lot to the story we don't know. Since she's a DEA agent, she knows more about bad seeds than you do," Violet called out to Lily's retreating back.

Fine, they wanted Lily to give her a chance? Then she'd give Morgan a chance — a chance to explain. "Morgan?"

The dark-haired beauty turned around, and in a split second looked fearful before her toughness fell back into place. In that one moment she looked eighteen and vulnerable, and that was all it took for Lily to change her mind about Morgan Hamilton.

"That night I caught you in my roses, what were you doing in my yard?"

Morgan took a deep breath and Lily listened to the young woman who had gone from being the town's bad girl to a woman who orchestrated takeovers in the corporate world. Long ago, Lily had accused her of purposefully ruining her rose bushes. Afterward, Morgan had painted the water tower and split town. Now she was back and Miles Davies, the stern ever-so-serious businessman, had lost his heart to her. So Lily listened to it all and felt something she hadn't felt in a long time — shame. She had been wrong. She'd been wrong for eighteen years about the young woman standing in front of her. How could she ever apologize?

Lily placed her hand on Morgan's arm as Morgan defended herself to Miles's sister, Paige. "I believe I — *we* — may have been too hard on you . . ."

"You ladies all look lovely tonight." The deep voice behind Lily had her spinning around to see John Wolfe looking ever so handsome in a suit. Long ago he'd lost his six-pack abs and was now rather portly. He still had the same twinkle in his eyes and strong arms that would keep her warm at night. Lily blushed. Dang, her sisters had been right. It wasn't as easy as it had been when she was younger. She was wiser now. She knew these feelings only opened her up to pain.

"Miss Lily, would you do me the honor of a dance?"

"I'd love to," Lily put her hand on his arm and headed for the dance floor.

John held her tight as they danced. "Lily Rae, I've been your friend since the sixth grade. We've always had this fond regard for each other, but I've discovered deeper feelings this past year as we fought for the town's gossip. I've had fun. Have you?"

"Yes, I have," Lily admitted reluctantly as John led her around the dance floor.

"Why don't we have dinner together at the Blossom Café tomorrow night?" John asked.

Lily's eyes widened in shock. "Are you kidding? That's the same as publicly declaring we're boinking!"

"Not that I'd mind boinking—it's been a while, and I sure do miss it," John grinned, "but I was thinking more like a date."

"No, John. You more than anyone should know why I can't."

"Won't or can't? Don't tell me you really loved Frank that much that you're still hung up on him after what he did to you."

"Of course not. It's the pain I remember," Lily admitted as the song came to an end, and she pulled away.

"Go ahead, Lily. Run away from another chance at love. I'm strong enough to follow. Just be prepared. I'm right about us just like I'm always right about what goes on around town," John said smugly.

Lily gasped. "How dare you? You know I am better at sniffing out gossip than you'll ever be."

"And I'm also better at loving you than Frank ever was. I'll give you all pleasure, with no pain, Lily Rae."

"We're not talking about love. We're talking about gossip," Lily huffed.

"You just keep telling yourself that," John chuckled as he walked away.

That man! He just, he just . . . oh fiddlesticks. She was going to have to confront the pain from that night at some point. It just wasn't going to be at that moment.

Now, Pierce Davies, the youngest of Jake and Marcy's kids, was looking rather tied-in-knots in love. What kind of good Samaritan would she be if she didn't help him out? And if it took her mind off her own love life, then so much the better.

Lily felt the crack of the broom reverberate up her arms. She heard the collective gasp of everyone in the Blossom Café the second she crashed her broom over John's head. But what was she to do? The man had kissed her in full view of the entire town after trying to out-gossip her! She had been the first to admit her mistake about Morgan, and now that sly fox was trying to claim it was him. On top of stealing her gossip, he kissed her to shut her up. Her first kiss in years, and he did it in front of everyone as if to prove a point. It didn't matter that she liked it. It didn't matter that her heart was pounding like she was once again a teenager. No, it didn't matter because he was now smirking at her.

With a huff, she spun on her orthopedic shoes and

marched out of the café. Lily walked back to her house and pulled out her notebook. She had crossed Julie off the top of Miles's page and had written Morgan's name instead. It would have been her one-hundredth match, but as much as she would like to claim it, she couldn't. She was still in search of that special couple.

Lily walked out onto her porch and took a seat on her swinging bench. Her lips still tingled from the kiss at the café. John had kissed her, and she had liked it. Her heart took time to slow back to its steady beat as she closed her eyes and relived the kiss. When had it happened? When had she and John gone from friends to kissing?

Taking a deep breath, Lily opened the book. All these couples, all this love. Was she destined to end up like them after all these years? But as soon as her heart fluttered, she looked next door and felt the panic rise from the pit of her stomach and take hold of her.

No, it wasn't meant to be. She would never find her happily-ever-after. But number one hundred could. Lily focused her attention on the book in front of her and pushed aside her own desires. She had to find her hundredth couple, and that would take her mind off what she couldn't have. It would mend her heart. She thought back to the reception the previous night and had an idea about who was next. Tammy Fields, the assistant for the only two attorneys in town, Henry Rooney and Kenna Ashton. Tammy was a sweet girl who had made the best out of a hard life, bless her heart. It also wasn't a secret she had a thing for Pierce Davies. Pierce just hadn't woken up to the treasure right in front of him. Rubbing her hands together, Lily got to work. Sometimes all it took was a little competition to make a man realize his feelings.

Chapter Twenty

L ily sat smiling as her one-hundredth couple kissed at the altar and pronounced Pierce and Tammy Davies husband and wife. From behind her, a hand settled on her shoulder. She knew who it was without turning around. Only one person had a touch so gentle and reassuring that she wanted to melt into it.

"Congratulations, Lily Rae," John whispered, his breath tickling her ear and sending shivers down her back.

"On what? Beating you again?"

"Don't you ever stop?" John chuckled. "Is this some kind of foreplay for you? You know I am not going anywhere. I'm a little too big for you to move. But no, congratulations on arranging one hundred happy marriages. Now, don't you think it's time to focus on your happiness?"

Lily stiffened. "I *am* happy."

"Liar," John whispered so softly she wasn't quite sure if he had said it or not.

Lily gulped and then stood and straightened her dress to follow the happy couple to the reception. She *was* happy. She had a full life. She helped others find happiness. Besides, she was too old to fall in love again. She was a senior citizen, for crying out loud.

"What did he say to you?" Daisy asked as soon as they were alone.

"Nothing," Lily muttered, and she went to put her wedding gift on the table.

"It didn't look like nothing to me," Violet smirked. "You turned all red and were breathing so hard I thought you were going to pass out."

"I said it's nothing," Lily spit out.

Her sisters stopped, and their hands went onto their hips in a way that reminded Lily of their mother. They weren't buying it, and she didn't want to talk about it.

"I think she loves him but is too much of a chicken to follow her own heart," Violet said casually to Daisy.

"*Bawk, bawk, bawk.*" Daisy flapped her arms like a chicken, and Lily turned red with anger.

"Don't you dare call me a chicken!"

"I'll call you an old cow if I want. Look, there's ol' Bessie put out to pasture," Violet challenged.

Lily gasped. "I don't see you two opening your hearts to anyone. How dare you call me a chicken for not wanting to get hurt again?"

"Because we don't have someone as wonderful as John Wolfe wanting to love us," Daisy shot back.

"Lily, we are matchmaking professionals and your sisters. Trust us when we tell you that man is head over heels in love with you."

Lily felt her throat tighten. She forced down a swallow as panic rushed back. Every time she thought she had moved on, she remembered the feeling of the door opening and the camera clicking. The pain and betrayal still had their claws securely hooked into her.

"Come on now, Lily Rae. You know you want to."

Lily clenched her jaw at the war raging inside her. She hadn't been able to turn her back on John, but she hadn't been able to open her heart to him either. Instead, she funneled her conflicting feelings into a race for gossip. It kept both her mind and her heart busy so she didn't have to come to terms with the past. Maybe, just maybe, her sisters had been right to call her a coward.

For months John had called on her every day. He brought her flowers, her favorite sweets, or a book he thought she'd enjoy. And damn her luck for actually enjoying the book and looking forward to his daily visits. They would sit and talk for hours. They talked about the old days, about the young couples in town, and the babies being born. She knew they were essentially dating, but this was just too much.

"You want me to move in with you?" Lily practically shouted. "We aren't even a real couple yet. And move in with you? Do I look like a milkman delivering free milk?" The rage that flowed through her had her wrapping her hand tightly around the broom handle.

The ol' goat smirked. "I think that ship has sailed, Lily Rae . . ."

Thwack! The broom crashed over his head before she even knew she had done it.

John shook his head to clear the cobwebs. "Now, Lily Rae, that wasn't very nice, was it?"

"Well," Lily sputtered, "that wasn't very nice of you to bring up such a delicate subject."

"You have to move past Frank and what he did to you. I know it was awful. I was there. But, Lily, for us to have a future you need to find closure."

Shameful old memories flooded her mind. She felt her

tears starting to prick her eyes. "Maybe I don't want closure."

John's head hung, and he let out a deep breath. "Did you really love him that much? Does his memory keep you warm at night like I do . . . or did? If you can't open your heart to me, Lily Rae, then what are we doing here?"

"That's a good question. I guess the answer is leaving." Lily opened the door and prayed he left before the first tear fell. Ever since the last of the Davies boys had been married off, she'd been a miserable mush of wild emotions. She hadn't felt this confused since menopause. No, if she were honest, it started before then, but she also knew she wasn't honest with herself.

"If that's what you really want, Lily Rae. Goodbye."

John walked out the door and Lily slammed it shut. She rested her back against the door and felt the tears start to fall. Golly, she needed something big to happen to take her mind off this, or she was going to fall to pieces.

"Lily Rae! Open the door at once."

Lily blinked her bloodshot eyes. She was sitting on her couch trying not to think about John and the fact that the last time she saw him he was at a tableful of women. She wiped at her eyes and straightened her hair.

"Now, Lil!" She heard Violet yell as she continued to hammer on the door.

"Hold your horses. I'm comin'," Lily shouted. She stood up and tried to straighten her dress. When she opened the door, her two sisters tumbled in.

Daisy sucked in air and Violet sighed. "So, it's true. You broke up with John and then went out on a date with Roger

Burns?" Violet asked.

"The ol' goat wanted to move in with me. Can you imagine?" Lily asked and stuck her nose up in the air. "Well, I showed him."

"Moving in with John sounds divine. Dating Roger sounds gross. I know we're old, but we're not *that* old! Why did you kick John out anyway? Whenever we ask, you refuse to answer. It's time we talked about this," Daisy said stubbornly.

"Why? Well, I . . . I . . . I'm not a hussy who just lives with a man. If he really loved me, he'd ask me to marry him."

Violet snorted. "That's what you're going with?"

"Lily, you need to move on —" Daisy started to say before Lily cut her off.

"Would everyone stop saying that?"

"Excuse me." Lily knew the sweet voice belonged to her best friend, who wasn't actually all that sweet. "I hate to interrupt Lily's much-deserved whiplashing, but have y'all heard the news?" Edna asked.

"Heard it? Shoot, Edna, I *am* the news," Lily spat at her best friend.

Edna shook her head. "No, dear, you're old news. I just got a phone call from John . . . Bridget has deployed to Rahmi to save Ahmed. That country is under attack, and Prince Mo is meeting with the president to ask for American help."

The sisters gasped. Bridget Springer was Keeneston's newest resident, and they already loved her as if she'd grown up here.

"Tell us everything," Lily demanded.

"She and her police dog, what's his name?" Edna asked.

"Marco," the three sisters responded immediately. Bridget trained police and military dogs for a living. Marshall Davies, the sheriff of Keeneston, got one of the dogs, and Bridget just never left after training the handler. She had fallen in love with the biggest, hottest badass of Keeneston, Ahmed. He was the head of security for the Prince of Rahmi and was feared worldwide. But not by their Bridget. She saw past the hard exterior to the loyal and loving man underneath.

"Yes, well, she and Marco are going to jump out of a plane and into the fight," Edna exclaimed.

"What should we do?" Daisy asked as she wrung her hands.

"I know what we should do," Edna said matter-of-factly. She opened her purse and pulled out her gun. "When's the next flight to Rahmi?"

"Oh, put that away Edna. We need to activate the phone tree. Casseroles, pies, blankets . . . they'll need them all when they get back," Violet told them, disappearing into the kitchen.

"I'll start on my cheese log," Edna said and put her gun back in her purse. "Although I still like my idea better."

Lily watched her friend hurry across the street with a cell phone to her ear. The Keeneston grapevine had been activated. Soon the whole town would be together, stocking food and holding out hope for Bridget, Ahmed, and the whole island nation of Rahmi.

"Daisy," Violet called out, "make a pitcher of our special iced tea. We need to take Lily to the woodshed while we're cooking."

Daisy smiled. Their dear sister had this coming. Although Lily sputtered her protest about needing to focus on the casserole for Bridget and Ahmed, she wasn't going to win that battle. Daisy pulled the bourbon out and went to work making a big pitcher. They would need every drop of it.

Lily sat at the kitchen table and poured her third drink. Her sisters had been at her since the first casserole, past the pies, and now onto the brownies.

"Lily Rae! Are you listening?" Violet asked as she poured herself another drink.

"I'm trying not to," Lily grumbled.

"Just answer the question," Daisy finally yelled. "Why are you messing up what could be the best thing of your life?"

"Because I'm scared," Lily screamed back as she slammed her glass on the table. "I'm scared I'm going to open up my heart, and it will just be ripped from my chest again. I survived that once, but I don't think I could survive it again."

Lily angrily swiped at a tear rolling down her cheek. Her sisters sat across from her, stunned. Violet picked up her drink and downed it in one gulp. "Get over it, you pansy."

Lily choked. "What?"

"You heard me. Get over it. Because you were a coward, the man you love is calling Edna. He's calling your best friend instead of you. She was sitting at that table with him the other day, too, wasn't she?"

Lily felt the blood drain from her face. "He wouldn't."

"And why not?" Daisy asked. "You've shut him down time and time again."

Lily's hands started to tremble. "Oh, no. I've made the biggest mistake." She shoved back from the table and ran from the room.

"Where's she going?" Daisy asked Violet.

"To get her man." Violet grinned as the front door slammed shut.

"John!" Lily hammered her palm against his front door. "I know you're in there. I hear your TV."

A couple seconds later, the door opened, and John looked down at her. He seemed upset, but Lily didn't care. She had finally decided to let herself love again, and she wasn't going to lose him.

"Lily Rae. Now isn't the best time . . ."

"It's okay, John dear. I have to get back and make a second cheese log since you liked this one so much. Oh, hi, Lily." Edna smiled at her from behind John's back. "I'll see you later, John."

"Sure thing, Edna. And thanks for the cheese log. It was delicious."

Lily watched in shocked silence as Edna walked off the little porch and headed back toward her house with a huge smile on her lips. Lily turned and looked at John. She felt her heart starting to break, but she was also stronger now. She wasn't eighteen, and he wasn't Frank. She had pushed him to take another woman's cheese log when he should have been eating hers all along.

"John, we need to talk," Lily said firmly, pushing her way into his house.

"What is it, Lily Rae?" John stood staring at her and put his hands in his pockets. "I'm trying to keep up to date on the Rahmi situation."

"How can you find that stuff out?"

"I'll never tell," John smirked.

"Even to your girlfriend?"

John's smirk faded. "I don't have a girlfriend."

"Yes, you do, if you still want her. John, I've been a stubborn idiot. I was too scared of the past to grab my future. Please tell me you still love me."

John let out a long breath and took the seat next to her on the couch. He lifted his arm, put it around her, pulled her against his chest, and placed his chin on her head. "Lily, I have loved you for years. And for months I have showed you how much you mean to me. I want to believe you . . ."

"Give me a week and I'll prove it to you."

"Lily Rae, you don't have to prove it to me," John whispered, and he tightened his arms around her.

"I need to prove it to myself. I need to put my heart out there again," Lily said softly. She leaned back against him. And in one week she would prove to herself, John, her sisters, and the whole town of Keeneston that she had opened herself up to love once again.

"*Psst*. Is the coast clear?"

Violet turned to look at the back door of the bed-and-breakfast where Edna was poking her head inside. "Yes, come in! How did it go?"

Edna walked in and dropped into the kitchen chair. "It took y'all long enough. I made poor John eat my whole cheese log while I waited for Lily to arrive. But, just like you said, she arrived and pounded on the door. I casually made my exit, and by the daggers she was shooting me, I would say she is well on her way to being in love."

"I can't believe it worked." Daisy shook her head. "It was just like with Pierce and Tammy. How did she not see we were using her own playbook against her?"

"Love blinds you. As we all know," Violet said as she frosted one of her cakes.

"Well, now we just have to see if she forgives me,"

Edna said. She stuck her finger in the frosting.

Violet gave it a playful whack. "You can't stop pretending until the deed is done."

"Got it. I haven't had this much fun since we got to shoot that awful man who was trying to hurt Miles and Morgan. Oh, and I looked it up. All flights to Rahmi have been cancelled. Well, I better go make my other cheese log for when the kids get home. I'll let you know as soon as I hear if they've made it. If there's anyone taking bets, I'd put money on Bridget and Ahmed."

Violet agreed. Those two would literally fight a war to be able to love one another. She only hoped Lily was prepared to do the same.

Lily breathed in deeply and smiled. The smell of freshly baked banana nut bread filled her nose as she pulled the pan from the oven. It had been a humiliating week. She'd made a fool of herself all over town trying to prove she loved John. She made him muffins and served him at the café in front of the whole town. She chased Edna away from him at Ahmed and Bridget's surprise engagement party. She made his favorite meals, rented his favorite movies, and even had a candlelight dinner at the pond. She was determined to make new happy memories for herself there.

A knock at the back door had her turning around with a smile on her face as John pulled open the screen door. "Is that my favorite bread?"

"You know it is," Lily grinned as she placed the steaming hot bread and some butter on the table.

"Lily Rae, you've been spoiling me." John laughed and sat down at the table. Lily poured him some orange juice before taking a seat across from him.

"It's only because I love you, you ol' billy goat."

"About time you realized that. I love you, too, Lily Rae. Which makes me want to ask you — "

Lily stopped him with her hand. "I've been thinking about this all week. I love you. I know that. But I'm scared, John. Last time I rushed into things and have lived to regret it every day of my life. So, if you will have me, I very much want to be your girlfriend."

Lily held her breath and waited as John stood up and walked over to her. He held out his hands, and she placed her smaller ones into his. Pulling her up, he leaned down and placed a gentle kiss on her lips.

"I love you, too, Lily Rae. And I'm proud to be your boyfriend and whatever else I might become in the future as long as it's with you by my side."

Lily sniffed, "Oh, John!" Before rising up on her tip toes and kissing him hard.

"Oh, Lily!"

Violet clamped a hand over her mouth as she pulled away from the open screen door. She motioned Daisy and Edna to move back. The giggle that was about to escape was held back with her second hand being placed over her mouth as they ran across their yard and over to Edna's back patio.

"What is it?" Daisy and Edna asked at the same time.

"We did good, ladies. When I left they had each said 'I love you' and were making out like teenagers."

"Are they getting married?" Edna asked after they all high-fived each other.

"I don't think so. And John said he was fine with that," Violet told them.

"That's okay, we have time to work on them now. I bet

that someday she'll be begging that man to marry her," Daisy predicted.

Violet hoped so, but only time would tell. A lot of time considering she knew how stubborn her sister was.

Chapter Twenty-One

Twenty years later . . .

Daisy took a seat on the white rocking chair she'd designated as hers when she was six years old. Violet sat next to her, and Lily gently swung on the hanging porch bench. They were creatures of habit; that was for sure. These spots had been theirs from when they had pigtails to white tufts of overpermed hair. Daisy looked at Lily who had been "dating" John Wolfe for almost twenty years. Lily had fluffed her hair and even had a little makeup on today.

"What's going on, Lily Rae? You look all dolled up," Daisy asked as she started to gently rock.

"You do look nice. Are you and John finally going to admit that you've been living together for almost two decades?" Violet asked with a snort.

"Even better. I've decided it's time he proposed. I'm ready to be a bride," Lily beamed.

"Wait . . . John hasn't asked you to marry him?" Daisy asked, trying to wrap her mind around this news.

Lily stammered, "Well, not exactly. I mean, he has before, but that was just, oh, seven years ago when he basically moved in."

Violet rolled her eyes. "You can't even tell the truth to your own sisters. That man moved into your heart and your bed close to twenty years ago!"

Lily huffed and crossed her arms over her chest. She looked down and groaned. She needed a push-up bra. "Fine, he moved in eighteen years ago, and we've been happy ever since. Now I've decided I'm not getting any younger," Lily paused when her sisters snickered, "so I think we should finally get married."

"So, ask him. It's the modern times. Women's rights and all that," Daisy said and picked up her crocheting.

"But I am *not* a modern woman. That man has had the best years of my life and I deserve a romantic proposal." Lily stomped her foot on the porch and let out an aggravated sigh.

Violet snorted and leaned toward Daisy. "I told you so."

Daisy reached into her bra and pulled out twenty dollars. "A bet's a bet."

Lily looked back and forth between them and narrowed her eyes. "What's that all about?"

"Oh, just a little bet Daisy and I made twenty years ago."

"A bet about me?" Lily asked.

"Uh-huh," Daisy said as she began crocheting again.

Lily grew impatient. "And what would that bet be?"

"Just that it would take you forever to realize you wanted to get married to John, and when you finally got your head out of your tush, you would be begging John to marry you," Violet said casually, sipping some tea.

"Begging? I'm not begging."

"Oh, you will." Violet smiled. "How else do you plan on getting him to marry you?"

"I'll bet you twenty bucks he'll propose to me by the end of the week." Lily stood up and stomped her orthopedic shoes right back into the house.

Daisy shook her head and smiled. "You'd think after almost ninety years she'd have learned we know her better than she knows herself."

"Put twenty on Lily proposing to John," Violet said. She set down her cup and handed the twenty back to Daisy.

Daisy pulled out her notebook and wrote down the bet. "I'm in for twenty as well."

"Miss Daisy, Miss Violet," Ryan Parker, the oldest son of Cole Parker and Paige Davies Parker called out. "I got your text. You need a lift to the café?"

"Aren't you a sweet boy?" Daisy grinned at the handsome twenty-year-old man in front of her with dark brown, almost black, hair and the Davies hazel eyes.

"Man now, I daresay." Violet beamed and opened her arms wide for the young man to give her a hug. She'd seen his mother born and held her as a babe. She'd helped his parents find love, and sometime soon, she and her sisters would help him the same way.

Ryan smiled at her, and Violet practically swooned. He was a looker all right. She stood up, and Ryan wrapped her in a hug. Violet pulled him down into one of her famous hugs. Daisy rolled her eyes over the top of Ryan's head, stuck in Violet's pillowy bosom, and Violet winked at her.

"Thank you for picking us up. Are you ready to head back to college at the end of the week?" Violet asked as she let Ryan up to breathe.

"Yes, ma'am. I do miss Keeneston when I'm away. It's been a nice spring break. Here, let me help you to the car." Ryan held out one arm for Miss Violet and one for Miss Daisy. "What do you need to do at the café?"

"Oh, we have some bets that need to be placed. How do you like the cook we hired?" Violet asked.

Ryan grinned again and even Daisy flushed.

"Not quite as good as you, Miss Violet, as you can tell when the whole town flocks to the café on days when you're cooking. Now, what's the bet?" Ryan opened the back door of the car and helped the ladies in.

"Whether, by the end of the week, Lily has proposed to John or if John has proposed to Lily," Daisy told him as she pulled out her notebook. "Would you care to place a bet?"

Ryan pulled out his wallet. "Put ten on Lily having to propose. Once a guy gets burned, it's real hard to put yourself out there again."

Daisy and Violet nodded their heads as Daisy recorded the bet. Ryan closed the door. And while he walked around the car, Daisy rolled her eyes at her sister. "You texted him for a ride? We may be in our late eighties, but we're perfectly capable of walking to the café."

"But it gave us a chance to see him and gave me a chance to hug him." Violet winked.

"For crying out loud, he's young enough to be your grandchild," Daisy hissed.

Violet just grinned. "But he's not, and you're just jealous I've had the hottest men of Keeneston between these puppies and you haven't."

"Violet Fae!" Daisy was cut off from scolding her sister by Ryan sliding into the front seat.

Lily fluffed her hair and put some lipstick on in the mirror. Today was the day. Today she was going to become engaged and be as happy as the bookcase full of couples she had helped find love. The back door opened, and Lily hurried to the kitchen to meet John.

"I have the groceries, dear," John called out.

Lily paused in the hallway right outside the kitchen and took a deep breath. She pushed back her shoulders, propped up her boobs, and sauntered into the kitchen swinging her hips seductively. She sent John a sexy smile as she saw his surprised look as his eyes roamed her body.

"Did you throw your hip out again? You're walkin' funny." John rushed forward and put his arm around her waist.

Lily swatted his arm. "No! I'm fine. I was just walking into the room. Don't you notice anything else?" Lily batted her mascaraed eyes at him.

John's brow creased as he looked into her eyes. "Do you have something in your eye?"

Lily growled. "Do you notice anything different about me?" Lily asked sweetly.

"Umm . . . oh! You got a new haircut. It looks nice." John smiled as if he was the smartest man on the planet, and Lily tried to control her temper. She was sure he'd take one look at her and go down onto one knee.

Suddenly John stood. "I have to go."

"What? Now?" Lily cried.

"Yes, uh, I need to change the oil in my car."

Lily rolled her eyes. "Your gossip radar is going off, isn't it?"

"No, I just remembered I've driven over five thousand miles and . . . yeah." John put the last of the groceries away and hurried for the door.

"We've been together almost twenty years. Don't you think you can tell me how you know all these things?"

John froze, and it would have been comical if it weren't about something she wanted to know.

"Maybe if I was your *wife,* you'd tell me." Lily tried the seductive smile again and ran her finger down his chest.

"Nope. Even if I had a wife, I wouldn't tell her," John said and leaned forward, placing a quick peck on her cheek before hightailing it out the door.

"I got twenty on John proposing," Henry Rooney, the town's defense attorney, called out and waved a twenty in the air. Daisy hurried over to grab it and record his bet.

"No way, I have twenty on Lily having to do it," Kenna Ashton, the town's prosecutor, said as she dug around in her purse for her wallet.

"Please, Mom. John is old-school. He'll be doing the proposing," Sienna, Kenna and Will's twenty-one-year-old daughter, said as she pulled out a ten.

Daisy ran between the tables of courthouse employees, sheriff deputies, the five Davies brothers, their wives, and some of their kids sprinkled around the room, collecting bets.

"Agreed. I have twenty on John proposing," Nabi, the head of security for the Rahmi royal family, called out. Hmm, Daisy needed to find a good woman for him. Maybe after this week she and her sisters would start looking again for him.

"Are you crazy? Lily's left him sitting for too long. She's going to have to propose," Cole Parker, Ryan's father and head of the Lexington FBI office, said as he pulled out his wallet.

"Lily's a tough woman. She won't stop until he has proposed. I bet John will fold and do exactly what Lily wants," Annie Davies said as she pushed the gun belt of her sheriff's deputy uniform out of the way to pull out her money.

"Exactly!" Tammy Davies and Morgan Davies called out as they placed their bets.

"Don't you all know anything? I agree with Cole. Lily will have to do it. John is too proud to do it after all these years," Ahmed, co-owner of Desert Farm and former head of security for the Rahmi royal family, told the patrons of the Blossom Café. Mo, the prince of Rahmi and Ahmed's business partner, nodded his head in agreement.

"Oh, Dad, you men are so dense," Ahmed's daughter, Abigail, said as she reached for her purse. "Here's five dollars on John doing exactly what Lily wants and not even knowing it."

"I agree with Abby and my mom," Sophie, Annie and Cade Davies's daughter, called from the table she sat at with her cousins, Sydney and Layne.

"Us too!" Reagan and Riley said as Daisy recorded their bets.

"We're for Lily proposing," Mo's twin sons, Zain and Gabe, called out.

"Yeah, Lily proposing . . . doesn't that make us Team John?" Pierce Davies asked his brothers.

Miles shrugged. "I guess. Team John all the way."

Layne rolled her eyes. "You're so uncool, Dad. That was so ten years ago."

"Well, then that makes us Team Lily," Gemma called from her table of her sisters-in-law, ignoring the way their children rolled their eyes.

Dinky and Noodle, two of the town's senior sheriff's deputies, placed their bets for Team John. "Lily will have to beg him . . ."

"Beg him to do what?" Lily asked as the café fell into total silence. The only sound was that of purses being zipped closed and forks clanging as they were dropped. "I'll have to beg who to do what, Dinky?"

Dinky cleared his throat. "You'll have to beg that fancy French chef of Mo's to give you the recipe for his, um, fancy cookie things.

"Macaroons," Noodle hissed under his breath.

"And why would I do that?"

Dinky flushed pink. "Violet won't talk to him cause he's so stuck up like . . . Sorry, Mo."

Mo shrugged. "It's true. And he's going to retire on me at the end of the year, so you better hurry to get that recipe," Mo said smoothly. So smoothly, in fact, that Violet actually believed him.

"He's retiring?"

"Yes. You'll have to find someone else to argue with," Mo teased.

Daisy's eyes narrowed at Violet, but Lily wasn't done with her rant. "So, I see how it is. Who placed a bet against me?"

"Even if they were betting on it, not that they would ever do something like that, but you know I can't tell you that, Lily Rae," Daisy chided as she tightened her grip on her betting book.

"*Humph!* Well, I'll prove you all wrong. That man will be begging me to marry him." Lily stormed out on a huff.

The screen door slammed closed and everyone sat in silence as they watched her march up the street.

"I believe her. I put twenty on Team Lily," Father James said. "Oh, and I'm also retiring in a couple years."

"What?" the town cried and all bets were temporarily forgotten.

Father James held up his hands to quiet the inquisition peppering him. "I'm not leaving Keeneston. I'm just retiring . . . kind of. I'll be around to perform weddings, funerals, and stuff like that. The day-to-day running of Saint Francis and the sermons will soon belong to another worthy gentleman."

"Who?" Daisy asked with concern. It had taken almost

six months to break Father James in when he came to Keeneston, and she didn't want to have to do that with another priest. After all, most might frown on the betting, gossip, and the occasional need to shoot a bad guy in Keeneston.

"I don't know yet. In fact, I don't even know how long it will be. The new father could show up tomorrow or in five years. We are spread kind of thin. After the larger parishes get filled, Keeneston will be up. But, like I said, it will most likely be years."

"We'll be sorry to see you retire but are very glad you are staying in town. It wouldn't be the same without you," Violet said and hugged Father James, pulling his head down to disappear into her ample bosom. Daisy rolled her eyes and crossed herself. Her sister was so going to hell in a hand basket.

Chapter Twenty-Two

Lily paced back and forth in front of Southern Charms as she waited for Paige Davies Parker to get back from lunch. What she needed to help prove everyone wrong was inside Paige's shop. And it wasn't one of Paige's famous Kentucky Derby hats.

"Miss Lily? Are you waiting for me?" Paige asked as she moved to unlock the shop door.

"I sure am. But first, how did you place your bet?"

"What bet?"

"Oh, not you, too," Lily groaned.

Paige smiled and pushed back the light brown hair from her cheek. "If there was such a bet, I would place money on you having John begging for you to marry him . . . that is, if such a bet existed."

"What about the other girls?"

"We're Team Lily all the way."

"I knew I could count on y'all. Now, I need help. I need to seduce John into marriage."

Paige alternately gulped, choked, and giggled. The Rose sisters were like her grandmothers and thinking of Lily seducing John was rather comical. She was in her late eighties, for heaven's sake. Did they even do it at that age? Well, she and Cole certainly still did and they were now in their early fifties and had no plans on stopping anytime soon. So maybe it wasn't so crazy after all.

"So you want to see my secret stash? There's a price for that."

"I'll pay anything, dear," Lily practically begged.

"I want to know how John knows everything."

"I would love to tell you, dear, but the ol' goat won't even tell me that. He said even if we were married he wouldn't tell me."

Paige shrugged her shoulders. "It was worth a shot. Come on into the back."

Twenty minutes later, Lily walked home with the sure-fire win wrapped up in a Southern Charms bag. John was listening to wire taps or communicating with aliens to sniff out his latest gossip, so she had the house all to herself. Or so she thought. Her two traitorous sisters sat on the porch, laughing and drinking her sweet tea.

"What do you have there, Lily Rae?" Violet asked, eyeing the bag.

"None of your beeswax. What are you two doing here?"

Daisy held up an envelope. "Look what we got in the mail today."

"What is it?"

"It's an invitation to our seventieth high school reunion," Daisy told Lily, handing it to her.

"Why do we need a reunion? There's only so many of us left, and we're all right here. We see each other every day."

Violet shook her head. "You know very well that over half our class left Keeneston."

Lily gulped. There were people from her high school class she never wanted to see again.

"Don't worry, we had Nabi do a little snooping for us. Frank won't be coming," Violet said gently.

"How do you know that?" Lily tried to be strong, but the memories of that night at the pond came rushing back.

"He died six years ago." Daisy held out her hand and took Lily's. Giving it a little squeeze to reassure her sister.

"He's dead?" Lily whispered. Was this the answer to moving on? She should feel sad, but all she felt was relief.

"Yes, dear," Violet and Daisy told her.

Lily sat down on the swing and let out a deep breath. "Then what are we waiting for? We have some shopping to do. We want to look our best for our reunion, don't we?"

☆   ★   ☆

"John! Darling, will you come into the kitchen please?" Lily called out. She looked down at the pink negligée, matching satin robe, and the miraculous pushup bra and smiled. Only three days into this bet and she would have her proposal in minutes. She couldn't wait to rub it in everyone's faces.

"Yes, darlin'?" John called as he walked into the kitchen. Lily leaned farther back from where she sat on the kitchen table and sent him a come-hither look. "Are you stuck up there? What are you doing on the kitchen table anyway?"

Lily felt steam pour out of her ears. "Stuck? You ask if I'm stuck? Look at me, you stupid man, and ask yourself what you think I'm doing up here laid out like a feast."

John looked at her again—really looked at her. "Oh . . . ooh. You're feeling frisky. Hold on, I'll be right back!"

Lily rolled her eyes as John hurried from the room. Finally. The dense man got it. Lily tapped her foot on the chair and took a deep breath. John came rushing back into the room with a goofy grin on his face.

"You're that excited to see me in this? If you married me, then you could have this every day," Lily purred.

"Why? I already have it everyday. But no, I finally did what we talked about. I went and saw the doctor and he gave me a certain little . . . I mean, *big* prescription. Look, look, it's working!" John said giddily as he looked down at his pants.

"Oh, John," Lily gasped and held out her arms. She'd tackle the marriage business during the afterglow, when his mind was so muddled he'd agree to anything.

"It's not going down," John said four hours later, waking Lily up from a little nap. She pulled on her robe and looked over at John.

"What?" she said sleepily. The damn ol' goat reverse-played her. As she lay in blissful happiness, he said how glad he was that they were living together in sin. It made things more adventurous. What was she going to do now?

"Mr. Happy is still happy and it's been four hours. What do I do? Or do I bother? I mean, look at it. I still got it." He grinned.

"Men. I guess we better call Dr. Emma. She's with her daughter, Ava, today. Ava's getting ready to go back to college after spring break so Dr. Emma took her shopping at Southern Charms before meeting Noodle for a family dinner."

"How do you know that?"

"I'm not the only one with secret sources. I'll tell you mine if you tell me yours. You know, if we were married, it would be covered under spousal privilege."

"Never . . . ow! This is starting to hurt."

"I'm going to call her."

"No! This is both embarrassing and impressive. Take a picture with your phone."

"I'm not going to do that!" Lily shook her head. Her life had been ruined over a picture, yet John wanted to show off for one. He'd probably text it to everyone in their senior group. But when John gasped in pain, Lily grabbed her phone.

"Dr. Emma, I'm so sorry to bother you, dear. We have a situation here." Lily hung up the phone and turned to John. "She'll be right over."

Lily looked at the needle and gulped. Dr. Emma had something akin to a bemused professional smile playing on her lips as sweat broke out across John's forehead.

"You're going to do what with the needle?" John asked as his voice cracked.

Dr. Emma just smiled serenely and snapped on her surgical gloves. Lily reached for John's hand. "I love you, you ol' billy goat."

"I'm reconsidering how much I love you if she sticks that where I think she's going to," John muttered. The pain of the needle was not as strong as the pain from back of his head being smacked.

Lily let out a huff and plopped onto the porch swing next to her sisters. Tonight was the dinner and dance for their reunion. It was also the end of her week. She was going to lose her bet. She had until midnight to receive her proposal, and there were no signs pointing to that happening.

"Do you have your outfit picked out?" Violet asked as

she worked on crocheting a blanket.

"Yes, I decided on the pretty pink one," Lily told her, gently swinging.

"I'm going with the white and yellow one." Daisy grinned.

Violet rolled her eyes. "We're so predictable. I'm going with the purple one. I can't wait to see everyone. I talked to Donna and she said there was going to be quite the turnout. People are coming in from all over the country. There will be close to twenty of us after adding in spouses and hosts."

"Wow. And I love that they made it a sock hop. It's going to be so much fun putting on those skirts again," Daisy said excitedly. "Look, it's later than I realized. I need to get home and change. Should we meet here and drive over together?"

"Yes. I have something special planned for our ride over," Lily grinned mischievously.

Daisy looked in the mirror and gave a little swish of her yellow skirt. She tucked her white shirt into the waistband and finished her outfit off with a yellow and white belt. She looked like spring and felt excited for the first time in a long while.

Violet, who lived a couple blocks away, knocked on the door. Daisy spritzed herself with perfume and went to meet her sister. Opening the door, Daisy's mouth dropped.

"Are you borrowing Lily's pushup bra?" Violet and Daisy asked each other at the same time and then laughed.

Violet looked beautiful in a dark purple skirt and a pale lavender top. She finished it off with a white cardigan. "Are you ready to go?" Violet asked.

"I am." Daisy shut the door and started the short walk to Lily's. "I don't know about you, but I'm really excited about tonight. I have a feeling it's going to be fun."

Violet stopped walking as she looked up the street at Lily's house. "What on earth?"

Daisy raised her head and looked at a shiny black stretch limo parked in front of the house. Lily and John stood in the yard dressed to the nines, talking to a sexy specimen of a man in a black suit.

"It's Nabi," Violet said on a sigh.

"How can you tell?"

"I'd know that backside anywhere," Violet snickered. "Nabi! Oh, what a dear you are to drive us."

Nabi turned around and walked to the sidewalk to meet them. "I'm not just driving you. It would be my pleasure to escort you to the dance if you ladies would agree."

"Of course! You're too sweet." Violet opened her arms and Nabi's head disappeared into her abundant chest.

Hell, Daisy mouthed pointing to Violet and then to the ground. Violet just winked at her over the top of Nabi's black hair before finally releasing the man.

Nabi took a deep breath, sucked in air, and smiled at the ladies. He opened the door for John to help Lily inside and then offered his arm to Daisy and Violet.

"Lily, what a wonderful surprise." Violet reached over and gave Lily's hand a squeeze. Lily had a pink skirt and shirt with a white scarf tied around her neck. She looked lovely and utterly miserable. Violet just widened her grin. Twenty years of dangling a great man like John was finally coming to bite her in the butt.

"Oh, look at the school. It's all decorated," Daisy exclaimed, pulling Violet's attention away from Lily.

Streamers, balloons, and signs with their names on

them filled the front lawn and decorated the entranceway. Daisy could hardly wait for Nabi to pull to a stop. She saw Donna's name, John's name, and all of theirs, along with several people she hadn't thought about since high school.

"Look, Daisy. Charles Lastinger is here," Violet teased and Daisy wanted to smack her.

"He always had the biggest crush on you," Lily said, joining in on the teasing.

"Charles was a good guy," John told them. "After high school, he went to some Ivy League college in New England and became a surgeon. I lost touch with him after that."

People from the class stopped to see who was getting out of the limo. John stepped out first and offered his hand for Lily. Daisy stuck her head out next and was met with Nabi's arm. Grabbing hold, she stood up and waited for Violet to take Nabi's other arm. Walking with Nabi in the middle of them was causing quite a stir, especially after arriving in the limo owned by the Prince of Rahmi.

Daisy had a hard time not looking awestruck. The gymnasium had been completely made over. Posters of all the singers and actors from their teen years lined the walls, along with big records and pictures of them when they were in high school.

Nabi let out a low whistle. "I'm escorting two of the most beautiful ladies from your class," Nabi smiled sweetly and nodded to the blown-up image of the three sisters arm-in-arm.

"You and me both," John chuckled.

"Look, John, there you are." Lily wrapped her hand around his arm and beamed up at him.

"Ladies, I believe our table is over there," Nabi said, leading Daisy and Violet to the table with the Jimmy

Stewart centerpiece.

"Daisy Rose?" a soft, deep voice asked from behind them.

Daisy turned around with a smile already on her face. "Yes?"

The man with a full head of white hair, except for the tiny spot on top that was hidden by a comb-over, stood tall in his black leather jacket and jeans. "I don't know if you remember me, but I'm Charles Lastinger."

Daisy felt her face flush when he caught her running her eyes over a surprising set of broad shoulders and sweet brown eyes. "Charlie, it's so good to see you again."

Charlie looked between her and her hand resting on Nabi's arm. "Is this your grandson?"

Lily smothered a laugh that came out more like a strangled cough. Violet and Lily winked at each other, and Violet wrapped her other hand around Nabi's very impressive biceps. Leaning closer to Nabi, she grinned devilishly. "No, Nabi here is my date for the evening. Daisy is here all by her lonesome."

Violet would pay Nabi back for this by finding him a wife. Somehow. She'd tried for years, but this summer he'd turn thirty-eight, and she was determined to find someone before then.

Charlie's eyebrow rose, and he looked at Violet one last time over the gold-wired rims of his glasses. "Good for you, Violet. Nabi, it's nice to meet you." Charlie shook Nabi's hand before focusing all of his attention on Daisy.

"You look like a spring bloom tonight, Daisy." He smiled and offered her his arm. Daisy hastily dropped her clutch on Nabi's arm and wrapped her fingers around Charlie's. "Would you care to accompany me to get a drink?"

Daisy's heart pounded. She couldn't remember the last time a man looked at her the way Charlie was. She felt eighteen all over again and loved every minute of it.

Chapter Twenty-Three

D aisy tuned out the sounds of her sisters whispering feverishly as she let Charlie lead her across the gymnasium. They stopped to say hello to Donna and some of the men who had been on the chess team with him. It seemed surreal to Daisy. Charlie was paying such close attention to her. He was asking about the café and told her how impressed he was when John had told him she had gone to college.

He handed her a glass of wine and gestured to an open table. "Would you like to sit and talk, or am I keeping you from someone?"

"No, you're not keeping me from anything. I would love to catch up." Charlie held out a chair, and Daisy sat down. She wasn't used to feeling like the center of attention. As the middle triplet, she'd always been kind of overlooked.

"So, did you ever get married?" Charlie asked, taking his seat next to hers.

Daisy fought the urge to duck her head. It was rather embarrassing to admit she hadn't been lovable enough for a man to stick around. She had taken time off from dating after having her heart broken, but then it just seemed the whole town had eventually decided they were to be spinsters. By that time, she just didn't feel the desire to put her heart out there again.

"No. I never married. What about you?"

Charlie nodded. "Yes, I was married for forty years. Jan passed away twenty years ago, and that's when I decided I should retire. I had given so much of my life to hospitals and patients that there I was, suddenly a senior citizen with no wife and two grown kids with children of their own, and I didn't even know them."

"You have grandchildren? How wonderful!"

Charlie took out his phone and pulled up pictures to show her. She saw his two sons and five grandchildren, now all grown with three children of their own. "Actually, most of my family has relocated away from Boston. They're all spread out, but generally in this region. My eldest son's family is in Cincinnati, and my youngest son is in Louisville. It's one of the reasons I came back for the reunion."

"It must be lovely coming back home to see your family." Daisy managed to grin and finally allowed herself to feel a loss for what might have been.

"It is. I wanted to see how Keeneston looked after all these years. Was it still as nice as I remember? I've missed it here and have been thinking of moving back. I would be an hour away from each family so I'd be able to see them more."

Daisy felt excitement the likes of which she hadn't felt since they took down the international arms dealer. "You're thinking of moving back? Well, I'd be happy to show you around town to help you decide."

Charlie smiled and placed his hand over hers. "I'd like that, Daisy Mae. I've heard nothing but excellent things about your café. How about I meet you there tomorrow for lunch?"

Daisy sucked in a breath. "I don't know about that . . ."

"Oh." Charlie sounded crestfallen.

"No, it's kind of silly, but it's a tradition here. You eat at the café with your date when you're declaring your intentions. It's so old-fashioned, but it's just kinda stuck. We like our quirkiness, and it helps us know who to place our wedding bets on."

"Bets?"

Daisy nibbled her bottom lip. "I'm kind of a bookie," she said hesitantly. As Charlie's face went from shock to a wide smile, Daisy relaxed.

Charlie squeezed her hand. "Now that I'm up on the Keeneston customs, I'll let you get back to the party. I've hoarded your attention, and there seems to be a lot of people who want to talk to you."

Daisy let out a long breath. It was over. For an hour she had experienced hope, but it must have been the magic of the night that made her feel eighteen again to give her those silly ideas.

Charlie helped her up and escorted her to where John and Lily were staring open-mouthed as Violet danced with Nabi.

"It was a pleasure seeing you again, Daisy. And I look forward to seeing you tomorrow for our lunch date at your café." Charlie sent her a wink before turning and walking away into the crowd.

Lily gasped and sent a look to John. "A date . . . at the café? Golly jeepers, Daisy Mae, what did you talk about? Don't you dare, John!" Lily's arm shot out and grabbed John when he had slowly been trying to sneak away. "She's my sister, and it's my gossip to spread."

"Just admit it, Lily Rae, you'll never be able to beat me," John said, slipping from his coat and rushing to the nearest group of people to share the news that Daisy and Charlie were going on a date at the café tomorrow.

Lily tossed the coat to the ground and balled her fists. "That ol' billy goat!" Lily looked frantically around before her eyes narrowed on the stage up front where the band played.

"You better hurry. At least you'll win this since you didn't get him to propose," Daisy taunted. Her heart was light, and she felt like singing.

Lily looked at her watch. "I still have five minutes until midnight," she called as she rushed the stage for the microphone standing on it.

Violet and Nabi headed their way as the band stopped playing. Lily pushed past them and snagged the microphone from the lead singer.

"What's going on?" Violet asked a grinning Daisy.

Lily tapped the microphone. "May I have your attention? It's so lovely to see all our classmates and their families here tonight. I want to extend an invitation for you all to join us tomorrow at the Blossom Café for lunch. When Charlie asked Daisy for a date there tomorrow, I thought it would be fun for the whole class to be there."

Violet and Nabi turned wide-eyed at Daisy who just smiled. "Who is this Charlie?" Nabi asked quietly, pulling out his phone.

"Charles Lastinger. He was a classmate of ours and had the biggest crush on Daisy in high school." Violet giggled. "I guess he still has a crush on her."

Nabi tapped on the phone's keyboard and then looked up. "Ahmed's running a check on him right now."

"Nabi! Don't you dare. You tell Ahmed to stop that or I'm cutting him off from chocolate chip muffins." Daisy stomped her foot like a toddler in a fit of anger.

Nabi just grinned. "I don't tell Ahmed what to do. Only Bridget does that." The phone pinged and Nabi looked down at it. "He checks out."

Daisy rolled her eyes. "I feel so sorry for Abigail when it comes time to date," Daisy said, referring to Ahmed and Bridget's daughter. It would be hard with a mother who trained police dogs and had served in the military. Add in a father who had been one of the biggest, baddest special operations men in the world and the poor girl . . . rather, the poor boys . . . didn't stand a chance.

"I am not Abby. I do not need you and Ahmed playing watchdog."

Nabi leaned forward and placed a kiss on her cheek. "It's just because we care for you." Nabi looked around and then winked at her. "You don't think he's going to call me out for kissing his woman now, do you?"

Daisy snickered as Violet snorted and John bellowed, "You cheated!" He lumbered up the steps and walked onto the stage.

"Oh no I didn't, I just took advantage of an open microphone." Lily crossed her arms over her chest and gave a sly smile.

"Sometimes you can't win everything, Lily Rae," John said and stopped in front of her.

Daisy nudged Violet. "And in fifty-one seconds I will have won our bet."

Nabi crossed his fingers. "Come on, John, propose."

Violet and Daisy smacked him. "Lily's going to propose. Just watch. Forty-six seconds."

John cleared his throat and reaching into his pocket. "Being a couple is about sharing each other's victories and losses. There's no one else I'd rather share mine with than you, and there's no one I'd rather lose to you than you. So,

Lily Rae Rose . . ."

The entire gymnasium gasped and leaned forward as John pulled his hand from his pocket.

"I have one of these for me, and one for you," John said, handing a piece of paper to her. "On the count of three open it, and read it out loud. One. Two. Three."

Daisy gripped her sister's hand as they watched John and Lily open their pieces of paper.

"Will you marry me?" John and Lily read together at the same time the first sounds of the church clock down the street started to strike midnight.

Daisy looked to Violet who looked to Nabi. "Wait, who asked who?"

"YES!" John and Lily yelled with smiles spreading across their faces.

Nabi just shook his head. "They won, and we all lost. He found a way for both of them to propose, thus negating the bet."

"Oh, look," Violet cried, clasping her hands to her chest.

John pulled a small box from his other pocket and opened it to reveal a ring. Smiling, he pulled it out and slipped it on Lily's shaking finger. "I love you, darlin'."

"I love you, too," Lily whispered before John enveloped her in a hug.

"I wonder if Charlie's going to do that with you tomorrow?" Violet asked without taking her eyes from the stage. "Oh, Charlie," she mocked in a high-pitched voice, dissolving into giggles as Daisy smacked her arm.

"I can't wait to tell everyone about this," Nabi said with a grin as he texted away on his phone.

In the early morning hours, Lily sat next to John on the porch swing. She rested her head against his chest, and he wrapped his arm around her shoulder and pulled her close. Edna had already been over to congratulate them as well as half of the town. Marcy and Jake Davies had already declared they would be hosting a cookout tomorrow night to celebrate their engagement.

"There's only one thing that would have made your proposal better," Lily murmured against his shirt and snuggled closer. "And that would have been to see everyone's faces when they realized none of them could win the bet."

John straightened. "*My* proposal. I believe you proposed to me."

"Me? You are the one who proposed to me. It was your idea . . . and you had a ring." Lily sat up and then noticed John was grinning at her. "Oh, you ol' billy goat!"

"And you're my beautiful rose blossom," John whispered, lowering his lips to hers. "I love you, Lily Rae."

"I love you, too. Will you now tell me how you find gossip out before others?"

"Ouija board," John whispered into her ear, his lips in a grin.

Chapter Twenty-Four

"What are you two still doing here?" Edna called aghast from the front yard.

Lily looked at her best friend but didn't bother to move from where John was snuggling her on the porch swing. "What does it look like?"

"You're going to miss it? It's almost noon. Daisy and Charlie will be at the café soon!"

"It can't be!" Lily jumped up as fast as she could. "Come on, John. We have to go."

"We're never going to get a table. The place is going to be packed." Edna fretted.

"There are some perks to getting to our age, Edna. Those strapping young men practically knock themselves over when they jump up to offer us their seats," Lily said. She took John's arm and headed for the car. "Let's take the car, it's quicker."

Daisy sat in silence. Her purse was at her side. Her hair was fluffed and styled instead of the usual tight, permed rings. She even had Sydney, who was a part-time model, bring her lipstick and help with her makeup. Sydney's parents, Sheriff Marshall and Katelyn Davies, had dropped Sydney off, claiming they needed to borrow their nineteen-year-old daughter's car to get the oil changed.

Sydney had rolled her eyes, and bless her heart, slammed the door in her nosy parents' faces before she got Daisy all glam. Or at least that was the word she used. She'd left fifteen minutes ago, and Daisy had been too nervous to even move ever since. Daisy didn't want to risk messing up any of Sydney's excellent work.

At the sound of the doorbell, Daisy closed her eyes and took three calming breaths. She could do this. She wasn't too old to get her own happily-ever-after. After all, age was just an external number. What really mattered was how she felt inside. And right now, she felt like a nervous and excited teenager. She couldn't remember when she'd felt so alive.

"Charlie, welcome." Daisy looked into his smiling face and felt her heart beat faster. "Are those for me?"

Charlie handed her the bouquet of flowers and then held out his arm for her to take. "You look lovely, Daisy Mae. I brought my car, and I thought before lunch you could show me around my old hometown."

"I'd love to." Daisy took his arm and allowed him to open the car door for her. She slid into the seat and watched Charlie walk around the front of the car. He waved to the people walking by on the sidewalk and smiled happily as he got in the car. It seemed right. He belonged here in Keeneston, and he belonged here with her.

"And that's the water tower where the bad kids would gather in high school. Do you remember?" Daisy asked, pointing out the tall structure on the far side of town.

"I do. I was never cool enough or bad enough to be invited. Are the kids still hanging out there?"

"Yes, but now it's not exclusive. Everyone in high school hangs out there. But it wasn't always that way.

Morgan, who is now married to Miles Davies, climbed up there and wrote over it once, causing a very interesting commotion before leaving town."

As he drove into town, she continued to point out the changes since he'd left Keeneston. "Oh, and there is where we stopped a group of dog fighters. And here is where Tammy, who is now married to Pierce Davies, was stuck on a bomb . . . Oh, and here is where Pam, the former president of the PTA, ran over a bad man who was shooting at us. Edna shot back. My sisters and I were throwing pots and pans—really anything we could find. And there is where an assassin shot Kenna and her best friend, Danielle. But we got the bad guys in the end."

Daisy stopped talking as Charlie pulled to a stop in front of the café. He looked slightly stunned, and Daisy wondered if she'd said too much. "Oh, but don't worry. We really don't have much crime here. Ever since Bridget and Ahmed stopped a revolution and Cy and Gemma put away an international crime lord who ran the black market, it's been down right boring here. It's been wonderful."

"I'm sorry, did you say revolution? International crime boss? I remember reading about that corrupt Senator Bruce in the paper, but I didn't know there was a Keeneston connection."

"Oh, dear," Daisy said worriedly. "I've scared you. Really, Keeneston has been positively peaceful for the past twenty years." *Unfortunately*, Daisy thought. Her sisters had all talked about how much fun they had during the wild years.

"No, it just makes spending time in Boston as the chief surgeon pretty dull," Charlie chuckled. "I can't wait to hear all about these events and meet all the people involved. I remember Jake Davies. He was a lot younger than us, but his mother would make the best apple pies. I still dream of them."

"Well, no worries then. Jake's wife, Marcy, knows the recipe and always bakes new residents one. You are a new resident, right?" Daisy asked as Charlie turned off the car.

"Um, why are there people pressed against the window of your café?" Charlie asked, instead of answering her question.

Daisy turned to look and saw her sisters, Edna, the Davies boys, their wives, and even some of their children peering out at them. The second they noticed Daisy had spotted them, they suddenly became very interested in something on the floor. Their heads all bent as one when Daisy looked at them.

"Are you sure you want to do this? After all, we've really only been talking for a day," Daisy said nervously.

"Daisy Mae, I am almost ninety years old. Does it look like I'm someone who wants to waste time? I want to live what's remaining of my life to the fullest. If that includes a second chance at love, then I'm going to take it. I think the question is—are you ready to take a chance?"

Daisy swallowed hard. She had thought she'd missed her chance at love. She'd given up hope of ever finding it. With Robert, she had sat back and waited. Waited on his career, waited for him to come home, and waited for a happily-ever-after that never came. No, she was done waiting.

Daisy leaned forward, and before she could worry about the properness of it, she placed her lips on Charlie's. Even through her closed car door, she heard the gasps come from within the Blossom Café. She pulled back from the kiss and looked into Charlie's smiling eyes.

"I take it you've decided to take a chance," he joked.

"I have. I may be old, but I'm not fast, Charlie Lastinger. You'll have to earn this, and it starts right now with lunch." Daisy got out of the car and looked into the window full of shocked faces. When the patrons noticed they were coming in, they dove for their chairs. She was surprised Miles was still so agile as he leaped over the table.

"Does that man have a gun?" Charlie whispered. "He looks dangerous. Maybe the sheriff should look into him?"

Daisy looked to where Charlie was staring and smiled. Marshall took a seat next to the dangerous-looking man. Or rather, leapt into the seat next to him. The dangerous-looking man did indeed have a gun on him — and probably a knife as well. He didn't bother to look ashamed at being caught staring. Instead, he narrowed his eyes at Charlie and slowly raised his hand. He pointed with two fingers to his own narrowed eyes and then to Charlie in a clear warning that he was watching.

"Oh, yes, that is a gun. But that's just Ahmed. He was the head of security for Mo, the Prince of Rahmi. But now he's just a racehorse owner and de facto guard for all of us here in town. I think he just misses torturing terrorists. If he doesn't shoot someone every so often, he gets cranky. I just feel sorry for his fifteen-year-old daughter, Abigail. Poor Abby will have one heck of time dating." Daisy slid her arm into Charlie's and heard him gulp as Ahmed gave him one of his patented looks that left arms dealers quaking.

"Still want to do this?" Daisy asked. She wasn't going to soften this for Charlie. If he couldn't handle himself with a roomful of people who loved her, then he wasn't the man for her.

Charlie patted her hand. "Of course. Any friend of yours is a friend of mine. Even if they're big scary mercenaries."

Daisy grinned. "And you haven't met his wife yet."

Charlie opened the door and the loud buzzing of eager conversation stopped suddenly. The sounds of wooden chair legs scraping on the hardwood floor filled the air as all the diners turned to stare.

Violet stepped forward and offered a smile. "It's nice to see you again, Charlie. I have a table for you both right here."

Daisy looked at the only open table in the middle of the room. Charlie must have noticed, too, because he took a fortifying breath before leading Daisy to the table and pulling out a chair for her.

"Um, what would you two like to drink?" Sophie asked. Annie and Cade's eighteen-year-old daughter was working as a waitress over her spring break to save money for a new car.

"Sweet tea for me. Daisy Mae, do you still like yours with a lime slice?" Charlie asked. Daisy nodded and there were murmurs of approval from a few of the tables as Sophie hurried to the kitchen to get the drinks.

All at once, there was another sound of chairs scraping. An entire table of Davies men stood up with arms crossed across broad chests. Sounds echoed from the other side of the room as John, Will, Mo, Ahmed, and Nabi similarly stood. Before she could blink, a wall of overprotective men surrounded the table.

"So, what are your intentions with *our* Miss Daisy?" Will Ashton asked.

Charlie cleared this throat. "We've had a lovely day together, and I would like to spend more time with her."

"Did you practice your manners with her?" Mo asked as he looked down his regal nose in a look that Daisy knew he used to get his way with government officials.

"Of course," Charlie said, offended.

Miles Davies stepped forward, and Daisy now understood why he had been a commander in Special Forces. Just standing there, you could feel power, control, and leadership emanating from him. "You see, the Rose sisters are Keeneston."

Marshall Davies casually slid his hand to his gun. "And we protect our own."

"Especially someone who has put her life in danger for us," Cy Davies said as he sent her a wink.

"And she deserves respect," Cade Davies said in a way that reminded Daisy he hadn't always been a laid-back football coach. He had served alongside Marshall and Miles in combat.

"And to be loved . . ." Pierce Davies continued.

"And cherished . . ." Nabi smiled, kissing her hand and sending her a wink before giving Charlie a glare.

"And cared for every day . . ." Cole Parker added as he similarly rested his hand on his FBI-issued gun.

"Because, if you don't . . ." Ahmed said, slowly smiling in a way that sent shivers down Daisy's back. Charlie turned white, and Daisy thought for a second he might pass out.

"Daaaaad, stop being so dramatic." Ahmed's daughter rolled her eyes as she pushed through the wall of men. "Hi. I'm Abby. It's nice to meet you. If you hurt Miss Daisy, it won't be my dad you need to worry about. My mom," Abby pointed to the beautiful strawberry blond standing with her arms crossed behind her husband, "taught me how to break every bone in a man's body. But you seem nice, so there's nothing to worry about." Abby smiled, and her blue eyes danced with mischief.

Charlie looked around the room at all the faces staring at him and pushed his chair back. "My name is Charles Lastinger. I am almost ninety years old. I graduated Keeneston High School with Daisy. She was my crush back then, and she's my crush now. I was a field surgeon during Vietnam and then moved to Boston as chief of surgery for Massachusetts General Hospital. My children and grandchildren are in Louisville and Cincinnati now, and I'm ready to come back home. I want to spend the rest of my days, however many that may be," he said with a pointed look to the men surrounding them, "with someone I can love and who can love me. I miss being part of a community like this. While it's scary as hell to have you all here, it goes to show me that Daisy Mae turned into the remarkable woman I always knew her to be. If she weren't, then you wouldn't be here looking out for her."

"So, have you decided to move to Keeneston then?" Jake Davies, the patriarch of the family, asked.

Charlie looked at Daisy, and she felt the affection growing between then. "Yes, I have," he said. Daisy smiled at him and took his hand in hers as the men grunted and the women finally pressed forward to introduce themselves.

"Welcome to Keeneston," Kenna Ashton said. She started the long list of introductions. How funny that she was taking control when twenty odd years ago, she was being questioned in this very café by the very same townspeople when she showed up from New York City looking for safety. But Keeneston had opened its arms to her, and as Daisy watched Charlie shaking hands with the most important people in her life, she knew that Keeneston was welcoming back one of its own.

Chapter Twenty-Five

D aisy took her spot on the front porch of her childhood home and shot her sisters a smile. John was off doing who-knows-what, leaving the three sisters the entire morning to gossip. So much had changed in just two months — the summer heat being one. Daisy poured herself a glass of iced tea and took a cold drink.

"What's Charlie up to this morning?" Violet asked as she crocheted.

"He's visiting family in Cincinnati. His granddaughter is graduating from college this week."

"Why didn't you go with him?" Lily asked.

"We've only been dating two months. I've met them all, and they're lovely, but I didn't want to interfere. Besides, there's an unresolved bet we need to take care of, and having Charlie gone for a week will let me give it my undivided attention."

"Demanding, is he?" Lily snickered.

Daisy shot her a look, but it was true. She and Charlie had been inseparable since he moved to town. Violet had taught her some special meals to make, and she enjoyed having him over to eat, play cards, or go to a movie. He even cooked for her and always took her to events she knew he might not enjoy, like the garden show, just because he knew she liked it. She had laughed more, loved more, and lived more these past two months than she had since college.

"As if John isn't?" Daisy teased back.

Violet smiled, but it was a shadow of her normal grin. "I'm so happy for you two." Violet reached out and clasped each sister's hand in hers. "To see you this happy after all these years warms my heart. So, when is the wedding, Lily Rae?"

Lily shrugged. "I was thinking late this summer, right before all the kids go back to school."

"You just tell us what you need us to do." Daisy grinned and secretly hoped there would be two weddings soon. While Charlie hadn't said anything about it specifically, he kept saying how wonderful it was Lily and John were marrying. She had a feeling if she gave a hint to being open to it, he would ask her. She'd wondered and waited for Robert, but now she didn't want to wait. She was in love and was ready to be a bride.

"I was going to plan it all, but the women kind of took it over for me. Paige is taking me dress shopping next week after that ball for the British prince at Mo and Dani's. Kenna is narrowing down a list of locations, and Dani said Anton, their chef, will cook—"

"What?" Violet asked incredulously. "You can't have Anton cook for you—besides he doesn't even really cook anymore. He's eighty years old, for Pete's sake. He just orders everyone around. Shoot, he's too stubborn to even retire. I think Mo and Dani are forcing him into retirement."

Daisy rolled her eyes. Violet and Anton Vasseur had a long-standing feud. He didn't believe Violet could cook, and Anton reminded Violet too much of the life she'd left behind when she came back home.

"*Humph*, I always thought he liked you," Lily tossed

out innocently.

"Like me? I'm nine years older than he is, and he hates me." Violet stabbed her crochet needle into the ball of yarn.

"Dear, what's nine years when you're as old as we are?" Lily chided.

"But he's the one nine years younger. It's just not done."

Daisy giggled. "Sure it is. You'd be the envy of all the women at seniors. It's very fashionable. Besides, you still have all of your curves . . . even if they're just a little lower now." Daisy squeaked when the ball of yarn smacked her face.

"I thought we were here to decide what to do about Nabi. We need to find him a wife," Violet said, trying to change the subject.

"Oh, wait a second." Lily looked down at her phone. "Abby's calling me."

As Lily talked to Abby, Violet fumed. Her own sister was ditching her for Anton. Sure, it would be hard on her to cook for so many people. But it was her sister. It was her right to do it. Would she even be able to make the cake? She hoped so. It would be something special, from one sister to the other on a day none of them had thought would come.

"What was that all about?" Violet asked when Lily hung up.

"That was Abby. She said all the kids are meeting here. They need our help."

"I'll get my spoon," Daisy said with excitement. "Do you want your broom, Lily Rae?"

Lily let out a sigh. "I don't think it's that kind of help."

"That's too bad. It's been kind of dull around here since we scared all the bad people away. So, if it's not something dangerous, then what is it?"

"I guess we'll find out. Did you all get your invitations to the charity ball Dani and Mo are hosting for Prince James?" Lily asked.

Violet nodded along with Daisy. Lily and Daisy started talking about bringing John and Charlie along with them and how romantic it would be. Violet chided herself for being envious, but it didn't work. She was happy for her sisters, but now she felt alone. She was the one without a date, without a second chance of love, and mostly, she was the one being left behind as her sisters moved on in their lives.

Her phone rang, and as her sisters continued talking, she stood up and walked to the other end of the porch to answer the call. "Hello, Dani." Violet tried to sound upbeat.

"Oh, Miss Violet, the most awful thing has happened," Dani, or Princess Danielle of Rahmi as she was more formally known, cried into the phone.

"What is it, dear?" Violet asked, worried. Dani was not one to get upset over nothing.

"It's the ball! Prince James just held a press conference about his visit to Kentucky, and all he could talk about was *Southern* cooking! Anton doesn't do *Southern* . . . he does French or nothing at all. What am I going to do?"

Violet pursed her lips. She knew what she could do. She just didn't like the idea. "Let me help, dear. I'll come and teach the kitchen staff all they need to know for a good old-fashioned Southern meal."

"Miss Violet, I don't know how to thank you. You'll be saving the ball. I'll see you soon to start the first lesson. Thank you." The line went dead as Violet imagined Dani running through their mansion to prepare Anton for her arrival.

Dani hung up the phone and turned with a satisfied smile upon her face. "Well, did she buy it?" Tammy asked as the roomful of women eagerly waited.

Dani put her hand on her hips. "Was there ever any doubt? She bought it hook, line, and sinker."

Katelyn pushed her long blond hair over her shoulder and frowned. "But now we have to get Anton to cooperate."

Kenna shook her head. "It's so obvious to all of us that they would be perfect together. How can they not see it?"

"Love is blind," Annie said and shook her head. "In this case, blind to the possibility of it."

"I don't understand why they fight so much. Are you sure this is the right match?" Paige asked.

Morgan nodded, her black hair streaked with silver strands swaying. "I'm sure it is. If I've ever seen a couple so similar to Miles and me, it's them. And we all know how we turned out," Morgan grinned happily.

"Oh, that's true." Gemma smirked. "There've been reports of strange sounds out by the water tower one night each year . . ." Gemma snapped her fingers, "and you know, it just happens to be the same day as your anniversary."

The girls all laughed before Dani marshaled the troops. They had a kitchen to storm, and a French cook to wrangle.

"*Non!*" Violet heard Anton Vasseur, the head chef for the Rahmi family, yell at his kitchen staff. "*Non! Non! Non!*"

Violet heard the sound of a pan crashing into the sink and smiled. It reminded her of her time back in France. Anton's accent, combined with the smell of braised duck, had her flashing back. When it came to cooking, there was no one more passionate than the French. Unfortunately, it was now her duty to convince Anton that her version of Southern cuisine was just as artistic and complex as French cooking.

"*Tsk, Anton. Na pas votre mere vous apprendre qu'il est impoli de jeter des choses?*" Violet asked in French. It felt good to speak French skills again.

She smiled as Anton spun around to stare in surprise at her. He was a handsome man who had aged well. His gray hair was cut short, and his face was clean-shaven. He was impeccably attired in his black pants and white chef's jacket. Anton's blue eyes glared in anger as he looked her over. Goodness, her sisters were crazy to think someone as young as he was would be interested in someone who was turning ninety next year. Sure, he had a rounded belly that showed he enjoyed eating the delicious pastries that he made. But he had a palate like no one she'd ever met.

"No, my mother did not teach me it was impolite to throw things. My mother was French. Where do you think I learned it?" Anton asked with his smooth French accent that slipped over Violet and caused her to smile. She loved the challenge he issued with those words. It made her feel alive to verbally spar with him.

"What are you doing in my kitchen?" Anton asked, stepping away from the sink. The kitchen staff all stared in wonder to anyone standing up to him. But, Violet was no shrinking violet.

"Until the ball, this is *our* kitchen. I've been hired by Dani and Mo to teach y'all about upscale Southern cuisine. Prince James stated in a recent interview he couldn't wait to have some *Southern* food on his visit to Kentucky. So, here I am. Let's get started."

The kitchen staff took a step back. They knew the fireworks were about to start. Anton didn't even look at them as he approached Violet and stopped directly in front of her. He stared down his sharp nose at her and sneered. "Everyone out. Now."

Violet smiled sweetly back at Anton as the kitchen staff fled. She was practically giddy. "Don't you want your staff to see how to make the food they are going to prepare?"

"I will not be preparing something as amateurish as Southern food. I will not serve fried chicken to royalty. I will quit before I do such a thing. And I certainly won't be taught by you."

"I am a classically trained chef. You do know that, don't you? In fact, I believe we graduated from the same culinary school." Violet smiled again and tried not to laugh at his shocked expression. "But, how about this? You take a break, do some deep breathing, and come to terms with the fact that you are going to learn how to make Southern food, while I prepare some of the plates I intend to serve at the ball. I'll call you when I am ready, and then we'll test your legendary palate. Blindfolded."

"What for? This serves no purpose. I will not be serving this food no matter how much you bat those beautiful eyes of yours."

Anton surprised her with the compliment. He thought she had beautiful eyes? His praise threw her off balance and caused her to stutter. When one side of his mouth quirked up, she stomped her foot. "Oh! You did that on purpose. You think false compliments will make me forget about my job—well, no way! I bet you won't be able to identify all the components of my meal. And furthermore, I bet you will love every bite of it!"

Anton shrugged. "I am French; seduction is in my

blood. I can seduce you and still hate your cooking. I'll take that bet. But when I win, you get out of my kitchen."

Violet felt herself blush as if she were a teenager again. "And if I win, you agree to be the Blossom Café's guest chef for two nights where you will serve a *Southern* menu."

Anton held out his hand. "Deal."

Violet placed her hand in his and shook it before he brought her hand to his lips. He placed a slow, lingering kiss on her knuckles, and Violet was robbed of the ability to speak. With a wink, he walked from the room, whistling. Violet was so surprised she didn't notice the nine smiling women looking in the windows and giving each other high-fives.

Chapter Twenty-Six

Violet felt naughty. Her heart pounded as she wrapped the blindfold around Anton's eyes. Her hands lingered, letting them fall to his shoulders. She looked at her hands and saw not the hands of an old woman, but of a young woman on an adventure. She knew she was the type who liked to be challenged and liked to stay on her toes. But until the moment Anton had told her she had beautiful eyes, she had thought the strong feelings she had for him had been hate, when they had been attraction all along. He stood up to her bossy ways, and there had always been a twinkle in his eyes when they argued. How could she not see the passion between them?

Easy, he was younger than she was, and she was raised in an era where men simply didn't date older women. She knew she could never act on these feelings, but the relief she felt just knowing she was capable of having them was enough to give her hope.

"Right this way, Anton." Violet steered him down the hall and through the kitchen door. She directed him to a stool and helped him sit down in front an appetizer, a soup, a salad, an entrée, and a dessert.

"Are you ready?" Violet asked. She picked up a country ham canapé.

"Ready to beat you, you mean," Anton grinned

devilishly. "Maybe I should have bet a kiss from you instead." He chuckled when he heard Violet gulp.

"Open up," Violet squeaked before clearing her throat.

Anton opened his mouth and Violet set the food on his tongue. He closed his mouth and slowly chewed. She saw him move the food around his mouth as every taste bud had a chance to identify the ingredients.

"It's a country ham canapé with a bite. The salt of the ham is balanced out nicely with the cheese, but it's not regular cheddar. Can I have another bite?"

Violet didn't say a word as she placed another bite in his open mouth. She grinned from ear to ear. She knew he would never be able to figure out the special ingredient. It was pure Kentucky magic.

"I taste cheddar, garlic, and something slightly hot. Cayenne?"

"Is that your final guess?" Violet asked with as much calm as she could.

She waited as Anton's lips thinned. He knew he was missing something. "*Oui*," he replied confidently.

"It looks like I've already won our bet. But let's continue playing, shall we?" Violet crowed.

"What did I miss?"

"Beer," Violet answered without restraining her glee.

"Beer?"

"Yes. You got the country ham canapé. And you were right; there was cheddar cheese and garlic. But there was also my own hot sauce that I knew you'd never get because of its complexity. And there was a can of Kentucky's best-brewed beer. We call it Beer Cheese, for the obvious reason. It adds just the right amout of kick to the canapés, don't you think?"

Anton snorted as he folded his arms over his chest.

"Next."

"Ready for the next one?" When he nodded she dipped her spoon into the soup. "Here you go."

Anton tasted it and smiled. "Another bite, please."

Darn, she knew she should have made this one harder, but this was a famous Kentucky dish, even if it might have French roots.

"I taste pork, beef, veal, and lamb. Knowing that everything is in it, if I had another bite, I am sure I would also taste chicken. It's not so much a liquid, but more of a stew. I tasted potatoes, onions, cabbage, and tomato, to name just a few ingredients. It's what you Kentuckians call *burgoo*."

Violet smiled regardless of the fact he guessed it. She'd already won. "But do you like it?"

"Unfortunately, I do. Just as I enjoyed the appetizer." Anton recrossed his arms, and Violet giggled when he gave a little pout.

"I'm glad. I won Anderson County's Burgoo Festival ten years ago with this recipe. Now, here comes the salad." She waited for Anton to cleanse his palate before handing him the fork with the salad on it.

"*Mmm.*" Anton groaned before realizing it. "It's chicken salad on a bed of living lettuce and kale, with pecans, a dash of red pepper, and I taste a hint of white pepper as well. The dressing, I must admit, is very good with the dry mustard added. It could be very easy to add too much, but it's just a hint that provides an excellent layer of flavor. I would suggest we offer two options of each course, so people may decide between the heavier options and a lighter one. You know too many of the women attending these things won't eat anything that has calories," Anton said in disgust.

"I agree completely. I was hoping we could work together on that part of the menu."

"*Oui*, now what is the entrée, and do I still have to wear this blasted blindfold?"

Violet smiled shyly. Without realizing it, he had accepted her menu thus far and agreed to work with her. Violet cut into the entrée and handed it to him. She waited as he chewed.

"It's fried chicken, but the flavor of the batter is unbelievable. Do I taste Mornay sauce?"

"Very good. Yes, it's fried chicken topped with a Mornay sauce, but can you get the rest?"

"You stuffed the chicken . . . what is this?"

"Do you like it?" Violet held her breath in anticipation. This was her favorite Kentucky dish. It was so complex that she rarely made it.

"I love it. It's very rich. To counter it, we will offer a tasteful Chilean sea bass for someone who wants something lighter. I know it's not Kentucky food, but we can pair it with a Southern vegetable."

"I love that idea. You know the open sandwich we call the Kentucky Hot Brown? The easiest way to think of this is as a cordon bleu, but stuffed with bacon, cheese, and tomato, then fried with a parmesan batter and topped with Mornay."

"I must admit it is great. Of course, I don't need to point out the French influence."

"I told you, I'm a classically trained French chef. Of course there is a French influence."

"Why didn't you tell me so from the beginning? We're essentially making a French dinner," Anton said haughtily.

"If that makes you feel better when you're cooking at The Blossom Café, then so be it." Violet laughed.

"I can't wait to taste dessert."

Violet felt as if she'd been handed the world when Anton complimented her cooking. She was going basic Kentucky for dessert, and Anton would know it in an instant since everyone on the farm had been begging him to learn to make it. It was her signature dessert.

"Here you go," Violet said and handed him the spoon.

"It's your blasted bread pudding with bourbon butter sauce. And some kind of candy topper — chocolate, walnut, with a sharpness to it? What is that?"

"I topped it with a bourbon ball. Do you like it?"

"*Merde*! Do you know how often over the years I have tried to make this? It's the sauce I can't figure out," Anton complained, taking off his blindfold. Appreciation and respect were now in his eyes.

"It's a simple sauce once you know it. You need fresh cream and the best bourbon to get the rich flavor."

Anton smiled down at her. "I was wrong, *ma chérie*. It is not as simple as frying food in butter. Now, what do you think about the sides for the sea bass?"

"What are they doing?" Gemma asked. "I lost sight of them."

"They just turned on the music. It sounds like the songs I heard in Paris when I was modeling," Katelyn whispered as she peered in the kitchen window.

"I can hear. I just can't see," Gemma complained.

"They're cooking," Tammy called to the women who couldn't see.

"Oh, he just tied an apron around her," Morgan told them as they each *awwed*.

"They are cutting up food side by side," Annie said and went up on her toes for a better look.

"She just fed him something she cooked," Kenna whispered a moment later.

"That's not all she's feeding him," Dani giggled. The women smiled and stepped away from the window.

"I think our work here is done." Bridget smiled, and they walked around the house to the front door.

The sound of a throat clearing spun them around. "And what were you ladies doing, spying in the kitchen window?"

"Nabi!" Dani gasped. "You startled me. Oh, we were just taking a walk and wanted to peek in and see how the dinner menu was coming along."

"And why didn't you just go through the door to check?" Nabi placed his hands on his hips and stared them down.

"Don't you know never to interrupt Anton when he's creating? Do you think we're stupid?" Bridget shot back. Nabi simply raised an eyebrow and shook his head before walking away.

"We really need to find him a wife," Dani muttered.

"What about Tiffany Sanders?" Kenna suggested. "She's the new president of the Keeneston Belles and is very nice."

"Ew, she's like Sienna's age. Would you want your daughter to date Nabi? Not that there is anything wrong with him," Annie backtracked.

The women walked in the front door and down the hall to Dani's private sitting room. Each woman had her own spot. It hadn't started out that way, but over the years they had each claimed a seat as theirs. There was a couch, a loveseat, and several comfortable chairs set up in a conversation square in the center of the room.

"What about Chrissy?" Katelyn asked.

"Who?" the rest of the women asked at once.

"My yoga instructor."

The women looked at each other and nodded their agreement. Yoga instructor it was.

Chapter Twenty-Seven

Violet smiled as Anton held the piece of éclair up to her lips. When had cooking become so sensual? Every day after the kitchen staff left, they spent hours cooking for each other. And when they fought, it was a passionate war of words, peppered with intellectual wit and sexual subtlety.

"What do your sisters think of us?" Anton asked as he filled another éclair.

"Umm," Violet stammered.

"You haven't told them about us, have you?"

"Have you told anyone about us?" Violet asked defensively.

"No, but I intend to tell the whole world tomorrow at the ball. Now that you, or should I say a bunch of *enfants,* found Nabi a girlfriend, I plan to be your next project." Anton slid his arm around her waist and fed her another bite of éclair.

"It was a group effort, not just the kids," Violet protested. "And what do you mean, project?"

Anton lowered his lips to hers and kissed off the cream that was on her upper lip. "Your next boyfriend project. I think I make a pretty good candidate. What do you think?"

"Oh, I think you have potential." Violet grinned, tilting her head and offering him her lips for another kiss.

"*Non!*" Anton crossed his arms over his chest and stared into narrowed eyes. "I will not make chicken fingers, Miss Cassidy. This meal is excellent. I made it for the King of Spain."

Cassidy, the youngest of Pierce and Tammy's children, stared at Anton as if he were growing horns. "It's slimy."

"It's a delicacy . . . do you know what that word means?"

"Of course I do. I'm nine, not three." Cassidy crossed her arms and stuck out her bottom lip.

"*Enfants!*" Anton cried and tossed his arms up in the air.

"*Têtu vieil homme,*" Cassidy said, sticking out her tongue. The patrons of the Blossom Café all looked at each other and then to their special guest chef.

"I am not a stubborn old man," Anton said and smiled. "But, for speaking my language of love, I will make you something special."

"Do you think if I told him I also speak Italian, he'd make me macaroni and cheese?" Cassidy asked Violet, who sat at the table next to them with her sisters.

Violet laughed and shook her head, and Lily placed another picture in front of her. "What do you think about this dress?"

Violet turned her attention back to Lily's wedding planning. They had two months to plan a wedding that had somehow turned into the event of the decade. Everyone in town had sent in an RSVP stating they would attend. Gone was the idea of a catered reception. It was now a potluck affair with four tents that were going to be set up at Dani and Mo's farm.

Violet's enthusiasm for the wedding had grown since she and Anton had become a couple. Now the idea of falling in love again and planning a wedding didn't bring on a panic attack. She loved Anton and had known it with the first bite of his cream puff. He was beyond passionate and wanted nothing more than to love her, care for her, and cook with her. Passion wasn't just in the kitchen either. No, it was in everything they did together. Since she fell in love, the trees were greener, the sky bluer, and her heart younger. Love had no age. Love had no number. Love was just magic, and everyone needed a little magic in their life.

Daisy flipped the page in the bridal magazine and couldn't help but imagine she was planning this huge event for herself. Looking up, she saw Charlie talking to John as they encouraged — rather, teased — Anton as he prepared food for the patrons of the Blossom Café. The three of them got along wonderfully, which only made Daisy's desire to marry Charlie deeper.

Daisy went back to the task of looking through bridal magazines for Lily's wedding, and her sisters talked about the plans the women of Keeneston were working on. Daisy was so caught up in the laughter and love filling the café she didn't notice Charlie standing next to her until he put a gentle hand on her arm.

"Ready, dear?"

Daisy folded down the corner of the magazine and smiled up at him. "Sure am."

"And where are you two lovebirds going this evening?" Lily asked as she sent a quick look to Violet whose smile widened. What did they think they were doing?

"Charlie is taking me on a picnic." When her sisters snickered, Daisy bent down. "Get your mind out of the gutters." Unfortunately that only caused them to giggle louder. Maybe they shouldn't have been sipping their special iced tea while going through the magazines.

Charlie placed his hand at the small of Daisy's back and escorted her from the café. His car was parked out front, and he opened the door for her. "Where are we having the picnic?" Daisy asked before he shut the door.

"It's a surprise."

Daisy sat back and watched Charlie walk around the car. They had talked of his family wanting to come see her this summer and of the gossip going around town about Nabi and Grace Duvall's wedding. The sweet kindergarten teacher had found her own second chance at love. Plus, Daisy and her sisters were trying to figure out what happened between Ryan Parker and Sienna Ashton.

"We had them pegged from the time they were babies together," Daisy sighed. "When he kissed her while they were playing hide and seek at age six, it was clear as day they belonged together."

"It doesn't appear that you and your sisters will get a match with that one. They didn't want to have anything to do with each other at the ball. Of course, they're young yet. Give them time, Daisy Mae. Kids don't have to get married at eighteen anymore," Charlie told her and reached over to pat her knee.

"I know they're just twenty and twenty-one, but I like to see everyone around me happily in love."

"Are you happily in love?" Charlie asked, pulling in front of Keeneston High School.

"You know I am. I've never been happier." And she hadn't. Daisy looked at the large brick building in front of them and felt at peace. It had all started here so many years ago.

Charlie turned off the car, and Daisy brought herself back to the present. "Is this where we are having our picnic?"

"Yes. I thought it would be nice to eat under the willow trees out back, just like we used to in high school." Charlie opened her door and gave her his arm. He then reached into the back seat and pulled out a picnic basket.

"Sounds lovely. I haven't been back there since high school. Oh! Look at the trees." Daisy rested a hand against her heart. The willow trees had grown and spread their weeping branches to form four leafy green fountains that swayed with the breeze.

Charlie reached into the leaves of the tree and pulled nature's curtain back. Daisy walked in and felt the temperature drop to a comfortable level. She looked up and marveled at the height of the tree and the swaying branches. When Charlie let the leaves fall back into place, it felt as if they were in their own world.

He spread the black-and-red checkered blanket on the ground and offered his hand to help Daisy sit. She watched as Charlie pulled out a black velvet box instead of food. His hand shook as he reached to open it. Daisy gasped at the small diamond band.

"Daisy Mae, my heart knew the first time I saw you sitting under this tree that we were meant to be. We both experienced life, and now life has brought us back together. Will you marry me?"

Daisy stared at the ring in his hand and then looked at his face. Fear, excitement, and, most importantly, love shone in his eyes. "Yes! Oh, Charlie." Charlie slipped the ring onto her finger and pulled her close. Daisy tried not to cry. She was too old for that nonsense. But her darn tears just wouldn't listen.

"You've made me the happiest man today. I hope you don't mind, but I thought I would come prepared."

Daisy pulled back from where her happy tears streaked the front of his shirt in time to see Charlie pull out a bottle of champagne. "I figured we could celebrate if you said yes, and if you said no, then I would drink it myself." Charlie chuckled.

"How could you think I would say no? I love you, Charles Lastinger."

Charlie poured the champagne and handed her a glass. "And I love you, too, Daisy Mae Rose."

Daisy clinked her glass with Charlie's and took a sip. The bubbles tickled, but her girlish giggles fled as soon as Charlie's lips met hers. Daisy wound her hand into his hair as his lips danced with hers.

"Okay, knock it off in . . . what the fu—!"

Daisy broke the kiss and looked up at their intruder. "Marshall Davies, watch your language!"

"Can we help you, young man?" Charlie asked as he removed his hand from Daisy's bosom.

Daisy almost felt bad for him. But he *was* interrupting a special moment. She watched as his face turned red and his eyes shot back and forth between the two of them before he cleared his throat. "Sorry, I got a call about some teenagers making out back here and . . ." Marshall just shook his head.

"A sheriff's duty is never done," Charlie said, taking pity on him. "But no worries, we're not some young teenagers engaged in some hanky-panky. We're a newly engaged couple making hanky-panky." Charlie sent her a wink and leaned forward to kiss her again. This time she didn't care if the whole town stormed through. Nothing was going to interrupt them.

"Is he gone yet?" she asked against his lips some time later.

"You didn't hear the tires squealing?" Charlie poured another glass of champagne and handed it to her.

"I guess it will be all over the town by the time we get home tonight. Too bad they won't have anyone to take their bets on when our wedding will be." Daisy laughed out loud. Her life was full with a town, her family, and now a fiancé. She'd never been happier.

Chapter Twenty-Eight

Violet sat on the stool in the Blossom Café's kitchen and watched Anton make a *tarte au chocolat*. His lost bet had been fulfilled, and his time as the guest chef at the Blossom Café had come to an end. He had flipped the Closed sign, turned out the lights in the dining area, and brought her back to the kitchen.

"I must admit, *ma chérie*, it has been fun cooking for the people of Keeneston. I feel ashamed that I have been here for over twenty years but never took the time to really get to know the town and her people."

"And now that you have, what do you think? Are you still going to go back to France after you retire?"

"Bah! Who wants to retire? What would I do with all that time? I'm a cook—I cook for people. If I go back to France, I will have no one to cook for."

Violet gave him a wobbly smile. She hated thinking of Anton leaving. "I understand all too well. I hate to admit I am getting too old to run this kitchen everyday, but the days I am here cooking are the best days of my week. To create a meal and see the moment they taste it is perfection to me. Their eyes close softly as they savor the food I make. I don't know who I am without cooking."

"You are a beautiful, caring woman, *ma chérie*. Now, here, taste this. It will solve all the problems in the world. It will make you give that seductive moan of yours, and it will spread love," Anton told her in a low voice, setting the *tarte au chocolat* in front of her.

"If only it could," Violet said a little melancholy. Once the reminder of being alone again hit her; it was hard to shake its lonely grasp.

Anton put his hand to his chest in mock exasperation. "You doubt my cooking? *Non!* Close your eyes, *ma chérie*." Anton picked up a fork, and Violet shut her eyes to the pain of knowing he was leaving in six months.

She opened her lips as Anton fed her his dessert. She moaned when she felt the chocolate melting over her tongue. The richness burst in her mouth, and she felt it all the way to her toes. Violet blinked her eyes open. Anton shot her a cocky smile.

"I take it you like it?"

"Love it," Violet practically purred. A man who made chocolate like this was such a turn-on.

"Ah, *ma chérie*, but who do you love more? The chocolate or Anton?"

Violet looked up at the ceiling in contemplation. "Maybe I should have another bite of the dessert before I answer," Violet quipped and picked up the fork, pausing midair. "What's that?" Violet asked as she stared at the plate in front of her. A square-cut chocolate diamond ring was placed in the center of the dessert.

Anton took the fork from her hand and placed it on the table before taking both of her hands into his. Violet turned wide-eyed and looked at him as he kissed her hands.

"Cooking has always been my passion. I thought my life would end when I could no longer create meals fit for royalty. But then I met a stubborn, vivacious woman who showed me that there could be passion both inside *and* outside the kitchen. You are not only my muse for cooking but my muse for life. I have fallen in love with you, *ma chérie*. Please say you will marry me so we can spend the rest of our lives sharing all our passions together."

Violet blinked and stared at Anton. What was happening? Lily was the one getting married. Anton was just another lost love. Wasn't he moving back to France?

"But, you're leaving at the end of the year," Violet stuttered, looking back and forth between Anton and the ring.

"I could never ask you to leave your family. I have none, and Keeneston has become more of a home to me than France. But that doesn't mean we cannot honeymoon there. Oh, the wineries and the restaurants we can tour together, *ma chérie*. It only holds appeal to me now with you by my side. So, what do you say, will you marry me?"

Violet squeezed his hands and smiled. "Of course I will. Oh, Anton, you have brought such joy to my life. I have found myself waking in the middle of the night with new recipes dancing in my mind — recipes for you. Your love has given me a new look at life. A spark that had been there once long ago is flaring back to life with your tender care. I love you, Anton, and I would be proud to be your wife."

Tears of happiness started to flow down her cheeks as Anton placed his lips on hers in a celebratory kiss. He pulled back and smiled, reaching for the ring and slipping it on her finger. Violet stared at it in amazement. She never would have believed she would have her own happily ever after.

Lily Rae sat on the porch swing with John's arm wrapped

around her shoulder, looking at the night sky. She rested her head on his chest. He gently pushed the swing in a slow rocking motion. The sound of crickets chirping and leaves rustling in the gentle breeze was broken by the sound of two cars speeding up the street.

"What in tarnation?" Lily asked. She and John leaned forward to see Charlie's car coming from the left and Anton's car coming down the street from the right.

"I think we're about to be told some news." John grinned.

"What do you know, John Wolfe? I'm going to be your wife. You tell me right now how you know these things," Lily demanded.

To her frustration, John just grinned wider and gave her a wink. "Just smile, Lily Rae. It's good news, and before you ask, I think it's a wonderful idea." John stood up and ignored her peppering questions.

The two cars slid to a stop nose to nose as the drivers' doors were flung open. Charlie and Anton got out to open the doors for Lily's sisters and shot each other a questioning look as they rounded the hoods. Lily watched her sisters step out of the cars and place their hands on their boyfriends' arms. From the porch, she could see it was good news. Her sisters were glowing.

Daisy and Violet looked at each other and, in an unspoken language the sisters shared, they understood exactly what was happening. Lily clutched her hands together in excitement. "Oh, this is wonderful news, John!"

"Let them tell you, Lily Rae," he said kindly and placed his hand at the small of her back.

Her sisters stepped onto the porch. They were practically bouncing in their orthopedic shoes. Wanting to jump in and demand they tell her their news, Lily gave way to her southern graces and instead sent John inside for some special iced tea while Charlie and Anton brought chairs over. It was one of the hardest things Lily had done when she offered tea to everyone as Daisy and Violet took their normal seats on the patios with their men flanking them.

Lily sat on the swing, and John sat next to her, waiting for them to make their announcement. She ground her teeth as they talked about the beautiful night, the fun time at the café with Anton cooking, and how good this batch of tea was.

John placed his hand on hers in silent communication to calm her. But when Violet waxed on about Anton's éclairs, Lily lost it.

"For the love of Pete, are you going to tell me why you're here so late at night?"

Daisy and Violet looked at each other in surprise and then at Lily. "We assumed John told you," Daisy said with a sly grin.

"Just say it, Daisy Mae! So help me, I'll wipe that smirk off your face. And don't you start, Violet Fae, or I'll tell everyone the secret ingredient to your fried chicken."

Her sisters rolled their eyes and held out their left hands. "We're getting married!"

Lily felt the tightness around her heart loosen as her smile grew. She held out her arms, and in seconds her sisters were in them. All the pain from the past fell away with the laughter and excited babble of the sisters. Gone were the years of broken hearts. Gone were the years of aging alone. Gone were the years of loneliness. Lily saw her sisters once again as young vibrant women in love—a love that would find them happier each day than the day before. Her sisters stepped back and each slipped their hands into their fiancé's hand. If only they could share that special day.

"John, what do you —?"

"I already told you I think it's a wonderful idea," John whispered in her ear.

Lily looked up at him and gave a thankful smile. "Daisy and Charlie, Violet and Anton, what do you think of a triple wedding? We have all the plans and the whole town is going to be there. Plus, it would just mean so much to me to have my sisters standing up with me. But, I leave it to you all to discuss. I'll understand if you want your own day."

Lily watched her sisters turn to their fiancés and then back to her. "We've already talked about it," Violet told her as she leaned forward and took Lily's hand in hers.

"And we would love it above all else. We're sisters and Mom did say we had to love each other," Daisy joked as she took Lily's other hand in hers.

The men each shook hands and greeted their soon-to-be brothers-in-law while the sisters wiped tears from their eyes. Anton cleared his throat. "We would like to make the cakes for the wedding. It is our gift and our pleasure to do so for you and the town."

"Oh, that's a lovely idea," Daisy said as she hugged her sister and future brother-in-law. "The town has been such a blessing and support for us. We should do something for them. After all, they are organizing all of this."

"But what else could we do?" Violet asked.

Lily pursed her lips. "I know what we can do. We can throw the best party this town has ever seen."

Chapter Twenty-Nine

Two months later, the three sisters were sitting on Lily's bed in the house they had grown up in. The sounds of women talking, laughing, and planning traveled up through the floorboards. The women of Keeneston were preparing three dresses and three veils for the wedding. They might have been generously partaking in some of their Rose Sisters Special Iced Tea as well.

"Can you believe after all these years we have found love?" Lily smiled as all three sisters linked hands.

"Together. We found love together," Daisy said almost in wonder.

"It makes sharing today all the more special. After going through heartbreak together and all the weddings of our matchmaking couples together, we can now start the second part of our lives together," Violet said with emotion cracking her voice.

"Second part, heck, this is our fourth or fifth part of life!" Lily laughed.

"Whatever part it is, it's the best part." Lily and Violet nodded in agreement with Daisy. This was certainly the best day of their lives.

"*Knock, Knock,*" Marcy Davies, the matron of the Davies family, called. "We have your dresses. Are you ready?"

The sisters gave each other one last meaningful look

before they opened the door and chaos reigned. Dani helped Lily with her hair, Tammy did Daisy's, and Katelyn worked on Violet. Kenna did makeup, Paige set the small veiled hats on their heads, and Marcy zipped dresses while Bridget and Annie fussed with jewelry.

"We have the flowers," Morgan called out as she and Gemma entered the room.

"Oh," Gemma gasped, "you ladies look absolutely beautiful!"

Lily turned from her corner of the room to see her sisters similarly turning to look at each other. Daisy's taller, thinner frame was beautifully displayed with a white, knee-length sheath dress finished off with a beautiful pale yellow silk scarf draped across her shoulders and hanging loosely from the crooks of her arms. Violet's curvy assets were highlighted by a white halter dress that tapered down to a tea-length wispy pleated skirt. Draped across her shoulders was a violet scarf.

Lily finally gave in and looked into the full-length mirror next to her. She stopped breathing. Her white A-line skirt with matching short-sleeved suit jacket was stunning. She couldn't believe it was her in the mirror. A teary-eyed Paige appeared in the mirror behind her holding a light pink silk scarf.

"I made these for each of you. Something new for your wedding day." Paige draped the scarf across her back, and Lily looked down to see her initials on one end and John's on the other. Her sisters each had a similar personal touch.

Marcy stepped forward and held out three silver bracelets with blue charms hanging from them. "These are symbols of love from each of the couples you played a role in helping. Here's Jake's and mine—a tractor. And here is

Louis and Bernadette—a bicycle. And there are so many more from so many thankful couples."

Kenna stepped forward. "Mine is the state of Kentucky with a heart in the center. You helped me find a home here."

"Mine is a crown, because you have taught me how to be gracious, loyal, and a proper princess for Rahmi. I couldn't have done it without your guidance," Dani told them, placing a kiss on each of their cheeks.

Paige smiled through her tears. "Mine is this bunch of grapes on the vine. It's for your leadership of the Keeneston grapevine you wield for the benefit of the community. We never need to worry about support, casseroles, or baby blankets when you three are in charge of the phone tree."

"I added a wooden spoon for when you taught me how to cook," Annie said as she pretended to not be tearing up.

"And mine is the spatula. You're never afraid to do what it takes to flip a bad situation to a good one." Katelyn stepped forward and hugged each sister.

Morgan grinned. "Mine's a pot for when you nailed that bastard for me. Even if you didn't like me, you gave me a second chance. And now you have your own second chance."

Tammy was still laughing as she pointed to the broom. "This one's for keeping our men in line and whipping them into shape for us to love."

"I think we all wanted the one I had made." Gemma chuckled. "Mine was a pitcher representing your *special* iced tea. I am pretty sure that drink has given way to half the marriages and most of the births in town."

Bridget pointed to the rectangular-shaped charm with three roses engraved on it. "This is for the café, the heart and soul of Keeneston, just like you three."

Violet and her sisters rushed forward. These special ladies were the new hearts of Keeneston. Violet wrapped each woman up in a hug as tears flowed. "Kenna, dear, I fear we've ruined all your hard work," Violet cried in dismay as she wiped her tear-stained cheeks.

"You arm yourself with kitchen accessories. I arm myself with makeup brushes," Kenna joked before blowing her nose. She grabbed her compacts and a large brush. In seconds Violet was all dolled up again and ready to be married.

Violet reached out and took her sisters' hands in hers. "Well, are we going to get married or what?"

A flurry of activity erupted as the flowers were passed to the sisters. Bouquets containing roses, daisies, violets, and lilies were tied in ribbons that matched each sister's scarf. As suddenly as they had invaded, the women hurried from the room, and the sisters were once again left alone.

"It's time," Daisy said, and she let out a deep breath.

The sisters looked at each other. They knew it was time for things to change, but the one thing that would never change was their love for one another.

Daisy was the first down the stairs. When she looked outside, she gasped. "Girls, I think our plan of taking our cars to the ceremony has been changed."

Violet stepped around where Daisy stood on the porch and looked in awe. She heard Lily gasp next to her. In front of the house was a black-lacquered open carriage adorned with flowers and hooked up to six white horses. Nabi's new trainee, young Nash, was at the reins. The men of Keeneston lined the walkway.

Will stepped forward and held out his arm for Lily. "Let me escort you to the carriage, Miss Lily."

Lily looked around as Cade took Daisy's arm and Ahmed took Violet's to lead each to the carriage. Lily choked up, and all she could do was give Will a nod of agreement as he placed her hand on the crook of his arm and led her to the carriage.

When the sisters were seated in the carriage, Nash lightly flicked the reins and off they went. The men and women who helped them get ready were ahead of them in their cars, driving across town to Desert Farm.

"Oh look!" Violet pointed to the balloons, ribbons, and lanterns lining the drive of Desert Farm.

"It's beautiful," Daisy said softly.

"Look at all the cars! I swear the whole town is here." Lily stared at the field packed with cars and finally started to feel nervous. When they were younger, they had all dreamed of their father walking them down the aisle and their mother sitting in the front row dabbing her eyes, smiling up at them. No one could have foreseen it taking them almost ninety years to find true love.

Nash pulled the carriage to a stop in front of Mo and Dani's mansion. The four tents formed a giant square behind the house in the gardens. Even from here, Lily could hear the string quartet playing music as the guests waited for their arrival.

"Our men will be lined up, waiting for us," Violet said with a wobble in her voice.

"In a couple minutes, we'll no longer be Roses," Daisy gulped.

"We'll always be Roses, just like we will always be sisters. Now, are you ready to walk each other down the aisle?" Lily asked. She linked arms with her sisters.

"I'm sorry, ladies. There has been a change of plans,"

Will said from behind them. The sisters turned to see a wall of men. Will, Mo, Cole, Cade, Marshall, Miles, Pierce, Cy, and Ahmed stood smiling at them.

"What's going on?" Lily asked as she looked to each man.

"We're here to escort you three down the aisle," Cade told them as he came up to kiss each sister.

"But . . ." Lily was speechless. And since her sisters stood next to her looking from man to man with a dumbfounded look on their faces, she guessed they were, too.

"Girls," Mo called out. The front door of the house opened as Mo and Dani's twelve-year-old daughter, Ariana, Cole and Paige's twelve-year-old daughter, Greer, and Pierce and Tammy's nine-year-old daughter, Cassidy, came running out.

Ariana's dress was the same pale pink as Lily's scarf. Greer's was the same yellow as Daisy's. Cassidy's the same purple as Violet's scarf. Each little girl held a basketful of pink, yellow, and purple rose petals.

"We're ready. We've been practicing," Cassidy said before the three girls took their places in front of their designated Rose sister.

"Then lead the way, our beautiful flower girls," Violet said and dabbed her eyes again. "Hurry before I turn into a watering pot."

The sisters followed the young girls around the side of the house. They stopped short of the tents, and Lily leaned forward to see Jake Davies, Nabi, Zain, and Gabe, Mo's nineteen-year-old twin boys, and Ryan, Cole and Paige's twenty-year-old son, busy ushering the last of the guests to their seats.

"I can't see our grooms," Lily whispered, peeking

around the corner.

"You'll see them soon enough." Ahmed grinned and sent a message on his phone before sliding it into his pocket. A second later, the sound of the wedding march began to play.

Lily took a deep breath and reached for her sisters only to be stopped by Will, Miles, and Cade. "We are escorting you, Miss Lily," Will told her as he took one of her arms and Miles took the other. Cade followed close behind them as they moved toward the tent and toward her future.

"You boys . . ." Lily started but lost the ability to speak when she entered the tent. The town of Keeneston rose to their feet, but she didn't see them. She only saw John standing at the other end of the aisle, smiling at her.

"Miss Daisy, are you ready to get hitched?" Cy asked and took her arm.

"More than you can ever know, young man." Daisy patted his cheek and ignored the gray hairs gracing Cy's temples before his brother, Pierce, took her other hand. Their brother-in-law, Cole, stepped behind Daisy and the little group started to walk toward the aisle.

Daisy closed her eyes as they paused at the entrance of the tent. She took in a deep breath and then opened her eyes. She watched Greer throwing petals in front of her. But then her eyes were drawn to Charlie, standing proudly at the end of the aisle.

"Okay, boys, get me to my groom." Daisy smiled, and the men she'd seen grow up, marry, and have children of their own escorted her down the aisle.

"My dear, you're ravishing. Anton is a lucky man. But you

tell me if he ever displeases you, and I will take care of it," Ahmed said smoothly as he raised Violet's hand to his lips.

Violet grabbed Ahmed and brought him down for a hug against her push-up-bra-enhanced bosom. She grinned to herself. Every bride was allowed one last thrill, and who wouldn't want dark, dangerous, and sexy Ahmed's head against their breasts?

Violet finally released him. As he sucked in air, she sent him a wink. "Let's go, boys."

Ahmed took one arm, Mo the other, and Marshall walked behind her as they guided her to the tent. Cassidy enthusiastically threw the petals in the air as she walked ahead of Violet and her escorts. In front of her stood Anton. He smiled at her, and she had never felt more beautiful than she did right then.

The Rose sisters stood with their grooms between them. Together they had entered this world. Together they'd had their hearts broken. Together they'd endured the pain of losing their parents. And together they'd eventually found peace in matchmaking. But today was the ultimate ending to their story. The Rose sisters were each getting their own happily-ever-after . . . together.

Father James cleared his throat. "And who gives these women to be married to these men?" His voice rang out across the tent as the sun began to set.

A warm orange glow was cast on the townspeople as they stood as one and said, "We do."

Chapter Thirty

The sun set as the couples said their vows. Cheers erupted from the guests as the brides and grooms were showered in rose petals. In a blink of an eye, the chairs were removed and a dance floor appeared. A band heralded the arrival of the three five-tier cakes Violet and Anton had made together. Violet and Anton stood arm in arm as everyone *oohed* and clapped.

"The cakes are gorgeous. This is the best gift you could give us." Lily leaned over and kissed Violet and Anton.

"I love the flowered toppers!" Daisy clasped her hands together and looked at the three cakes. "I'm guessing the one topped with daisies is mine," she teased as she hugged her sister and brother-in-law.

The three cakes were set on tables in front of each couple as cameras flashed. One by one, each couple cut their own cake. Amongst cheers, the band struck up a slow song.

"Shall we dance, my bride?" John asked. He held out his hand for Lily.

Lily took his hand, and he guided her onto the dance floor. Violet and Anton joined them, and Daisy and Charlie followed as well.

"I've never been happier," Lily said, smiling at her new husband. "But, have you seen Ryan and Sienna? There's trouble there, and I have plans for those two."

John chuckled. "My dear wife, they are still so very young. Give them time to grow up. They'll figure it out."

"I don't know about that." Lily saw Sienna staring longingly across the floor to where Ryan stood. Just a couple months ago, Ryan was the one staring longingly at Sienna. And who wouldn't? She was smart, tall, and curved in all the right places.

"We're not seventy anymore. And look at them all." Lily glanced over to the children. Well, some of them were already adults, standing with their parents. "I still have a lot of work to do before I leave this earth."

"Don't you mean *we* have a lot of work to do?" John asked, gesturing to her sisters and their husbands dancing around them. "We'll just take a little honeymoon while they grow up. Then we'll play matchmaker."

"A honeymoon? Aren't we too old for that?"

John ignored Lily's question and nodded to Charlie who nodded to Anton. Each man reached into the pocket of his tuxedo and pulled out an envelope. Lily took hers and with a quick glance saw that each of her sisters was holding the same envelope.

"What's this?" Lily asked. She stared at the envelope in her hands.

"Open it and find out," John urged.

Lily tore open the white envelope, letting it drop to the ground in shreds. She stood frozen, staring at the ticket in her hand. "You're giving me the world," she gasped.

"You always said how much you loved Keeneston but had never had the chance to see the world. So we are all going on a world cruise. And before you say anything, we already have the bed-and-breakfast and café covered for our journey. And when we get back, you'll be fresh and ready to play matchmaker again. Let's just start with someone a little older that Ryan and Sienna."

Lily didn't have to say a thing — Daisy was screaming in excitement loud enough for all of them. Lily looked down at the ticket and back up at her husband. She was about to embark on a wild adventure. She thought she should be nervous, but she wasn't. Exhilaration with this new chapter of her life filled her.

"Lily Rae," her sisters shrieked in delight. "Can you believe it? All of us together, exploring the world!"

Lily held out her arms, and her sisters were there, hugging each other in return as their husbands slyly high-fived each other. The band struck up a fast dance, and the dance floor filled with couples.

"We will miss you while you're gone," Gemma said as she hugged the sisters and their husbands. "But, I've set up an email account for you and will keep you updated on all the latest happenings."

Lily took her hand. "Gemma, you'll have to go back to your tabloid reporter days. I want pictures, and I want gossip."

"I won't let you down," Gemma said seriously before the sisters and their husbands were swarmed by well-wishers.

Abigail Mueez rolled her eyes as she danced around the floor with her younger brother, Kale. It was so embarrassing to be stuck dancing with her brother. Nolan, her first real boyfriend, was out of town. Eww, double barf. Her father, Ahmed, and mother, Bridget, were dancing way too close.

"You don't have to dance with me. I promised Ariana and Greer I would dance with them," Kale tried to say nonchalantly.

"You can dance with them next. I don't want to be the loser with no one to dance with for the first dance."

"Jackson would dance with you, but then you would turn pink and stammer like an idiot. So I guess I can see why you made me dance with you."

"Just because you're almost as big as I am now doesn't mean I can't still beat you up," Abby shot back to her brother.

"Please, your days are limited. And besides, if you do that I'll just hack your computer and send anything embarrassing on it to Jackson. Dad would flip if he knew you liked someone who was seventeen."

Abby punched her brother in the stomach hard enough to make him bend over, but light enough for him to laugh it off. "Or maybe you have something on there about Dylan. Maybe you like bad boys? At least he's your age, and he totally likes you."

"He does not."

"Does so."

"Does not." Abby let out a breath. "Okay, enough. I have no plans to date my friends. I turn sixteen in two days, and then I'm just two years away from college. I can't wait to leave town and find someone without you and Dad and, most importantly Mom, spying on me."

"Whatever. I'm going to dance with Ariana now."

The music ended and Abby watched her brother ask his best friend to dance. She didn't know why, but she had a feeling the equilibrium of Keeneston had shifted. Only time would tell if it settled back down.

Sienna Ashton saw her father, Will, coming toward her. He and her mother, Kenna, had just danced the first dance together. She had to tell him what she'd done. She hadn't told anyone yet. She was sure her parents would be supportive. They always were, but it was her dad she was most worried might think her a kook.

"You look beautiful tonight, sport," her father said as he kissed her cheek. "I still have trouble looking at you and not seeing my cute redheaded baby girl. And now you have a college degree and work in the real world. I guess I will have to admit you're all grown up."

"Daddy," Sienna said as she hugged her father, "I've been grown up for years."

Will placed a kiss on the top of her head. "You'll always be my baby girl. Now, are you too grown up to dance with your father?"

"Never. And there is something I want to talk to you about," Sienna told him with false bravado.

"What is it? Is it about your job with Lexington's new NFL team?"

Sienna nodded her head. "You know I love football, and basketball, and hockey."

"You sure did take after your ol' dad."

Sienna swallowed hard. Her father had been a quarterback in the NFL before he took over her grandparents' horse racing farm. Which is how she probably got her job at the newly formed Lexington NFL team. She wasn't naïve. She knew her father was an investor, and that got her foot in the door. But she was going to work hard to deserve her job.

"Well, I've already talked to the front office, and I am going to be working part-time in the front office for the next—"

"Part-time? Why?" Will almost stopped moving, but she urged her father to continue to dance.

"I'm going to work weekends and some evenings. During the day, I am going to earn my doctorate in sports psychology. I want to help athletes." Sienna grimaced as she looked up at her father.

"Sports therapy, huh? Could be a great fit for you. You understand the demands on professional athletes, as well as amateurs. Your years of being around football and then playing collegiate tennis will be a big help. How did you think of it?"

Sienna let out a breath she didn't know she was holding and suddenly felt foolish for ever thinking her father wouldn't approve. "You don't think I'm a kook?"

"A kook? You? No way. Other so-called professionals tried to have my receivers carrying around eggs like babies to help with their catching. Now those are a different story. But you're a professional like your mother. You will take it seriously, and I will be happy to hand out your card to every athlete I know. I'm proud of you, Sienna. I always will be. Your mother will make you buy more suits, you know."

"I know. She has a thing for them. I think she's been a lawyer for too long," Sienna said dryly.

"Not too much longer. She wants to retire in a couple years. After your brother graduates from college."

"Really? Mom? I don't know what she would do if she wasn't the town prosecutor."

Her father smiled. "We are going to travel like the Rose sisters, and I'm sure she will inappropriately interfere with your love life. Carter has been horse-crazy since birth. I'm sure he told you he's making equine business his major. Last night he even mentioned getting his MBA. I'm sure when we decide to retire, your brother will take good care of the farm."

Sienna agreed. Her brother had been working on the farm since he could walk. He rode like the wind, had some way to communicate with the animals through touch that amazed the whole family, and was a good leader with the people who worked on the farm.

"Oh, there's Mo and Ahmed. I need to talk to them about something we're working on." Her father leaned forward and wrapped her in a tight hug. "I'm proud of you, sport."

"Thanks, Dad." Sienna watched her father join his friends and decided to head to the bar.

"Oh, there you are, dear." Miss Lily and her sisters appeared out of nowhere to surround her.

Sienna gave each bride a hug. They'd been like great-grandmothers to her, and she loved seeing them so happy. "Congratulations to the brides! You ladies look lovely."

"Thank you, dear." Lily patted her hand and smiled to her sisters. "We wanted to see how you were doing. Here, have a drink."

Daisy shoved a glass of punch into her hand. "A toast! To men. They have some good points."

The women all raised their glasses, and Sienna took a drink. Oh crap, it burned. She coughed and the Rose sisters looked momentarily concerned. "Did we put too much lime in it?" Violet asked.

"Does lime burn?" Sienna asked as she cleared her throat.

"Oh, dear. You don't like it?" Daisy said sadly. "We made it ourselves."

Sienna looked at the three disappointed faces and took another sip. It still burned, but not as badly. "No, it's excellent," she choked out.

The three faces lit up in smiles. "Good, have some

more." Lily filled her cup to the top. "So, what's going on with you young people?"

Sienna took another sip. Hmm, not so bad after all. "I'm going back to school. I'm going to get my doctorate in sports psychology."

"That's wonderful, dear. Cheers to that!" Violet held up her glass and the four of them clinked their glasses and took a drink.

"And your brother has gotten so big. I can't believe he's almost nineteen. He's so tall already. Looks just like your daddy," Daisy told her before looking around the room. "Oh, and there's Abby. Isn't she lovely? Poor Ahmed is really going to have a problem when she goes away to college and he can't scare her potential suitors."

Sienna looked to the beautiful dark-haired, blue-eyed girl. "And she's smart and full of confidence. Her father won't have to keep the boys in line. She'll do it herself. But I don't really know what everyone was up to over the summer. I was so busy working. While it doesn't seem like much, there's a big difference between twenty-one and fifteen. That six years isn't much when you reach your mid-twenties, but it is right now. So I really feel bad I'm not up on the current gossip with the younger kids."

"Oh, well, then you know about Ryan. He's your age." Lily smiled innocently as Sienna choked on her drink.

"That's right. He just got back from his summer with the FBI and DEA. I heard they both want him to join after graduating. Such a handsome man. Don't you think? I hate to think of him in harm's way."

Sienna risked a glance across the tent toward Ryan. He was the boy who'd always had a crush on her. He snuck kisses while they played hide and seek or Marco Polo as kids. He always made an effort to open doors at school for her or to walk her home — because he was a gentleman who respected women, and he believed no one should walk home alone when he could walk with her. Not that Keeneston was a crime center, but what had been annoying as a teenager suddenly shifted earlier this summer.

They had been helping Nabi and Grace find love when he had surprised her. To stop her from screaming, he wrapped his hand around her mouth and pulled her tightly against him. Suddenly Ryan wasn't so little anymore. When she turned and really looked at him — his desire to go into law enforcement, his respect for women, his kindness to his younger siblings, and, okay, the smoking hot body he'd developed — didn't hurt either. But add these all together, and Ryan Parker was a catch.

And when all six foot two inches of broad chest, muscled thighs, and bone-melting hotness kissed her that night, Sienna realized Ryan Parker was a game-changer. Unfortunately, she'd missed the game. He claimed to be over her and left her flushed and breathless from their kiss. Since then, he hadn't so much as given her the time of day.

Sienna tossed back the rest of the drink. Bastard. He made her fall in love with him and then just left her high and dry. Miraculously, her glass was full again, and she downed it. Well, she'd show him she didn't need him. She could just as easily fall out of love.

"Psst." Sienna leaned toward the sisters. "Who is Mr. Tall, Dark, and Handsome over there?" Sienna tried to drop her voice, but since everyone around her looked, she must not have lowered it as much as she thought.

"That's Matt, dear. He's the new state trooper assigned to our area. He's a good, small-town boy and had the manners to come into the café the other week to introduce himself."

Sienna shoved her glass into Lily's hand. "Well, I better welcome him to Keeneston."

"Oh dear," Daisy whispered to her sisters. "I thought twenty-one-year-olds could hold more liquor than that."

"We better hurry up with our plan," Violet whispered. "Our husbands are looking at us curiously, and we did promise to give the kids time to grow up."

"Fiddlesticks. We're not matchmaking. We're just setting things right. Oh!" Lily gasped. "We really need to hurry. Sienna just ran her hand down Matt's stomach and is letting it rest on his waistband. Her father doesn't look pleased."

"But neither does Ryan. He can't take his eyes off them," Daisy said with glee. "Let's go!"

The three sisters casually walked across the tents to where Ryan stood with a death grip on his cake plate, his eyes narrowed like knife blades as he watched Sienna and Matt.

"Ryan, dear, how are you this evening?" Lily asked, casually glancing back at their husbands talking. Their time was limited when she saw their heads all turn and look at them.

"Great, Miss Lily. You ladies are the most beautiful brides I have ever seen." Ryan leaned forward and kissed each of their cheeks.

"Aren't you sweet?" Miss Daisy patted his scruffy cheek.

Violet looked behind her and then quickly turned to Ryan. "That's why we need one last favor from our favorite young man. See, poor Sienna accidently drank some of our special iced tea thinking it was punch. As you can see, she's a lightweight."

Having seen their husbands walking toward them, Lily hurried their plan forward. "And we can't leave on our honeymoon without knowing she's safe at home—you know, since we accidently are responsible for her condition."

"And we know Matt would take her home in a heartbeat . . ." Daisy added and then held her breath.

"No!" Ryan said harshly before reining in his temper. "He's new. Let him enjoy getting to know everyone else here. I'll take her home right now."

The three sisters jumped when hands were suddenly placed on their shoulders.

"I thought you all agreed to no more matchmaking," John said behind them as Ryan stalked across the dance floor.

"So that we can leave for our honeymoon with no worries," Charlie lectured.

"Because we will be keeping you too busy for any more mischief," Anton whispered into Violet's ear.

"Yes, dear," all three sisters said together, and they watched Ryan drag Sienna from the tent.

Chapter Thirty-One

R yan Parker had spent the summer interning with the FBI and DEA. He'd sat in on criminal profiling, engaged in the day-to-day training of their special operations divisions, and gone on drug busts. Of course, he was in the surveillance vehicle until the all-clear was given, but he had shown enough intelligence and ability that both divisions wanted him upon college graduation.

Through all of this, one person was always in his thoughts. Sienna Ashton and her shocking green eyes, light auburn hair, and curves that kept him up at night. But, she had brushed him aside. Then, at the beginning of summer, Sienna told him she'd only ever thought of him as a little kid. Ryan's young love had been spoiled. Out of anger, he'd kissed her just to prove he was a man. And it had worked. Unfortunately, he was still mad, and his pride a little too hurt to care.

But she found a way to tug at his heart once again. She was pawing on the new state trooper. He was twenty-two and "old enough" for Sienna. But Ryan sure as hell wouldn't let her make a fool of herself. Or so he justified it as he pried her off a very pleased-looking Matt.

"Ryan! Have you met Matt?" Sienna giggled.

"Yes, and if Matt will excuse us, I'm here to take you home," Ryan said tightly as he stared Matt down. Most of the time, he could literally look down at the people he was intimidating. But Matt was eye to eye with him.

Matt looked at Ryan and then Sienna and simply took Sienna's hands from his chest and placed them on Ryan's arm. "She's all yours, for now."

Ryan's lip twitched into a sneer at the implied threat. "Come on, Sienna."

"Are you going to kiss me again?" she asked about five notches above a whisper.

Ryan shot Matt a grin. Matt simply raised an eyebrow. "Aren't you leaving to go back to college, Parker?"

"Soon, but not tonight. See you around, Matt." Ryan placed his arm around Sienna and dragged her from the tent.

"It's good to see you again. I haven't seen you since you got back from your internship," Sienna said as he started the car.

"I got back last week. What were you doing tonight?" Ryan asked. He drove out of the farm and turned down the street heading to the neighboring Ashton farm.

"What do you mean? I was just making a new friend."

"No, you were making a fool of yourself."

Ryan almost winced when he heard Sienna suck in an angry breath. "A fool! Me? I don't think so, Ryan Parker. You're just upset it wasn't you I was dancing with!"

"You call that dancing? You were feeling the man up." Ryan pulled into Ashton Farm and drove past the moonlit horse pastures.

"Jealous?" Sienna shot back.

"Hardly," Ryan scoffed. There was no way in hell he'd tell her he'd do anything to have her touch him like that.

He pulled to a stop in front of her parents' house and opened his door. "Fine! Then you have no objection to me calling Matt," Sienna yelled as he got out of the car.

Ryan let out an aggravated growl and walked around the car to open her door. "I don't care what or who you do, Sienna."

"And I don't care who you're with either," Sienna spat back. She took his arm and let him escort her to the front door. He reached into the mouth of the knee-high horse statue and pulled out a key to their house. He unlocked the door and swung it open.

Ryan leaned forward. He wanted one last taste so badly. He smelled the sweet scent of her perfume and was nearly drawn in by her eyes. Slowly, he bent his head so his lips were close to hers. Sienna tilted her head up, closed her eyes, and licked her lips. "You keep telling yourself that, sweetheart."

Sienna's eyes popped open, but Ryan didn't see the glare she gave him or the look of desire as he drove away.

The next morning, French toast, pancakes, eggs, bacon, and sausage were all served at the Blossom Café. Sophie delivered breakfast to the depressed patrons. The café was full. People had been drawn to it to witness the absence of the Rose sisters, who had departed for their world cruise earlier that morning.

"I don't know if this is right. I was told to speak with Miss Violet about my diet. I don't want to disappoint Nabi," Nash Dagher, the newest member of the royal family's security team, said worriedly.

Sophie looked down at the pancakes and bacon that filled two plates. Nash needed to gain weight, and he had in the past couple of weeks he'd been in town. But she thought he worried too much until Nabi and Ahmed came in and sat down with him.

"Is that all you are having for breakfast? Did my ten-mile run with you this morning not make you hungrier?" Ahmed asked, looking disappointedly at the plates in front of Nash.

"Don't worry, Ahmed. I have already talked to the substitute cook, and Miss Violet left a weekly meal plan for Nash." Sophie smiled at the tableful of lethal men. They didn't intimidate her. Her mother had been an undercover DEA agent and had taught her how to hold her own.

Nash sent her an appreciative smile. "Thank you. I refuse to fail in my mission."

Sophie took Nabi and Ahmed's order and left, shaking her head. Nash had joined the security team as a short waif of a man with superior intelligence. Nabi and Ahmed were now working with him on an athletic program. Whatever they were doing was working. It looked as if he'd already grown an inch and gained ten pounds of muscle. She knew when she came back from her last year of college he'd look completely different. As she went back to work, she had a feeling a lot was going to change.

"Wyatt, she's a bimbo," Sydney said in the typical big-sister voice as she took a bite of her bacon.

"I don't care about the boys you date. Well, Edwin was a douche, but I don't bug you about the rest of them," Wyatt said in his smooth Southern voice.

"But you can do so much better. You're seventeen. Don't get too serious too fast. You'll be in college next year. Enjoy it. I'm having a blast." Sydney shot him a wink and Wyatt groaned.

"Don't make me bring dueling back into fashion."

"Please, you know I can take care of myself. It's you and that Paisley chick I'm worried about."

"I promise. I won't get too serious if you promise not to do any more lingerie ads. Do you know how embarrassing it is to have my sister plastered on billboards in her underwear?"

"Oh, grow up. It's no big deal." Sydney took a sip of her orange juice. She had followed in her mother's footsteps and modeled while attending college. It paid for her private education, and it also gave her the connections necessary to launch a career after school.

"You wouldn't think that if you had to put up with the crap I have to listen to from my lacrosse teammates," Wyatt grumbled. "Do you know how many punches I have thrown defending my big sister?"

Sydney's shoulder's slumped as the fight went out of her. "I'm sorry, Wyatt. I never thought how hard it is for you and Dad. Mom's used to it, and she's always with me at every shoot, making sure it's on the up and up. I never thought of you defending me. I should have, though. You're the best brother a girl could have, and I love you."

"So, you'll stop doing those photos?"

Sydney smiled. "I promise, in three years I won't be doing them anymore. I already have two shoots lined up. They're overseas so you shouldn't see them. You'll be happy to know that most of my new hires have been for designer clothes. So you don't have to defend me anymore."

"You're my sister; I will always defend you. Now, did you hear that Great-grandma Wyatt is making the farmhands drive her down to the stables to kiss all the horses?"

Sydney let out a worried sigh. "She's doing too much.

At least she's letting Dad take over the farm somewhat. And you . . . Mom said you've been working there everyday after school and this whole summer as well."

"I like it. The business side is fascinating and so is the training. Mom has taught me all about the physiology of horses. I think I may study large animal medicine."

"You want to be a veterinarian like Mom?"

Wyatt looked contemplative. "I think so. She said that during the school year I can work with her in the clinic to see if I like it."

"I'm proud of you, Wyatt." Sydney smiled and lifted her orange juice to toast her brother.

Sophie set breakfast onto the table and Zain Ali Rahman thanked her. He and his twin, Gabe, had found themselves, along with the rest of the town, at the Blossom Café that morning.

"It's so strange the Rose sisters got married and then left town on a honeymoon. It seems too empty without them here," Gabe said as he dug into his food.

"What will we do without their care packages when we go back to school next week?" Zain asked. He and his brother lived for those care packages full of cookies, copies of the *Keeneston Journal*, and other treats.

"I didn't think of that. But at least they are happy."

"True, but it's all so much. I still can't believe our Anton took early retirement and fell in love. For nineteen years, he's been yelling at us in French when we sneak into the kitchen to steal sweets," Zain said, shaking his head in wonder. Their French chef hadn't been happy a day in his life until Miss Violet bulldozed her way into his heart.

Gabe leaned forward. "Did you see those girls at the party last night? They were hot. Who are they?"

"Of course I saw them. I don't know who they are, though. Could they be part of Charlie's family? If they are, I sure hope they visit more often."

"They didn't seem to know who we were. I'm not looking forward to going back to college," Gabe groaned.

Zain nodded his head. They were royal heirs. They were down the line of succession a bit but were heirs to the Rahmi crown nonetheless. They were princes to the small Middle Eastern island nation and had spent every summer for eighteen years there, learning how to be princes and, in case of some horrific incident, how to be kings. This was the first summer they had been allowed to stay in Keeneston, and it had been the best summer yet.

But now it was time to go back to school. And at school, the guys tried to be their buddies to latch onto their money and fame. And the women all wanted to be a princess. What they both wanted was to find someone like their mother, Dani, who hadn't wanted to be a princess. Instead, she put up with being royalty in order to be with their father because of who he was as a person. So far they hadn't found anyone like that outside of Keeneston.

"I'm not looking forward to it either. Maybe we should spend this year being what they all think we are," Zain said mischievously.

"I like that idea. This could be fun." Gabe sat back and laughed.

"I always worry when he laughs like that," Dani said to the table filled with her friends.

"And without the Roses and John, how are we to know what they are up to?" Katelyn asked the group.

"Finally! I have a reason to use my wiretaps. Just get me their phones and I'll have them bugged in seconds." Annie rubbed her hands together and smiled. "Come on, Bridget, you know you want to."

Bridget looked up at the ceiling and refused to meet Annie's gaze.

"Oh my gosh," Annie cried as she gave Bridget's shoulder a little shove. "You already have!"

"Shh," Bridget lowered her voice. "Our kids are right over there. Keep your voice down."

Morgan just shook her head. "What's the big deal? Miles did that years ago."

"I can't believe it. I'm the last one to do this? Tammy, you haven't, have you?" Annie asked the little pixie across the table from her.

"Well, I didn't do it," Tammy said guiltily. "I had Cy do it when he was getting phones for his girls."

Gemma just rolled her eyes. "I swear if anyone needs to go on a world tour it's my husband. I can't pry Cy from his encrypted computer. He runs backgrounds on every person coming to our house. He needs a hobby."

"Tell me about it," Morgan said, exasperated. "Miles has been having panic attacks about Layne at college. I keep reminding him he's trained her to kill someone over fifty-eight ways."

"Marshall hasn't done any of that," Katelyn said in wonder before the girls at the table all broke into laughter.

"Are you kidding? He's the one who told Mo some things he could do to keep an eye on the twins," Dani laughed.

"And you better believe Marshall needs his own hobby," Kenna said as she nodded to Katelyn. "He's decided to recruit some more deputies since Noodle wants to retire soon. I've stopped by to ask him to serve warrants, and he's obsessed with finding the perfect replacement. I've decided I should be jealous of you."

"Me? Why?" Katelyn asked.

"Because you should see the list he has for this new deputy. If it's that long for a coworker, I can't imagine what his wife list was like."

The girls laughed. Paige leaned forward and whispered, "Maybe we should send them on one of those guy trips into the woods where they hunt, forage, and build shelters to survive."

"That's a great idea." The table of women turned to look at the other large circular table in the café.

"I have a feeling they're talking about us," Miles said dryly as the men looked at their wives who were all staring at them.

Will shook his head. "I don't want to know."

"I don't either. Annie has that *I'm about to do something illegal* look on her face," Cade muttered.

"Tell me about it. So does Bridget," Ahmed said and shook his head.

"I don't want to hear that," Marshall groaned. "I hope they don't make me arrest them again."

"Want to break out the drone to see what they're up to?" Cy asked gleefully.

"Hell no. Bridget would shoot it down. Do you know how hard it is to get a government-grade drone?" Ahmed shook his head.

"I wonder if I could build a mini drone?" Pierce pondered.

"I just think they need a hobby," Cole told the group, who all nodded their agreement.

"Goodness knows what's going to happen when my kids get old enough to start seriously dating. I think Dani is already having Nabi run backgrounds on all single royalty around the world." Mo shuddered. "Can you imagine our wives as matchmakers?"

The table groaned again. "Don't bring it up. My daughters are never getting married," Cy whined.

"Sienna has a boyfriend. Shoot me now, someone, please. He's so stuffy and *wrong*. At least he wasn't there last night." Will took a sip of his iced tea. "I think Cy and his super computer are better matchmakers than our wives. Let's only hope the Rose sisters get back soon. But a hobby would be good for the girls."

"What about a cooking class or a pottery class? Those are popular, right?" Cole asked the table.

"Dude, do you really want to relive the infamous vacuum cleaner incident? Have you not learned anything?" Will shook his head at his friend.

Cole cringed. "Maybe someone else should suggest a hobby to them then."

Miles let out a sigh. "How much longer until the Rose sisters get back?"

"One hundred eleven days," the table responded instantly.

Chapter Thirty-Two

5 years later . . .

"Sienna Danielle Paige Ashton," the dean of the university's psychology department said into the microphone, "has been a distinguished student these past years. Her passionate commitment to fight for patients' rights and to develop better treatment in applied psychology has helped her reach the top of her class. She has a bright future ahead as a sports psychologist that will not only help athletes and coaches of all ages, but I am sure will change the industry as a whole. And now, without further ado, I present Miss Ashton."

Lily, Daisy, and Violet dropped their husbands' hands as they stood to applaud. Sienna's parents, Will and Kenna, and her brother, Carter, clapped madly next to them. Sienna stood and walked toward the podium to give her speech.

"Oh, look at her, John. She's all grown up," Lily whispered.

"Lily Rae, for goodness' sakes, let her get settled before you start to meddle."

Lily put her hand to her heart. "Me, meddle?"

John just shook his head and clapped as Sienna finished her speech. "Interesting that you told Ryan to come over this afternoon when you knew darn well he and Sienna aren't speaking to each other for some reason."

"Please, everyone knows they love each other and just don't know what to do about it."

"And that was reason to call the poor boy on his vacation and tell him you need help moving something."

Lily shrugged. "I *do* need help moving the table outside for the party. And he needs something to do. I'm worried about him working so hard. He just got back from LA, and Paige complained he's heading back in two weeks."

"It's none of your concern, Lily Rae," John reminded her as the graduates walked across the stage to receive their diplomas.

"*Humph.* So says the man who wanted to help Nash with his date the other night. How was that any of your concern?" Lily raised her eyebrow in victory.

"Just clap, dear. They finished while we were arguing over it. Let's get back to the house and get ready for the party."

John, Lily, Charlie, Daisy, Anton, and Violet all gave Sienna a brief hug and kiss before leaving. Lily didn't let John know it, but months ago she had set a whole plan into motion, and today it was about to start spinning.

"Where do you want the table, Miss Lily?" Ryan asked and picked up the old farm table in the kitchen.

"Right outside, dear. Under the large maple tree would be perfect," Lily directed as Daisy gave her the thumbs-up sign from her position at the dining room window.

"What kind of party are you having? It's the perfect day for it," Ryan asked as he maneuvered the table through the door.

"Oh, just a little graduation party," Lily called from

where she was scooping ice into a large metal bucket.

"Is it for Wyatt? I know it's not for Jackson. We had his two days ago," Ryan said as he walked back inside.

"Oh, um, here dear. Can you carry this ice bucket?"

Ryan narrowed his eyes to where Miss Lily stood with bags upon empty bags of ice at her feet. How did she get all those bags of ice into the tub so fast? There had to be eighty pounds of ice in that thing.

"Sure thing, Miss Lily."

He bent down and easily lifted the tub of ice. Miss Lily held open the back door, and Ryan went through it sideways, right into the path of Sienna Ashton. He hadn't seen her since Christmas. Ah, graduation party. He should have known. So, she was Dr. Ashton now.

The kitchen door slammed shut, and they were alone. Ryan told himself his heart was beating harder because of the heavy load he was carrying, but he knew that was a lie. He benched three hundred pounds regularly, which meant it was the woman standing in front of him who caused it.

"Congratulations, Doc," Ryan said coolly with a quick nod of his head. He turned to take the ice under the tree when he heard her gasp.

"You're bleeding!" Sienna rushed over and shoved up the sleeve of his gray FBI T-shirt.

Ryan shivered at her contact and then pulled away. "It's nothing."

"What do you mean, it's nothing? You're bleeding through a bandage on your arm."

"It's just a scrape. Let it be, Sienna."

Ryan set the large ice tub down and shook her hand off. It really was nothing, but the gunshot had been enough for his boss to send him on vacation. His cover had been blown, and the group attempting to blow up the sports arena hadn't been too pleased. He'd received a bullet to his arm, but they were facing terrorism charges.

"How did you get that? I thought you sat at a desk in the FBI's field office in LA?"

"You always see what you want to. Tell me, Sienna, do I still look like a kid to you?" Ryan stepped so close that if she took a deep breath, her breasts would brush against his chest.

Sienna's mouth went dry. She looked up into his hardened face and steady hazel eyes that told her he'd already seen more than he should have. Standing just over six foot two inches, Sienna guessed he was close to two hundred pounds of pure muscle. The tight T-shirt showed off powerful biceps with a chest wide enough to envelop her. From there, she took in the jeans that seemed to hug thighs she suddenly envisioned pushing her knees apart as he . . .

"You okay, doc? You seem a little flushed." His deep mocking tone had her snapping her eyes back up to his.

"Well, it's summer in Kentucky. Of course, I'm flushed." Sienna motioned to his arm. "So, what happened?"

"I was shot in the line of duty, and this is my recuperation time."

"Oh my gosh," Sienna put her hand on his chest and then snapped it back as if it were on fire, "are you all right? Do your parents know?"

"Of course, I'm okay. I'll just have Dr. Emma check my stitches. I probably popped one when I picked up the tub of ice. No big deal. And of course, my parents know."

"Did they freak out?" Sienna asked. Her dad would have locked her in the basement if she got shot.

Ryan's mouth tilted into an amused grin. "Nah, when I got home my dad showed me his first gunshot scar. To tell you the truth, it was a bummer to know your dad was shot with a bigger caliber bullet than you. He has a cooler scar than I do."

Sienna laughed, and in that split second, all the tension from the past years fell away. They were the two kids who had grown up together. But then the door opened and the guests to the graduation party spilled out. The spell was broken as Dr. Emma zeroed in immediately on the bloody arm.

"Violet, what the heck?" Daisy hissed.

"Yeah, you were supposed to hold them off a little bit longer," Lily whispered.

Violet tossed her hands up in the air. "I tried. But they got me with the casseroles. There were just too many of them, and then the door somehow got opened and well . . . I failed." Violet let out a sigh. They looked out the now open door. Ryan and Sienna were as far apart as they could be.

"What happened to his arm?" Lily asked. Dr. Emma and her retired sheriff's deputy husband, Noodle, sat talking to Ryan across the way at the picnic table.

"Gunshot," John said from behind them.

Lily shook her head. "I knew he was running from his feelings, but I didn't think he'd run into a bullet."

"I can't help but agree with you, Lily Rae. He's been taking increasingly risky jobs for the FBI's special operations division, including undercover work. It's time our boy came home," John said, watching Emma restitch Ryan at the picnic table.

"How do you intend to do that?" Charlie asked.

"And what can we do to help?" Anton wondered,

sliding an arm around his wife.

John shook his head. "I don't know yet. But we'll work on it together."

Violet looked out at the crowd gathering in the back yard and let out a low whistle. "If I loved you any less, honey, I would be out there getting my hugs from Zain and Gabe."

Lily looked where the two twenty-four-year-old playboy princes were sauntering into the party. Their skin was tanned, showing their Middle Eastern heritage. Their glacier-blue eyes were straight from their mother. The combination was deadly. Women collapsed into fits of vapors when the boys put the two attributes to work. Since college graduation, they had been serving in the Rahmi Air Force. They had just arrived home the week before and were now ready to start their own lives — or as much of their own as they could, being royalty.

Anton just shook his head at his wife. "What about little Sophie? I remember her as an *enfant,* and now she's twenty-five."

Sophie Davies had inherited the Davies hazel eyes, but the quiet beauty exuded confidence as she hugged Sydney. "Well, at least Sydney has stopped modeling. It's nice to have her back in town," Lily said, watching the two girls laugh.

"It's just so wonderful to have everyone home for the summer. I miss them when they are away. And too many of them are getting ready to leave in the fall for college again," Daisy complained.

"It's what happens when they grow up, dear," Charlie said and patted his wife's hand. "Now, should we join the party or continue standing here gossiping about them all night?"

Lily watched her sisters and brothers-in-law step out into the yard. She looked at her watch. The wheels she'd set in motion would be at full speed soon.

Chapter Thirty-Three

"I still can't believe Edna and Tabby ran off together to Florida six months ago," Marshall said as he looked at the now empty house next door.

Kenna nodded. "He said it was getting too cold for him here. His winky got frostbite the last time he tried to write his name in the snow."

"But Edna? Where did that come from?" Will asked as he grabbed a beer from the large ice tub under the maple tree in Lily and John's backyard.

"They fell in love over bingo," Dani told them.

"How will we ever defend ourselves now?" Cy grinned.

Paige's phone pinged and she looked down at it. "Speaking of the devil." She held up the phone for everyone to see.

"Is that Tabby's pig on the beach?" Miles asked slowly.

"Is it wearing a bikini?" Ahmed marveled.

"Oh no," Katelyn giggled, "that's not just a bikini, that's one from Sydney's new swimsuit line."

Tammy snorted and then covered her mouth. "Well, Tabby's pig is very fashionable this season."

"Let's hope Sydney doesn't see it," Annie said. She shook her head a moment before a screech filled the afternoon air.

"Too late," Bridget cringed.

Morgan looked at the picture and smiled. "Tabby's pig has her own Instagram page?"

"The better point being that my sister follows Precious Piggy on Instagram," Pierce teased.

"What? You should see the things Tabby, Edna, and Precious do. It's the best page to follow. They took her to a nude beach last week," Paige said as she scrolled through the pictures and then held up her phone.

"Oh, that's just wrong," Cade gagged.

Mo leaned closer before jumping back. "Damn, you could have warned me it was a family photo. I can't un-see that."

"Hey, guys, what's going on?" Trey Everett asked as he and his wife, Taylor, walked over.

Trey had grown up in Keeneston and had been the star running back on Cade's state championship team. He'd met Taylor, an actress, through Cy's work in Hollywood. They'd been college sweethearts. While he had gone on to play in the NFL, she had started to direct and act in movies again. About five years ago, he, Taylor, and their two kids moved from Hung Island, Georgia, back to Keeneston after he retired.

Paige flashed them the camera, and Trey's look of horror cracked up Taylor and the rest of the group.

"What are you looking at?" Henry Rooney asked as he and his shiny slacks sauntered over. "Nudie pics?"

"How did you know?" Tammy asked with mock innocence. Her boss was the town's defense attorney and reigning leader of the worst pick-up lines in the entire state.

"I've got to see. Is it a new sex tape of that reality star?"

Paige held out her phone, and Henry rushed forward. He closed his eyes and covered his mouth with his hand.

Everyone took a giant step back, fearful he might hurl. Henry shook his head and cracked open one eye. "I can work with that. Baby, are those defibrillation paddles because you just stopped my heart?"

The group groaned.

"Don't encourage him," his wife, Neely Grace, begged.

"I'll show you my artificial hip if you show me yours," Henry continued, ignoring the continued protests. "Your beauty is more than my pacemaker can handle, so it's a good thing you look like an angel."

"Henry!" Tammy cried.

"Are those earmuffs? Cause I'd love to have them wrapped around my head," Henry rolled on as everyone made a dash for the other side of the yard.

"Wait, I've got more," Henry called out.

The pony-tailed woman looked out the window of their convertible and took in the black four-rail fences lining the road. Large, leafy trees branched over the winding country road, forming a green tunnel as they drove toward Keeneston, Kentucky.

"I still can't believe we are doing this," her sister said for the hundredth time as she fidgeted in her blue sundress.

"What do we have to lose?"

"True. We needed to start over, and this just landed in our lap. But don't you think it's strange?"

She didn't bother to answer her sister as she navigated the twisting road. Horses ran in pastures and bluegrass danced in the wind, creating ripples of dark blue. It was certainly different from their small coastal town of Daphne, Alabama.

"I sure hope this works out. We can't go back to Daphne, ever," her sister said seriously.

"No one knows we're here. It will be our chance to start over. Let's just hope they don't pry into our past too much." Her brown eyes eagerly sought out the houses that started to appear after a sharp turn in the road. "This must be Keeneston."

"It's even smaller than Daphne." Her sister's matching brown eyes widened in wonder as they drove up Main Street.

"Mechanic's garage, insurance, antiques . . ." she said, glancing at the storefronts along Main Street.

It was certainly beautiful. Bourbon barrels, cut in half and filled with cascading greenery, stood in front of some of the shops. Baskets overflowing with colorful flowers were on every post, and American flags fluttered in the warm summer air. The buildings were old, the paint was new, and doors were open. They slowed in front of what looked to be the only place to eat.

"The Blossom Café," her sister read aloud.

"Let's go," she said, continuing to drive. "There's a lawyer's office and a feed store.

"And a cute shop, Southern Charms. Oh, that's the place I read about that makes those fancy hats," her sister said suddenly excited as she fluffed her long blonde golden hair.

Soon the town trickled to a stop and fields of cows, crops, and horses took over again.

Lily signaled her sisters, and they gathered around the kitchen table Ryan had carried outside earlier. The sun was starting to lower in the sky, and Will had fired up the grill for dinner. Groups of people stood or sat in her yard. The women had taken over setting up folding tables and putting casseroles, salads, and fruit on them while the men all advised Will how to grill hamburgers. The younger kids were playing football and the older ones sat on a picnic blanket talking.

"What is it, Lily Rae?" Daisy asked as she took a seat.

Violet sat down and poured them all some iced tea.

"As much as I hate to admit it, I think we need to come to the realization that we're old," Lily started. She was suddenly nervous. Had she done the right thing?

"Do birds lay eggs? Of course we're old," Daisy said in that sisterly voice that annoyed Lily.

"Go on, Lily. What's sparked this realization?" Violet asked.

"It's getting hard for me to keep up with the bed-and-breakfast. And I know it's been hard for you two at the café," Lily said sadly.

Daisy and Violet both nodded.

"I can't stand and cook that long anymore. And that sweet girl who has been helping us went off and got married. I'll just ignore the fact that we are the ones who set them up. I don't know what I'm going to do," Violet confided.

"Charlie and Anton have helped us some, but we didn't know you were having the same problem," Daisy said and reached out, taking Lily's hand.

"I hate to admit it, but we are," Lily told her sisters.

"I just don't know what we can do other than close the café. It just doesn't seem right not to be run by one of the family. And since we never had children . . ." Violet looked thoughtfully at the kids running around the yard.

Lily took a deep breath. "That's what I wanted to talk to you about. John and I bought Edna's house."

"Why would you do that?" Daisy asked in surprise.

"Well, we had the money, and it's smaller than our place. I had an idea and didn't want to risk losing the house, so we bought it."

"What's your idea?" Violet questioned.

"It's an either-or situation. Edna's house is smaller, so John and I could more easily keep up with it. I could sell our family home and move into Edna's."

"Or?" Daisy and Violet asked at the same time.

"Or I thought about this big house we have and how there would be plenty of room for guests and my family. How would you like to move back home?" Lily put it out there and held her breath.

"Home? All of us?" Violet pondered. "I'd love to, but all those stairs."

"There's not enough room in the downstairs master," Daisy pointed out.

Lily nodded. "Well, there's room, but not as it's currently laid out. A builder could reconfigure the downstairs pretty easily to give every couple their own room."

The three sisters looked at each other, and Lily knew it was going to happen the second they smiled.

"I can't believe we're all going to be living together. That gives me such peace of mind. I'll talk to Anton tonight."

"And I'll talk to Charlie. Now if only you had a solution to the problem we have with the café."

Sienna stood from the red-and-white checkered blanket. She needed space. Ryan had been sitting directly across from her for the past hour, and she could feel every time his gaze brushed over her. It was pathetic. She had been dating someone for three years. They had even been talking about marriage. But while Ryan was being restitched, she'd called her boyfriend and told him she needed to see him tonight to talk. If he were smart, he'd know what was coming. Her heart just wasn't in it, and that wasn't fair to either of them.

Sienna reached the beer cooler at the side of the house and flipped the lid open. "Excuse us, is this Mrs. Rose-Wolfe's house?"

Sienna looked up and saw two younger women standing there. They were shorter than she was, probably five-foot-four. One was svelte, while the other was a bombshell with curves that would start Henry on a pick-up line marathon. Both had golden hair; however, one was redder and the other more blond. Both had the deepest brown eyes that looked rather wary at the moment.

"Yes, this is Miss Lily's place. I'm Sienna, may I help you?"

The svelte one gave a weak smile. "Thank you, can you point out Mrs. Rose-Wolfe?"

Sienna turned around and pointed at the trio of white-haired ladies sitting under the tree. "She's the one in the middle."

"Thank you," they both said, taking off across the yard.

Lily noticed the sudden silence first and the two young women second. Their strappy sundresses had also attracted the attention of the three husbands and all the younger men. John, Charlie, and Anton moved to stand behind their wives as the ladies stopped at the table.

The town gathered around Lily, who looked the two strangers over. If her senses were right, these two ladies might need her as much as she needed them.

"Mrs. Rose-Wolfe?" one of the young women asked nervously as she saw the whole party suddenly surrounding them.

"Yes, dear?" Lily smiled reassuringly.

"I received your letter. And if it's all right with you and your sisters, we'd like to accept." Her eyes darted to Daisy and Violet before settling back on Lily.

"Agree to what?" Violet whispered to Lily.

"Sisters," Lily said with a satisfied look, "meet our new help. They're going to help us with the bed-and-breakfast and the Blossom Café."

"Help us how?" Daisy asked.

"By running them for us," Lily answered.

"I'm sorry, but who are you?" Violet inquired.

"Please excuse my lack of manners, ma'am," the young woman said apologetically. "I'm Poppy Meadows, and this is my sister, Zinnia. We're your cousins."

The End

New Release Notifications for Kathleen Brooks,
Sign Up Here:
www.kathleen-brooks.com/new-release-notifications/
Subscribers will be the first to learn about the new
Forever Bluegrass series coming soon.

Other Books by Kathleen Brooks

The return to Keeneston is almost complete! The Forever Bluegrass Series will begin in October or November of 2015. Ryan and Sienna's story is already unfolding, but the first book in the series will give all of the details of their time together. And you'll still have the same loveable Keeneston, but now with a whole new crop of characters to know and love.

www.kathleen-brooks.com/new-release-notifications/

If you are new to the writings of Kathleen Brooks, then you will want to try her Bluegrass Series set in the wonderful fictitious town of Keeneston, KY. Here is a list of links to the Bluegrass and Bluegrass Brothers books in order, as well as the separate New York Times Bestselling Women of Power series:

About the Author

Kathleen Brooks is a New York Times, Wall Street Journal, and USA Today bestselling author. Kathleen's stories are romantic suspense featuring strong female heroines, humor, and happily-ever-afters. Her Bluegrass Series and follow-up Bluegrass Brothers Series feature small town charm with quirky characters that have captured the hearts of readers around the world.

Kathleen is an animal lover who supports rescue organizations and other non-profit organizations such as Friends and Vets Helping Pets whose goals are to protect and save our four-legged family members.

Email Notice of New Releases:
www.kathleen-brooks.com/new-release-notifications/

Kathleen's Website:
www.kathleen-brooks.com

Facebook Page:
facebook.com/KathleenBrooksAuthor

Twitter:
twitter.com/BluegrassBrooks

Goodreads:
goodreads.com/author/show/5101707.Kathleen_Brooks

24716044R00185